"Hi, Julie."

Reagan's voice cracked. *Get it together, Harrison, you're not sixteen.* He cleared his throat. "Nice to see you again."

"Hi." She went to the back door to let her son out of his booster seat. "Thanks for arranging this. Aiden's really excited, so I hope you're ready. He may give you a run for your money."

"I'm ready for anything." His wide smile might seem too eager, so he dialed it back a notch. Spending time with her son would remind him of why he didn't date single moms. Although he was incredibly attracted to her, he figured a widow with a young son was too much responsibility. At this point in his professional career, he was very careful of who he let into his life. He didn't need any distractions. This tour with Aiden should shake loose any romantic notions he had toward the kid's mother.

Praise for Laurie Winter

Home Field

by

Laurie Winter

Warriors of the Heart Series

Home Field

Cover Art by *Tina Lynn Stout*

The Wild Rose Press, Inc.
PO Box 708
Adams Basin, NY 14410-0708
Visit us at www.thewildrosepress.com

Publishing History
First Sweetheart Rose Edition, 2017
Print ISBN 978-1-5092-1484-6
Digital ISBN 978-1-5092-1485-3

Warriors of the Heart Series
Published in the United States of America

Dedications

To my family, who've inspired me to chase my dreams
~*~
A special thank you to my early readers:
Kailey, Carolyn, Sharon, Tara, Jill, Joe, Marie,
and Colleen, whose invaluable feedback
helped bring *Home Field* to life
~*~
To my super agent, Jessica Schmeilder,
and my Golden Wheat family,
who have believed and supported my writing
through every twist and turn
~*~
And most of all to my husband, Paul:
You are my happily ever after.

Prologue

Camp Dorstal, Afghanistan
May 22, 2012

A million stars must be out tonight. In the desert, without the city lights, the darkness was only interrupted by white points of light, which spread over John Ellis like a blanket. Tonight the moon waned into a small sliver, which would provide good cover for their mission tomorrow night.

Long after the sun had set, the heat lingered on. A refreshing breeze carried with it the mingled scents of gasoline, roasted lamb, and sewage. The juxtaposition of a modern military base erected in the middle of a primitive desert.

Sitting in the darkness, John continued to be haunted by last night's dream. He'd been with his wife in the place she called Cottonwood Field. She clung to him like a scared child, asking why he'd left her. He looked at her tear-stained face and felt her breath heavy against his neck. The memory was almost too much to bear.

Julie had asked him to stay, and he wished he could have remained in that dream forever. But something called him back. He'd told her not what she wanted to hear but what she needed to hear. When he'd awakened in his barrack, he was shaking and dripping with sweat.

Tonight, as he sat in the cool night air, he tried not to think about what his dream could mean.

Heath walked over to the grungy sofa where John sat. He plopped down next to him and tossed over a cold bottle of water. Worn springs groaned beneath them.

"Thanks." John twisted off the plastic cap and took a long drink. "You think they'll give this mission the green light tomorrow?"

"Who knows, but I'm itchin' for a fight. It's a prime opportunity to get this guy. We may not get another shot."

"Yeah, but Central Command might not have the stomach to let us do our job."

"Well, you've done this long enough to know the drill. We prepare…regardless."

John finished off the water and crushed the empty bottle in his palm. The crinkle of plastic temporarily drowned out the hum of choppers in the field nearby. Soon, he'd be boarding one of those birds. For the first time, the idea of going up in the air made him nauseous. "I don't have a good feeling about this mission."

"Your imagination messing with you, huh?" Heath laughed. "After some of our other exploits, this one should be a walk in the park—easy in, easy out."

"It looks simple on paper, but I can't stop feeling spooked." John rubbed a hand along his rough, brown beard. "What would happen to Julie if I didn't come back?"

"Stop talking like that, man." Heath kicked John's leg. "You're not going anywhere, okay."

"I need to take care of something." John stood, and then strode toward the barracks, leaving Heath sitting alone in the dark. John walked into his room and looked at the pictures taped up to the wall. Photos of his life back at home—his mom and dad, Aiden, and Julie. He studied the wedding picture he'd tacked up right next to his bed. That was the happiest day of his life and the image he wanted to see first thing when he woke up. Their wedding day was when he'd finally realized his life was about more than just guns and military operations. She became his family, and she gave him a purpose.

He reached into his foot locker and found the paper and pen he used for writing letters. Taking out two pieces of crisp, white paper, he went to a quiet corner to write. The first letter would be easy. He always knew what to say to Julie. The second one would be a great deal harder. His hand shook as he wrote the words he hoped no one would ever have to read. This one was placed in a blank envelope he'd hand to Heath before they left for their mission tomorrow. Heath might resist John's instructions at first, but he ultimately trusted Heath would see his wishes carried through.

John returned to his cot and placed both envelopes in his footlocker for safe keeping. But then again, in Afghanistan, nothing was ever safe.

Chapter One

Timber Lake, Wisconsin
July 26, 2013—14 months later

Just as Julie couldn't imagine taking one more step, she stumbled up to her front door and stepped into the refreshing, cool air of her house. Her body screamed that running today might have been the world's dumbest idea. But as dumb ideas went, agreeing to attend the banquet tonight with a bunch of pro football players tipped the scales.

A shiver of exhaustion ran up her body. The late July heat and humidity extracted its revenge on anyone who dared to be outside. That "easy" three-mile run had quickly turned into a struggle. She must look like a newborn giraffe, all wobbly knees and shaking legs. Running used to be fun. Now, that form of exercise felt like a punishment. But then again, that was kind of the point.

Her self-inflicted misery only went so far, though, because today she'd avoided going anywhere near Cottonwood Field. As she wiped sweat off her brow, an image materialized in her mind of wildflowers mixed with the sweetness of first love. Contemplating the past would have to wait for another day, when her heart could handle the memories.

After moving to the stair banister, she held on for

balance and began to stretch, working out the cramps that threatened her lower body. Her stiff muscles tightened in full-on rebellion.

She walked into the kitchen and shook her head at the card lying by her purse. "I can't believe I agreed to go to this dinner," she mumbled under her breath and tossed her cell phone on the counter. She'd been seconds away from declining the invitation when Aiden spied it sitting on the kitchen counter. Sometimes, she wished her little guy hadn't started reading so early. Aiden had bounced up and down, beside himself with excitement at the thought of his mom getting to meet the Timber Lake Warriors pro football team.

Where was the little munchkin now? Julie opened the back door to glance around the backyard. "Aiden," she said to the little boy with a mop of brown curls covering the top of his head. "Tell Grandma I'm home. I'm going upstairs to get ready for tonight."

"Okay," Aiden called back. He darted over to a bright, sunlit patch at the back of the yard. "Grandma, Mom is back from her run," he yelled out to Julie's mother, who was on her knees, weeding the small vegetable garden she'd planted in the spring. "She's going to make herself look beauuuuutiful for tonight."

Her precocious son was always so happy and full of life. Somedays, she wondered where all his energy came from. Maybe he had a secret stockpile tucked away. She loved being his mother, he was the axis her world turned upon and the glue that kept her from shattering apart. There wasn't anything she wouldn't do for him. Run across burning coals, or even go to a banquet with professional athletes, just to bring a smile to his face.

The screen door banged closed behind her, and she gingerly walked upstairs. Her laptop sat open on the desk, beckoning her to come on over and check her email one more time. Maybe, just maybe, Senator Guidall's office would finally have responded. When she'd phoned and emailed his office, she'd hoped to enlist his help in discovering the cause of her husband's death. A US Senator could provide the influence needed to break through the walls the Army continued to erect.

Her whole body sank with disappointment. A "0 new messages" icon mocked her from the screen. Zero, a perfect description of her irrelevance. One more person giving her the silent treatment. She slammed her fist onto the desk. The action reignited her anger. The Army stole her future with John, and now they denied her closure. Someone would eventually give her answers.

Even after a year, emotions were too close to the surface and threatened to bubble over with the smallest provocation. But she would never give up. She owed it to John to see this through.

She let out her breath, her lungs exhaling the burn of failure. Then she noticed the time. *Shoot.* Where had the afternoon gone? She shut off the computer and hurried down the hall to the bathroom, needing to get ready for the event that started in less than two hours.

The thought of attending this banquet alone, without John by her side with his steady support, caused her apprehension to shift into overdrive. Fear turned her normally steel spine into putty. Layers of stinky, sweaty clothes landed on the floor before she stepped into a hot shower. Julie rested her hands on the cool shower tile and let the water run over her body. Steam rose and twirled around her. Very slowly, she relaxed.

Much too soon, she climbed out of the shower, wrapped herself into a fluffy towel, and made the short march to her room. She still hadn't decided what to wear. After a brief inventory of her closet, she chose a simple, black dress looped with a gold belt. Black sling-back heels and small gold hoop earrings completed the ensemble. She sat in front of the mirror and pulled her hair into a soft bun. The humidity made corralling her stubborn curls difficult. They'd much rather behave like Medusa's snakes. After a touch of makeup and a dab of her favorite rose perfume, she was ready to go.

Julie hustled downstairs and through the kitchen, before stepping outside through the back door. "Mom, I'm leaving for the country club."

"Have fun, dear." Mary brushed her dirty hands over her shorts and slowly stood. "Aiden and I will have a wild and crazy night, so don't hurry home on our account."

Grandma's idea of a wild night equaled ordering pizza, dancing to silly songs with Aiden, playing Chutes and Ladders, and finally crashing at nine pm. Her mom, at fifty-three, had a youthful look and spirit. Julie noticed her chin-length brown hair had picked up more gray, but her skin was still smooth with only a few laugh lines around her eyes. Hopefully, time would be as kind to Julie. "I'll try to have fun, but I'll be a fish out of water. I don't expect to be gone too long. Can't imagine I have too much in common with a bunch of millionaire football players."

Aiden ran around the backyard, carrying a football

and dodging invisible defenders. When he saw her, he hurried over and gave her a big hug, his hand splayed out, being careful not to dirty her dress. "Don't forget to get lots of pictures with the Warriors. Autographs, too, but I really want pictures." His wide eyes and firm set of his lips told of just how seriously he took this opportunity. "Make sure to get Sam Matthews!"

"I'll try, Aiden, but I'm not walking around bothering people during dinner."

"You look so pretty, Mommy, those guys will want their picture taken with you!" he said with a crooked grin.

Julie's heart squeezed in her chest as she leaned down to kiss the top of Aiden's tousled hair. Inhaling the smell of him, she wished she could bottle it—a mixture of shampoo, sweat, and sunshine. She saw John's spirit reflected back in Aiden's smile…a reminder of everything still good in her life. Going tonight meant so much to her son, offering him some excitement and bragging rights with his new friends.

Waving goodbye, she walked through the back gate and toward her red Jeep parked in the driveway. Halfway there, Julie stopped, her high heels skidding on the pavement. Panicked, she checked her purse to make sure it contained the lapis lazuli bird John had given her after his first Afghanistan deployment. The stone bird was her security blanket and went with her everywhere.

After a bit of digging, a flash of blue at the bottom of her purse caught her attention. When she pulled it out, the cold stone bit into the soft flesh of her hand, its sharp edges solid and real. The physical discomfort served as a distraction of the constant pain that tore through her heart.

She got into the driver's seat and grasped the steering wheel with shaking hands, knuckles turning white. Anticipation rose in the pit of her stomach, snaking its way up her throat. She hadn't experienced a case of the butterflies this bad in a long time. Taking a deep, calming breath, she backed out of the driveway, put the Jeep in drive, and started forward down the road.

****

Reagan Harrison tossed the keys of his white Range Rover to the skinny, adolescent boy serving as valet.

The valet caught them and darted over to the driver's side of the vehicle. "I'll take good care of her, Mr. Harrison."

"Thanks, man." Reagan gave the kid a sincere smile.

The familiar entrance of Hidden Creek Country Club stood before him. The late-day heat radiated off the cement sidewalk, and small beads of perspiration emerged from his forehead. Slung over his shoulder was his expensive wool suit coat. He wanted to delay putting on the confining thing until absolutely necessary. Most of his formal attire needed to be custom tailored to fit his size and build, which was another reason why he hated having to dress up. The whole ordeal was a huge pain in the butt.

Reagan strode up the stairs, and then through the front door. A blast of air conditioning hit him like a welcome kiss. Straight ahead stood his teammate and fellow linebacker, DeMarcus Wagner. "Hey, D." Reagan gave him an easy punch on the arm. "How you feeling after practice?"

"I could hardly bring myself to come tonight." DeMarcus' deep laugh echoed off the marble floor. "I should be sitting in our room with my feet up, playing Xbox."

During training camp, the team stayed in a college dorm. The coaching staff proclaimed living together built camaraderie and helped the players focus. Reagan thought the tradition was a cruel form of torture. Not only did he have to live in a dorm for two weeks, but he had a roommate. DeMarcus snored like an old bear.

"Yeah, today was a rough one, but no training camp practice will keep me down." Reagan's deltoids begged to differ. But, if he wasn't sore then he wasn't working hard enough—and that was not acceptable. The whole season hinged on the success of training camp. These early weeks set the precedent for the challenges to come. "A bunch of us plan to hit Ed's bar after we're done here, since we have tomorrow off. You in?"

DeMarcus shook his head. "No way. You're crazy to even think about going out tonight."

"Just let me know if you change your mind. After sitting in there for a couple hours, you may feel differently." He looked at the ballroom doorway. Not that he minded spending time with the military guests of honor, but after a grueling week of training camp, he looked forward to going out and blowing off some steam. "Come on, brother, let's get a drink."

Reagan stepped into the ballroom and took in the view. The room stretched on and on, the white marble floor extended out to a wall of windows, which overlooked an emerald green golf course. The large mural painted on the wall by the dance floor showed a deep woods illustration, reminding him of his favorite hunting spot back home. Sunlight filtered through the windows, adding to the cheerful atmosphere.

The men strode over to the highly polished walnut bar. "Double whiskey on ice," Reagan told the bartender.

"Yes, sir." The young man quickly went about pouring the drink and slid it across the smooth wood toward Reagan's waiting hand.

The beveled shape of the glass fit his hand like a comfortable friend.

"Make that two," DeMarcus said. Soon, they both held cold glasses of amber liquid.

Reagan swallowed the liquor, which quickly went to work. A warm relaxation filled his body, starting from his stomach and radiating outward. His sore muscles immediately loosened. He glanced around the room, full of his teammates, both old and new, along with coaches and other Warriors staff. Mixed throughout the crowd were military service members, active duty and retired, many in full uniform.

After the off season, seeing the team back together felt good. For better or worse, they were a family. Sometimes a dysfunctional one, but a family nonetheless. The start of every season brought new members, working for their place. And old vets, like him, who balanced their time between mentoring the newbies and fighting to keep them from taking their hard-won spot on the team.

Standing around a large sign at the far end of the room were several of his teammates, locating their assigned tables on the chart.

When Reagan and DeMarcus walked up to the

group, DeMarcus found his name and scoffed at the placement. "Why do I get stuck at a table with Coach Grant and some rookies?" he asked the group. "I never bother to learn their names until after training camp. What's the point, if in the end they get sent packing?"

"That's exactly why they put you at the rookie table," answered a man's deep voice.

Robert Pappas looked like a giant teddy bear, but Reagan knew better. He was one of the best offensive linemen in the league. You were in for a fight if you played against him, or stood in his way at the food line. "Big Pappy." Reagan extended his hand.

The two men shook hands, a greeting of mutual respect.

"How about Coach Perry laying into Josh today?" Robert asked with a deep chuckle. "I thought he would cut him right then and there."

DeMarcus shook his head. "Man, I don't know how many times you can drop the ball and still expect to play professional football?"

Reagan smiled at the memory. "My pounding him into the ground over and over might be responsible for Josh's lack of success." Training camp was rough, and every guy played for himself. Josh might be his teammate, but on the practice field, Reagan's job was to make him pay for his mistakes.

"You here alone?" Robert asked Reagan. "No hot date tonight?"

Shaking his head, Reagan laughed and looked around the room. "No date...flying solo. I'm a sucker for a woman in uniform." In reality, dating was the last thing on his mind. No time. And, he already had a girlfriend, well sort of, if that's what you'd call Brynn.

She was more like a pretty distraction. Most women didn't want to play second to his passion for football, and his football career would always take top priority. He'd learned over the years to keep his relationships easy and light, especially after what had happened with Sarah.

"Only you would pick up women at a military appreciation banquet." Robert shook his head in amusement.

Realizing the event was about to begin, the small assembly of players broke apart. Most went to find their wives or girlfriends to escort them to their tables. Reagan started toward his assigned table situated across the room by the wall of windows. After stopping to talk with a few service members, he was approached by a Marine who was missing his left leg and awkwardly standing on crutches. The young man didn't even look old enough to buy a drink. He imagined himself in that situation and shuddered.

"Excuse me," the Marine said to Reagan, his face lit with awe. "I just wanted to tell you I'm a big fan. You're amazing, the way you run down the other team's quarterback. Like you're breathing dragon fire."

"I try to earn my nickname every time I step onto the field. But you're the real hero, man. Thank you for your service and your bravery." He gave the guy's shoulder a squeeze. Men like this US Marine, one who barely needed to shave, gave him pause. During the same months Reagan was out trying to score, both on and off the field, this young man had sacrificed a lot, including his leg, in service to his country.

Pride flushed on the guy's face, and he started hobbling back over to his seat.

A glance over at his assigned table showed it was almost full. Reagan noticed two other Warriors players, along with their wives, and three service members and their guests were already seated. Beside the only empty chair, he saw a mass of curly red hair, pulled up to reveal a feminine, ivory neck that led down to delicate shoulders draped in black. The woman appeared to be sitting without a partner, and the thought of being next to her made his chest tighten. He'd spent time in the company of some of the world's most beautiful women. Why was this one making his nerves ping with anticipation?

As he pulled out his chair to sit, the faint smell of roses washed over him, and when the woman turned slightly to face him, he realized his body's initial reaction had been correct. His suit jacket tugged at his shoulders, like it had suddenly shrunk, now feeling four sizes too small. He lifted his hand to loosen the knot of his tie.

Her light auburn hair was pulled away from her face, but a few wavy pieces refused to stay in place. This woman was incredibly attractive, with caramel-colored freckles sprinkled over her nose and high cheekbones. Her large blue-green eyes gave him an uneasy look, but rosy lips offered a slight smile. Reagan set down his glass on the table, realizing his night had just gotten a whole lot more interesting.

Chapter Two

Julie felt the man's presence before she saw him. His deep voice couldn't be missed, even over the hum of the crowd. She realized he meant to sit in the empty chair next to her, and a shiver traveled over her skin. The chair slid back, and Julie turned to get a look at who'd she'd be sitting beside for the next hour. From her seated position, he towered over her. Well over six feet tall, he had a solid build that looked somewhat dangerous. Her second impression was he was way too good-looking and seemingly well aware of that fact.

"Hi." He flashed a million-dollar smile as he sat. "I'm Reagan Harrison."

"Hello." Her voice cracked, suddenly flustered by his closeness. Her heart pounded as fast as a hummingbird's wings in her chest. "My name is Julie Ellis. It's nice to meet you." When she reached over to shake his hand, she noticed he smelled of peppermint. Maybe from the muscle rub athletes were so fond of or the lingering scent of gum. For some reason, she found the smell relaxed her strained nerves. His large, rough hand embraced hers, holding firm and warm. The contact made her body buzz. Startled by her reaction, she tugged back slightly.

He let it drop. "You here alone?" His wide mouth curved in a grin.

"Yes," she answered with an ache in her heart. In a

perfect world, she wouldn't be here alone.

"You can't be a member of the Warriors team, because I definitely would've remembered seeing you on the practice field. You must be a member of the military." His smile widened while his gaze roamed down her neck, before lingering on her breasts.

Seriously...is this guy for real? Her face tightened, and she crossed her arms over her chest, before noticing she'd inadvertently lifted her cleavage, giving him an even better show. Sighing, she lowered her hands, where they sat clenched on her lap. "My husband was a member of the Army Special Forces, a Green Beret," she said in a tight voice. "He was killed in Afghanistan last year. John grew up in Timber Lake, and I was invited to represent him. He was a huge fan of the Warriors football team."

Reagan's easygoing smile evaporated, his lips now firmly pressed in a tight line. "I'm sorry for your loss." He turned his attention to the glass of whiskey on the table before him.

"Thank you." She softened slightly as he acted like he understood the reason she came by herself, which wasn't to be hit on by an oversexed football player.

The sudden sound of laughter from across the table captured their attention.

Julie sat quietly and observed the wide variety of people with them. She was an outsider here...and very much alone. Reagan must have felt bad about their earlier, awkward exchange, because he began making introductions, helping her feel at ease.

The other Warriors players at their table all sat beside an elegant woman. She wondered why Reagan had come alone tonight, imagining he would have no trouble finding a date. He possessed a magnetic quality that she knew other women would find irresistible. Judging by his demeanor, he was well aware of his affect on them.

Reagan glanced over and caught her eye, another warm smile spreading over his handsome face. A smile that could bring a weak woman to her knees. His bright blue eyes sparkled with a vibrant light as he held her gaze. Before looking at the approaching waiter, she observed his sandy blond hair was slightly overgrown and unruly. The light stubble covering his strong jaw line revealed he'd been too busy to shave. The carefree look didn't match his clean-cut suit and tie. She pictured him being more comfortable kicking back in shorts and a T-shirt.

The waiter made his way around the table and approached Julie, asking for her drink order. "May I have a glass of wine, please? Do you have Riesling?"

The waiter nodded and turned to Reagan. "Another double whiskey on ice." Reagan pointed to his empty glass. The waiter scurried off to the bar to fill their requests.

"I can't get into wine, but could be I've never given it a chance."

"Wine is my best friend after a long day. I see you prefer whiskey. One taste makes my stomach turn. A bad experience…many, many years ago." Her stomach turned sour as she remembered the feeling of whiskey churning up her insides and the hangover that followed.

"Sounds interesting." Reagan set his elbow on the table and leaned in her direction. "I've got to hear this."

Did he really, or was he only being polite? Probably just being polite. Well, he had asked so she better oblige. Not like her story was anything too embarrassing. "One night during final exams, a group of us were bored and didn't want to study. Someone suggested we play poker, and after every hand, the losers would take a shot of whiskey. Not being a very good card player, I lost every game. I don't remember anything after the fifth hand."

"One bad experience can ruin a drink forever. The body has a long memory."

Yes. And those carefree, college days seemed like a lifetime ago.

"Reagan," said a man in a blue suit sitting a few chairs over. "No date tonight, huh? Was Brynn busy? Last I heard you two were a hot item."

"She's off on some movie shoot, and I didn't feel like tracking her down. Less complicated this way."

Even though Julie was now chatting with the woman sitting to her right, she listened to every word of Reagan's conversation. So, he dated the likes of Brynn Campbell, which made sense. A famous, beautiful woman to match Reagan's own striking looks.

"Yeah, enjoy the freedom while you can," the man said. "Sandy almost didn't come tonight, because one of the kids is sick. She's been checking her phone every five minutes."

"I don't know how you parents do it. Kids are way too much responsibility for me," Reagan said, before turning his attention back to Julie.

Inside, Julie cringed. Men like Reagan didn't see the value of children and, therefore, didn't deserve them. They spent their lives too self-absorbed to be bothered with a child, only to never know the joy they missed.

Noticing the Warriors' General Manager taking the podium, the conversations quieted. "Welcome, honored guests. The Warriors team is grateful to have this opportunity to acknowledge your service to our country. Through your brave sacrifice, we all enjoy the freedom you've afforded us. We would also like to thank the many family members who stay behind while their loved ones are away. The Hero's Recognition Banquet is an opportunity for our organization to connect with the community. We're pleased to have so many decorated service members in our midst. The Warriors appreciate your loyal support, even when you're stationed thousands of miles away. I thank you for attending and hope you enjoy your evening."

A round of applause followed, and servers brought out dinner plates.

After the speech, Reagan turned to face her. "That's the man responsible for drafting me." He motioned to the podium. "He's a genius at picking players who best fit together. Each position needs depth. It's what makes a team run smoothly throughout the season. With the team we have this year, we have a real shot at winning the Super Bowl."

"My husband was a big fan of the Warriors, but I never understood the appeal. Watching overpaid, pampered athletes run around the field seems pointless," she said without much thought, before sipping her wine. Realizing what she'd just said, she snapped her mouth shut. The whole table looked her way in stunned silence. She wanted to crawl under the table with embarrassment.

After a few seconds, an amused grin crept across Reagan's face. "Why don't you tell me what you really think?" he teased. "I understand how we get that reputation...we can act like a bunch of whiny overgrown children."

The other people at their table laughed along with Reagan then returned to their previous conversations.

"Compared to a military member, we are definitely overpaid. To a military wife, I'm sure that fact doesn't seem fair."

He had no idea of the struggle to pay the monthly bills with a part-time paycheck and Army survivor benefits. She looked down, hiding her reddening face. "That wasn't very nice of me to say. I'm sorry." On her lap lay a gray piece of paper, folded into a wrinkled mess. Her bad habit of nervous hand wringing had created a mangled event program.

"It's fine. You should hear the things fans yell while I'm standing on the sidelines. What you said would be considered kind."

Raising her head, she met his gaze. *Good grief...could it be humanly possible to be that good looking?* Her proximity to Reagan had turned her brain to mush. Did he realize with one look he melted her from the inside out? *Hope not.*

The guy was being nice and making her feel included. Meanwhile, she continued to stick her foot in her mouth. "Since we've already established I don't watch Warriors football, I need to ask...what position do you play?"

"I'm a linebacker. Basically, I make sure the opposing team's offense can't move the ball forward down the field. Not a very glamorous job and a bit rough...taking a pounding play after play. I may be a little crazy in the head, but I love the game."

"He's the reason our opponents have such a hard time scoring against us," the man seated on the other side of Reagan said to Julie. "They hate to see him standing across the line of scrimmage. He's a quarterback's worst nightmare."

"We all work as a team," Reagan told her. "When the defensive line and linebackers do their job, the quarterback will have a tough time getting rid of the ball. We all work together to make an unbreakable chain." While he was talking, he lined up various salt and pepper shakers, and other tableware, to demonstrate a typical defensive lineup.

Julie smiled at the passion in his voice when he talked about football. In some ways, his enthusiasm reminded her of John and how he had talked about his duties in the Army. He would've loved to be here and gotten a chance to meet the players he had enjoyed watching. He'd even followed the team while stationed in Afghanistan.

A dinner plate was placed before her. The food looked and smelled delicious. By now, her nervousness had given way to hunger. Made sense, considering she hadn't eaten anything since breakfast. Maybe that's why she felt so lightheaded. Not because of the man sitting next to her. She savored everything on her plate—ahi tuna steak, with French green beans and red potatoes.

"Stop being humble," another man said and turned to Julie. "This guy is the league's sack leader. His nickname is Reagan the Dragon for a reason. The quarterback may be the knight in shining armor, but my man Reagan is the beast who hunts him down."

The crowd around them laughed and nodded their

heads.

"So, here comes a dumb question." She looked hesitantly at Reagan, hating to sound like an idiot, again. "But what's a sack? I really should have quizzed my son about football before I came."

"I'm happy to help with your growing knowledge of football. A sack is tackling the quarterback when he still has possession of the ball. For the offense, sacks are not good because they lose yardage. They'll have farther to go to get a first down."

"I think I need to ask Aiden for a lesson. He's seven and knows so much about football. He started playing on a peewee football team this summer. I really have no idea what's going on during the games, so I just cheer along with the other parents. It's really quite embarrassing." Despite herself, she began to like talking to Reagan. Maybe, he wasn't a mindless jock after all. What if he was just a regular, nice guy?

"Football's a fun sport, I'm glad your son's playing. What position is he?"

"I'm not sure, to be honest. Aiden's the reason why I'm here tonight. Ever since he started playing football, he's become the Warriors' number one fan, just like his dad. He instructed me to get pictures with as many players as possible."

"I can help. After dinner, I'll take you around and introduce you to the guys on the team. Parading around the ballroom with such a beautiful woman will do my ego good."

Julie's face heated at the compliment. "That won't be necessary. I don't want to bother you." Hopefully, her tendency to turn red when embarrassed wasn't too noticeable. Fair skin and red hair were a deadly combination.

"I insist." Reagan's jaw was set tight.

Oh boy. She knew that look well. She'd seen it enough times with John. Both he and Reagan were men who saw the word 'no' as a challenge. Julie fought the urge to smile. "We'll see." No sense in arguing. But when their meal was done, she planned on taking a few pictures from afar and getting out of there. Home and comfy pants were calling her name.

"Have you lived in Timber Lake all your life?" Reagan asked.

"Aiden and I moved here from Fort Bragg, North Carolina last year. I wanted to be closer to family. Having been born and raised here, I knew Timber Lake is a good town for Aiden to grow up in. There's something special about a Midwestern town." She paused for a second to look out the window, seeing the sun set over a darkening golf course. Timber Lake would always hold so many special memories.

When she returned her attention back to Reagan, she saw him gazing back at her, absorbed in his own musing. How did he do that? While she held his attention, she felt like they were the only two people in the room.

Julie looked away and took the napkin off her lap, setting it down on the table as her empty dinner plate was cleared. A new glass of wine was placed in front of her, and she took a calming drink. In her purse, she heard her cell phone chirp. Since she had it set to alert for a new email, she pulled it out of her purse. Checking a phone during dinner was rude, but if the senator finally got back to her, she needed to know.

The notification said—one new email. Pushing

down any expectation, she opened her email. The subject line read—twenty percent off your next meal at Culvers. Her mood soured. What did she expect on a Friday night? The senator's office was working late?

She watched as a sharply dressed woman approached the podium, beginning a series of short speeches.

Reagan shifted his body to face the front of the room but not before giving Julie a quick wink.

She forced herself to return the smile.

The Warriors' head coach, Bill Grant, gave the concluding remarks and by then, Julie was ready to get up and move around. The cramps in her legs begged to be stretched. Finally, Coach Grant wrapped up his comments. "Please stay for another drink, enjoy the music and dancing, and have a wonderful night."

"Okay, let's go get those pictures your son asked for." Reagan stood and looked around.

"I don't want to inconvenience you," she said in a hushed tone. "I really should get going." As much as she had enjoyed herself tonight, all she wanted to do right now was crawl into bed.

"Kevin. Come over here and take a picture of the two of us."

Kevin, a stout man standing several feet away, walked over. "You sure you want a picture with this guy, ma'am?" he asked with a laugh. "I'd be willing to act as a stand-in."

"I bet you would." Reagan's lips twitched with a smile as he turned back to Julie. "Do you have a camera, or are we using your phone?"

"My phone should work." Observing the way people responded to Reagan Harrison, she knew he was a man used to getting what he wanted. She pushed back her chair to stand. The combination of tired legs and sitting too long made her lose her balance.

Reagan reached out and took hold of her elbow, capturing it in one quick motion. He helped her stabilize, and drew her up.

His touch spread a sensation of warmth, which stayed with her for the rest of the evening.

****

Reagan took hold of her arm, noticing the glow of pink spread across her cheeks. Was her blush a reaction to his touch or the result of too much wine? Hopefully he was the cause.

She was pretty, in a girl-next-door kind of way. And every time she graced him with a smile—well, his pulse kicked up a notch. His body had gone rogue, responding to the nearness of her, to her floral scent, to the stray copper curl of hair that stuck out in defiance.

As the night wore on, he noticed sadness behind her brightest smile. Those green eyes stood guard over the windows to her soul. He sensed her loss, the pain of her husband's death hung over her like the black dress she wore.

They stood side by side as someone held her phone and took their picture. He wanted to reach over and grab her around the waist, to pull her close and shield her from the world. Instead, he listened to his head and kept a respectful distance. What he felt was only a physical attraction. Tomorrow, he'd probably wake up and forget all about Julie Ellis. If he was lucky. If not, he was in for a world of trouble.

A few clicks of the phone's camera and they were done. On to the next player.

For the next half an hour, he guided Julie around the ballroom, introducing her to his teammates and getting autographs and pictures for her son. Every member of the Warriors they approached treated Julie with kindness. Reagan had noticed the questioning glances from his teammates, and he chose to ignore them. Those guys might be as close as brothers but this was none of their business. As she chatted to Robert Pappas, Julie looked like a porcelain doll standing next to the large man. Reagan stepped back to talk to DeMarcus, who stood nearby.

"Thought you'd be out of here by now." DeMarcus elbowed him in the ribs. "Some of the guys left for Ed's already."

"I've changed my mind." Reagan's gaze stayed transfixed on Julie, who looked wide-eyed at big Robert. "I need to catch up on my beauty sleep." Each day of training camp, the coaching staff dialed up the heat. Most could take it. Some broke under the pressure and jumped off the flames.

"Sure." DeMarcus bobbed his head and smirked. "And that hot little number in the black dress? She's got nothing to do with you wanting to hang out here?"

"No." He clamped his lips shut.

"Then why have you been following her around like a puppy?" DeMarcus yipped and began to pant.

"Shut it," Reagan grumbled. "Julie's a war widow. She wanted some pictures for her kid. I'm just being nice."

DeMarcus' eyebrows shot up, and he glanced at Julie. "You...nice? That would be a first. Hey, don't you think she kinda looks like Serena from Gossip Girl?"

"You watch that show? When did you turn into a teenage girl?"

"What?" DeMarcus crossed his arms. "I watch it with Angie sometimes."

"I'll have to take your word." He would happily stay single, if that meant never being forced to watch those chick shows.

"Well, you two enjoy the rest of your evening. I'm heading home and hitting the sack." DeMarcus reached out to shake his hand. "And, man...don't mess this up." He looked pointedly at Julie and smiled. "There're not many women who can tolerate looking at your ugly face for this long." He laughed and started toward his girlfriend, who stood by the door.

Reagan remained still, caught between wanting to go after DeMarcus and punch him in the face or stay close to Julie. That man knew how to rile his last nerve. Still, he and DeMarcus were tight after playing six years together. They'd survived as professional athletes, the ups and the downs. Very few people understood the pressure. DeMarcus knew. The media, the fans, the coaches. One big mistake, and your career would be finished, just like that. The public had a short memory. Hero today, disgraced tomorrow.

In that moment, Julie's gaze drifted toward him, lingered there. Heat rose in his chest. He went back to her side and made their excuses to Robert. She had a few more players to get to before everyone left for the night.

"It's okay if I don't meet every member of the team." She tucked a stray strand of hair behind her ear. "I should really be going home."

Her hair glowed like molten copper in the low light

of the ballroom. "If you're sure." He hated for her to go, knowing he would never see her again. Asking her out was out of the question. She hadn't been receptive to his stupid advances earlier, and she most definitely hadn't changed her mind as the evening progressed. If anything, she seemed more withdrawn. Plus, there was no way he'd date a single mother. Not even a beautiful one. And especially at the beginning of the season, when every single brain cell needed to be on the game of football, not on the pair of shapely legs standing before him.

"Thank you."

Her hand rested like a feather on his arm.

"For taking the time to introduce me to the team. Aiden will be thrilled I got to meet so many members of the Warriors."

An idea struck him, surprisingly simple. "How would your son like a tour of Warriors Stadium? I could make the arrangements. Maybe some afternoon after practice."

Her eyes opened wide, like pools of green under her arched auburn brows. "*Ummm*, are you sure that's okay?"

"Of course. Your son will love it. Just give me your number, and I'll contact you with the details." Her cheeks flushed pink, accentuating the tiny freckles dotting her nose. She was so different. *How refreshing.* When they talked, he was reminded of the man he used to be, before the eight figure football contract and the transforming fame that followed.

Taking out paper and a pen from her purse, she wrote her name and number then handed it to him. "Please don't feel obligated. I wouldn't hold it against you if you change your mind."

He took the paper, folded it, and slid it into the front pocket of his pants. "I won't." They walked side by side in silence to the main entrance of the country club, said goodbye, and Reagan watched her move toward her car, into the muggy heat of the night.

Chapter Three

Rolling over in bed, Julie looked through squinted eyes at the digital clock on her night stand. The early morning sun filtered through the delicate curtains that covered the east-facing windows. She wished she could stay in bed a little longer, but Aiden had Sunday morning football practice, and she needed to get moving. Slowly standing, she eased her bare feet to the cool wooden floor.

Given the choice, she would have stayed asleep, lost in a memory from long ago. But reality crashed in like an unwelcome guest. Her dream last night had felt so real—her past with John had been real at one time.

In her dream, she'd been with John, together in Cottonwood Field, the smell of grass and flowers drifting through the air. The date was the Fourth of July, the sun had started to set, and it was time to go home. Earlier, they'd shared a picnic by the creek. She packed up the leftover chicken and fruit salad. "The fireworks are starting soon." She grabbed his hand, pulling him toward the path home. "I don't want to miss them."

"I'm not ready to go yet." As he moved his head, his brown hair flopped over his eyes. Drawing her close, he began kissing her.

The kisses held a delicious enchantment, which left her seventeen-year-old body hungry for more.

"We've got to talk about what will happen next month. I need to know you'll be okay."

"I don't want you to go, but I understand why. I've always known you'd enlist in the Army, and the day would come when you would have to leave me to start your training. I want you to live out your dream." She rested against his chest. He was solid and lean, almost a foot taller than her. Because of their height difference, her head came to rest perfectly over his heart and she felt its steady, reassuring rhythm.

"Basic Training's just the beginning. The recruiter told me to expect three to four more months of extra instruction before deployment. Then, I can be sent anywhere in the world." John ran his fingers through the curls in her hair. "The worrying will be hard on you, and I don't like putting you through that."

She raised her head, looking deeply into his dark brown eyes. An inner strength bubbled up, almost taking her by surprise. She would survive this. John would have enough obstacles over the next few months without worrying about her, too. "I still have my last year of high school. Plenty of people will watch over me while you're gone. We won't be apart forever."

"I'm afraid to say goodbye," he whispered in her ear. "What if I fail and never pass the Special Forces assessment? Would you still want me?"

"No matter what happens, I'll always love you. Don't ever forget." She stood on her tiptoes to bring her lips to his.

Their tender kiss turned urgent as their time together was coming to an end. He pulled her down onto the grass, and they lay side by side. Their young love felt as powerful as a summer storm. She sought sanctuary in John's protective embrace. He wrapped his arms around her tightly, and rolled her to lay over him. A moment she'd wished would never end.

But those peaceful days would soon be over. They'd be separated indefinitely. Julie didn't want to think about the future. In that moment, she was living for the here and now. She would stay dedicated to John and to the promise of their life together.

John reached over to pick a flower off the ground and placed it in Julie's hair.

"I'll wait forever. Our souls are connected. You may be on the other side of the world, but you'll always be here." She pointed to her heart. "I know you'll come back to me." Standing, she held out her hand to pull him up then they started on the path that led home.

That was the last thing Julie remembered before waking. Ten years had passed since she and John shared that moment in the field. So much had changed since then. His death brought an end to all those young hopes and dreams of living a nice quiet life, raising their children, and growing old together. She'd been robbed.

Now, showered and dressed, she pulled her hair into its usual ponytail. Julie moved downstairs to find Aiden sitting in front of the TV, eating a bowl of Fruity Flakes. His usual early morning position. "We need to leave for practice in forty-five minutes," she called out as she headed into the kitchen.

"Yeah, I know," he replied, not taking his gaze off his cartoon.

Julie smiled and hit the brew button on the coffeemaker. She was very lucky to have Aiden. He was the light of her life, the reason she got out of bed each morning. Aiden was a perfect example of a child's resiliency. She knew he missed his father, but John had been absent for over half of his young life. In some ways, their life now wasn't much different from when John was deployed, only Aiden's dad would never come home.

If only she could step into the past and stay there. More than anything, she wanted to turn back the clock and be a whole family again. She could pretend—trick her mind into thinking John was only deployed. But that was a temporary fix. Reality could be as painful as a knife, ripping through her fantasy and piercing deep in her heart. Her grief needed an outlet. And that's why she wouldn't stop pushing for the Army to be held accountable for John's death. She'd never give up.

From the kitchen, she looked into the family room to see Aiden still hadn't moved from his spot on the sofa. His eyes stared unblinking at the TV screen. Hadn't he already watched this episode like a hundred times? Drying her hands on a towel, she went over to the doorway that separated the two rooms. "Aiden, go now and get changed for practice," she ordered. Her exciting news would have to wait. Once he found out, he wouldn't be talking about anything else.

He gave her a quick look and pushed the remote to turn off the TV. "Going, Mom," he replied and ran upstairs.

****

"Harrison," the linebacker coach hollered across the practice field. "Stop daydreaming and get started on those drills."

Reagan spat out the water he'd squirted in his mouth only a few seconds earlier. The water was warm and sour on his tongue. He played on an NFL professional team. Somebody get him some cold water. He jogged toward the twenty-yard line and led the group of linebackers on a backpedal weave. Knees bent and hips in position, he shuffled back, following the white line on the grass until he reached the other side of the field. He turned, bent his knees, and made the return trip.

Meanwhile, the linebacker coach continued to shout from the sidelines.

He blocked out the useless noise and focused on listening to his body. Muscle memory remained a loyal friend. After years of training, his body knew the drill. The muscles in his legs and hips strained with exertion, but he kept pushing—faster and faster, not losing form.

When he finished, the small group of men huddled to get instructions from the coach before getting in line to run up against the one-man sled. The bodies around him radiated heat and smelled awful. Every face looked flushed and wet. Air that had been cool hours before now sizzled under the hot sun. Add humidity to the mix, and they had a recipe for a miserable morning practice.

A cold shower and calorie-laden buffet awaited him across the street, in the team's facility inside the stadium. But first, he had to get through the training camp session. On cue, his stomach clenched then rumbled.

"Looks like Harrison's ready for a break," the coach said, standing next to the sled. "Complete this drill to perfection, and you can take ten. And I mean perfect." Spit flew out of his mouth with the word 'perfect.'

Internally, Reagan groaned, but he lined up, got into a six-point stance, and launched forward until his body impacted the foam body on the sled. He pushed against it, using his weight to move the heavy sled ten yards.

His quads and glutes burned with the effort. Stepping off to the side to watch his fellow linebackers complete the drill, Reagan allowed his mind to wander. He wondered what Julie was doing right now. How many times already that morning had he gotten distracted by the memory of auburn hair and green eyes? Too many.

Had she had a good time two nights ago at the Hero's Banquet? He hoped so. And when he called her later, he hoped she'd agree to meet him for a tour of the stadium. She'd have her kid along. That would be okay. He could handle being with the kid for an hour or so.

"Man, what's going on with you?" DeMarcus came up to stand next to him on the sidelines. "You're over here in la-la-land with a stupid grin on your face. Why are you smiling? You should be over by the coach, yelling at the rookies."

Reagan turned his attention to the sled and a rookie linebacker, who'd just lost his footing. Instead of pushing the sled forward, he kept his body too high and fell back.

"At this rate," DeMarcus went on, "we'll be here all day."

Normally, this situation wouldn't bother him. Sure, he was hungry, hot, and tired, but he loved being out on the field, even for training. Today, though, he had other things on his mind. For one, the piece of paper with Julie's number, back in the locker room. He wanted to call her now and hear the sound of her voice.

Julie Ellis had gotten under his skin. Luckily, his attraction to her was just a little itch, nothing more.

****

Julie was already seated when Chrissy entered the Gingerbread Café. "Over here," Julie said over the noise of lively chatter, waving her hand in the air.

Chrissy walked over to their table, and her curly brown hair bounced up and down around her smiling face.

The aroma of roasting coffee and baked goods filled the air. Customers occupied almost every table, drinking coffee and chatting—lazily spending their Sunday morning.

"I'm getting a coffee, be right back." Chrissy went over to the counter to place her order.

Chrissy Taylor was five-feet-two-inches of pure energy. She still had a cheerleader's body, small and compact, something Julie envied. Some people called her hyper, but Julie figured she was so full of life that, on occasion, her energy just burst out.

Moments later, she joined Julie, a steaming hot, extra large ceramic coffee mug and a blueberry scone perched precariously in her hand. She set them on the table, pulled out an empty chair, and made herself comfortable. "What ya working on?" Chrissy asked before taking a bite of scone.

"I'm updating patient logs." Julie pointed to the stacks of papers placed before her. She loved her job as a Pediatric Physical Therapist, and the kids she worked with made all the extra effort worthwhile. "I can't get caught up. I was wrong when I thought only working part-time would mean less paperwork."

Chrissy gave a sympathetic smile. "My students think I go home after school and sit around and watch TV. They don't understand all the homework they complain about needs to be graded by someone, and that someone is me. I can't tell you how many nights I grade papers until bedtime." She stopped talking long enough to take a sip of coffee. "Being a grown-up stinks!"

"I agree." Julie laughed out loud. "What I wouldn't give to be sixteen again. Not a care in the world. But we were in such a hurry to grow up and become responsible adults. What were we thinking?" Funny to think her wild-child friend had grown up to become a responsible fourth-grade teacher. Now, she was in charge of a classroom full of kids, keeping them out of trouble.

Chrissy's blue eyes peered over her large cup of coffee. "Obviously, we weren't."

The two friends engaged in small talk around their table. They were seated before a window, which overlooked the park where Aiden had football practice. Outside, people strolled past the café, enjoying the beautiful, summer morning.

Julie gazed out the window, watching a couple walk by, hand in hand. They were young and in love. Their happiness burned like a shot of whiskey, and the sting traveled straight to her heart.

"Hey, Jules, you okay? You look a million miles away."

Sighing, Julie turned her attention to her friend. "I'm fine," she insisted. "Sometimes I get lost in my own head."

"Just don't go too far." Chrissy reached across the

table to take hold of her hand. Moisture shone in her eyes. "I love you, Jules."

"Love you, too, Curly-Q."

Chrissy's giggle cleared away their sober mood. "You know I hate that nickname. Now...tell me about the banquet. I bet the country club was gorgeous. Did you get to meet many players? How was the food?"

"One question at a time." Holding up a hand, Julie laughed. Chrissy always knew how to pull her back into the sunlight. "Actually, the banquet was better than expected." She watched as Chrissy's face lit up with excitement. "The club was very nice, and the food was amazing. John would've loved it."

"I know you wish he had been there with you." Chrissy patted her hand.

Julie paused for a few seconds to tuck away her grief like she'd done so many times before. Her dark moods concerned her friends and family. She understood that. So, she painted on a smile, like a shining masquerade mask, and told Chrissy every detail—what she ate, what she drank, which famous Warriors players she met.

"That's so cool. I'm glad you decided to go. Did you get autographs for Aiden?"

"I got an autograph and picture of almost every Warriors player there." Julie remembered the man who'd made Aiden's wish possible. At the thought of him, a smile naturally formed. "I had the good luck of sitting next to a player who, after dinner, spent the rest of the night tracking down his teammates."

"Wow, that's fantastic! Who's your knight in shining armor?"

"Reagan Harrison." His name on her lips sent a

small thrill up her spine.

Chrissy let out a loud whoop, which attracted the attention of the people seated around them. "Holy smokes, girl, he's the hottest football player in the country. You're so lucky. Did you get a picture taken with him, too?"

Julie nodded and pulled out her cell phone. "Here are the pictures." She showed Chrissy the screen. "This first one is of Reagan and me."

Bug-eyed, Chrissy nearly choked on a bite of scone. She recovered and gave the picture another look. "You two make a super-cute couple. I bet his girlfriend was jealous."

"He came alone. I overheard him talking about his girlfriend, Brynn Campbell, you know the movie star. She was off somewhere on a shoot."

"You look so pretty." Chrissy's gaze stayed focused on the picture. "I bet he didn't want to let you out of his sight."

"Don't let your imagination run away with you. Reagan just felt sorry for me, a war widow, sitting at the banquet all alone. He was kind, even if he was a shameless flirt and slightly self absorbed." His attention had made her feel alive for the first time in a long time. "He offered to take Aiden and me on a tour of the stadium."

"Wow."

Julie had made her best friend speechless. "I haven't told Aiden yet. I'm waiting until after I hear from Reagan. I'd hate for Aiden to be disappointed if the tour doesn't work out." Noticing the time, Julie took one last drink of her coffee then gathered her papers into a neat pile.

Chrissy stood to get ready to leave. "My dear, dear friend," she said in her best teacher tone. "After looking at the picture of Reagan standing next to you, and seeing the look in his eyes, I don't think you'll be disappointed."

Chapter Four

Thursday afternoon, Julie moved through the house, mindlessly picking up the toys scattered around. Toys multiplied almost like mosquitoes every time she turned her back. She really needed to do a better job of teaching Aiden to pick up after himself. After putting away small cars, plastic army men, and wooden train tracks into their appropriate containers, she picked up the phone to call her mom. "Hey, did you get that clog out of the drain?" Julie asked, with her cell phone cradled between her shoulder and ear. She brushed on sparkling sea green nail polish onto her right thumbnail.

The sound of her mom's laughter came through the phone. "I tried the Plumber Gel stuff, but the darn thing won't budge. Time to call a real plumber. What's the name of the outfit you used for the leak in the bathroom?"

"Down The Drain. I have their card somewhere," she said, before glancing at her shiny nails. *Don't want to mess up all my hard work rummaging through my purse for a business card.* "I'll give it to you tomorrow." Having Mom live right down the block was wonderful. When she lived at Fort Bragg, she'd missed having her close by.

"Oh, that's right. You're not coming for dinner tonight. I bet Aiden's excited to see the inside of Warriors Stadium."

"It's all he's talked about for the past few days. I've learned more about the Warriors football team than I ever thought possible. Aiden thinks he's meeting a real life superhero."

"To a young boy, Reagan Harrison probably is a superhero." Her mom paused. "Chrissy told me you declined her invitation to the party this weekend. Honey, you need to get out there and live your life. Ever since you've moved back to Timber Lake, you've become a hermit, isolating yourself. I'm glad you went to the banquet last Saturday. Meeting new people is good for you. I love you, and John loved you. He'd want you to live your life to the fullest."

Julie sighed in resignation. "I know, but right now I'm doing the best I can. My focus needs to stay on Aiden. I don't have time for a social life."

"I know your life hasn't been easy lately. You've persevered through tough times, and you're an incredibly strong woman. I just don't want you to wake up someday, regretting that so many good things passed you by. Don't lose any more precious time to grief. Now go and have fun, and I'll see you tomorrow for our lunch date."

"Thanks, Mom, I love you, bye."

"Love you, too, baby. Bye."

Julie pressed End, but remained seated at the kitchen table. Her mother was right, of course, but she didn't have the energy to fight through her sorrow. She missed John every minute of every day. At times, she'd go over to her computer to write him an email, wanting to share some news then remember he was gone. That realization always hit her like a physical blow to the heart.

Don't lose any more time to grief, her mom had said. So far, nothing had given her any reason to expect a good future. A void in her life existed that she couldn't imagine being filled. But if she wanted to really start living again, she needed to find a reason for hope.

Would she ever get a straight answer from the Army? They were acting as slippery as a greased pig. And while she ran around after it, the truth remained just out of reach. Bringing home his body to lay him to rest in Arlington National Cemetery wasn't enough. Why was he dead? And who was responsible?

Aiden rushed into the house through the back door. "Mom, when do we leave for the stadium?" His eyes shone wild with excitement.

"In two hours. You need to shower before we go. You're a mess." She grinned at her son, who was covered head-to-toe in dirt.

"Okay, but I want to finish mine and Mike's race track in the yard."

"You have thirty minutes, then it's upstairs with you. We need to make you look presentable for Mr. Harrison. I don't want him thinking I have a mud monster for a son."

"Yippee!" Aiden shouted. "I can't wait to meet him. I bet he's as big as Mr. Miller from school. Mr. Miller told us that he could've played football in the pros if it wasn't for his bum knee. Can I get ice cream from the truck when it comes by?"

Her son's mind worked like a crazy train, jumping from one thought to another. She shooed him outside. "Go outside and finish your track."

Aiden bolted out the door and jumped high up into

the air, like he was part kangaroo. Julie heard him tell his friend Mike they had to hurry—he needed to take a shower before he met Reagan Harrison.

Her son was her biggest blessing—more valuable than all the money and fame in the world.

****

The time was a few minutes before four o'clock, and Reagan roamed past the staff entrance of Warriors Stadium. He'd paced back and forth for the past fifteen minutes. Every so often, he would look out the glass doors for Julie's car. If not for seeing Julie, he would've been in a crappy mood. Today had been a rough practice, with the coaches running the team ragged. Their tough love was part of training camp, getting men in shape for the season—the pain came with being a professional athlete. But tell that to his body, which ached like he'd been run over by a herd of buffalo. And tomorrow he'd go through the process all over again.

At four o'clock on the dot, he spotted a Jeep drive into the staff parking lot, Julie's distinct red hair unmistakable through the windshield. He opened the door to meet her.

She stepped out of the car as Reagan approached.

"Hi, Julie." His voice cracked. *Get it together, Harrison, you're not sixteen.* He cleared his throat. "Nice to see you again."

"Hi." She went to the back door to let her son out of his booster seat. "Thanks for arranging this. Aiden's really excited, so I hope you're ready. He may give you a run for your money."

"I'm ready for anything." His wide smile might seem too eager, so he dialed it back a notch. Spending time with her son would remind him of why he didn't date single moms. Although he was incredibly attracted to her, he figured a widow with a young son was too much responsibility. At this point in his professional career, he was very careful of who he let into his life. He didn't need any distractions. This tour with Aiden should shake loose any romantic notions he had toward the kid's mother.

Suddenly, seemingly out of nowhere, a dark-haired boy sprung out of the back seat and landed directly before Reagan. The kid was struck speechless. His wide, round eyes mirrored his gaping mouth.

"Hi, Aiden." He shot him a friendly smile. He bent down and held out his oversized hand to shake Aiden's. "I'm Reagan Harrison. Your mom told me you're a big Warriors fan. Would you like to come with me and take a look inside the stadium?"

Aiden gave a slow nod and looked over at Julie.

She took hold of Aiden's hand and gave him a soft nudge with her elbow. "He's usually not this quiet. Enjoy the silence while it lasts because once he finds his tongue, he'll be talking non-stop."

Laughing, Reagan motioned for them to follow him toward the building. They walked to a large, glass-fronted visitor's entrance. "The stadium is pretty quiet right now, but during home games the parking lots fill up with fans for their tailgate rituals. This place can seat seventy thousand people, and the stadium can get unbelievably loud." He held open the door for Julie and her son.

As they entered, their footsteps clicked on the black granite floors. Historical Warriors photographs surrounded them. The team colors of red and silver were everywhere, from the paint on the walls to the modern lobby furniture.

"I'm taking you to the front offices first," Reagan said.

Julie and Aiden followed along into a large central room, with a half dozen office suites attached to this main hub. Behind a glass-topped desk sat a petite, dark-haired woman whose fast clicks on the keyboard sounded like a snare drum. She raised her gaze as the door closed behind them, her pink reading glasses perched on the tip of her nose.

"Julie and Aiden, I'd like to introduce you to the person who makes this organization run, Rosalie Turner. Rosie, these are the friends I was telling you about earlier. I'm showing them around the stadium."

Rosalie came from behind her desk, approached them with her short stride, and gave Reagan a hug.

She was just shy of five feet tall, and Reagan knew he looked like a giant in comparison.

"Very nice to meet you, Julie and Aiden. I work as the office manager for the front office staff. That includes the General Manager, Vice-President and all other operational management. My job is to make sure things run smoothly around here."

"And she does it well. Thanks for letting us bug you for a few minutes." He had a lot more to show them.

"I'm glad to meet you. Aiden and I are very fortunate to have Reagan showing us around. You have a beautiful office."

"Well," Rosalie said, walking over to Julie. "He may try to hide his soft side, but under that rough and tough exterior is a heart of gold. Don't let him try to pretend otherwise." As she went back to her desk, she gave Reagan a quick pinch on the arm.

He let out a loud laugh. *Time to move along.* "That's enough destruction of my bad boy reputation for one day. See you around."

"Bye." Julie followed him out the door, still holding onto a silent Aiden's hand.

As soon as they exited the room, Aiden finally piped up. "I'm almost as tall as her."

Reagan and Julie's eyes met. Her smile felt like a full force kick to his chest, rattling something inside him he'd thought was long dead. "Come on, kid." He put a hand on Aiden's shoulder. "Let's go see the locker room."

That was all the encouragement Aiden needed. The next hour was filled with questions, comments, and even suggestions on how Reagan could improve his game.

By the time they got to the field, Reagan wondered how to get back that shy, quiet boy he'd met in the parking lot.

As soon as their feet touched the grass, Aiden took off running across the field. He zigzagged toward the end zone and finished with a touchdown dance.

Reagan did spend some time around kids and loved his nieces and nephew. And then he made visits to the Children's Hospital. But being around them was exhausting, and Aiden possessed an endless energy supply. Where was the sign-up sheet for that?

Overall though, this tour was going better than he'd expected. Aiden seemed like a good kid, and Reagan really wanted to keep seeing the beautiful smile on Julie's face. Plus, the kid knew a lot about football for someone who was growing up without a father.

"I'm sorry about Aiden." Julie shook her head. "He's just so excited to be here, and you're a larger-than-life hero to him. Thanks for being so kind and patient."

"I remember being young and idolizing my sports heroes. I'd do the same thing if I was in his shoes."

Julie's gaze followed Aiden around the field, a wide smile lit up her face.

Outside, under the late afternoon sun, she was naturally lovely. Her glossy hair was pulled up in a high ponytail, and her navy shorts weren't too long to hide her shapely legs. He had a sense that she was unaware of her affect on men. She had an effortless style that didn't try to attract attention, but did anyway.

Reagan shook those thoughts out of his head. The way the soft curve of her neck beckoned him to go over and plant a kiss on the soft spot behind her ear shouldn't be such a strong temptation. He needed to focus on something else. Anything else. Focus on her kid—that should break the spell. So, he watched Aiden run around the football field, in all his pretend glory.

Julie walked across the field, and then took a seat on the home team bench.

He followed her lead and sat next to her, making sure to leave at least a foot of empty space.

"I can't believe how big the stadium looks from here." Julie's gaze roamed around at the green field spread out before them.

A large, dark scoreboard was set off to one side, and tens of thousands of stadium seats surrounded them.

"Playing in front of a full house must be exciting. I can't even imagine what that must feel like."

"At my first pro game, I was so nervous I threw up right before running onto the field. I still get amped before every game. It's pretty exhilarating…the crowd and the noise. I'm very lucky to do this for a living."

A football bounced off of his feet, and he heard a small voice pleading to play catch. How could he say no? He picked up the football and told Aiden to start running. Reagan passed him the football, but it slipped through Aiden's outstretched hands and fell to the ground. He laughed as the kid scooped the ball and held it to his chest then took off toward the goal posts, going in for a touchdown.

****

As Julie watched them play, her eyes welled with tears. Her heart warmed to see Aiden so over-the-moon happy.

Reagan instructed Aiden on how to catch the football with his body, instead of just with his hands. Both their faces were tinted pink. Reagan's from a slight sunburn that tipped his nose and cheeks, while Aiden's was from pure exertion.

Frowning, Aiden listened to the instructions. His whole body glowed with awe and adoration.

Reagan threw the ball gently to Aiden. For the tenth time in a row, the ball slipped from his grasp. Reagan's display of patience was award-worthy. Even a saint would be frustrated, but time after time, he only yelled back words of encouragement.

While they played, she noticed Reagan looked more natural today, in the khaki shorts and blue button-down shirt, rather than the expensive suit he'd worn at the banquet. The light cotton, short sleeve shirt accentuated his wide shoulders and thick arms. His blond hair was messy but still looked stylish. Chrissy was right—he was hot. Over six feet of all-American hunk. Luckily, she was just experiencing an innocent physical attraction. No danger of a broken heart. At this point in her life, she wouldn't fall for any man, let alone a football star with a Hollywood girlfriend.

Noticing the time, Julie got off the bench and walked in the direction of an outsized Aiden tackling a much-larger Reagan. "Aiden," she shouted, waving to get his attention. "We should probably be going now. Mr. Harrison had a busy day, and I'm sure he's ready to go home."

Reagan lay flat on his back with Aiden pinning him to the ground. With one motion, Reagan stood and brought Aiden along. He walked over to Julie, carrying her son safely tucked under his sturdy arm.

"Awwww," Aiden said in a fit of giggles. "We're having so much fun."

"Yeah, I can see that." Maybe too much fun. Aiden would soon be a sleepy puppy.

Placing Aiden back on the ground, Reagan came over to stand next to her. "I heard the kid's stomach growl and I'm getting kinda hungry, too. How about you two join me for dinner? There's this burger and custard place a few blocks from here…Fuzzy's. The joint isn't fancy, but they have the best burgers in Timber Lake. What do you say? I hate to eat alone."

"Can we, Mom?" Aiden asked while hopping around, pulling on her arm. "Reagan doesn't want to eat alone."

His concern for his new friend was endearing. She was outnumbered and knew it. "All right, let's all go to Fuzzy's. We wouldn't want poor Mr. Harrison to eat alone."

Reagan and Aiden high-fived, and Aiden raced toward the tunnel.

As they followed side by side, Julie turned to Reagan. "Thank you for doing this for him." She touched his arm, sending an electric charge surging through her, multiplying as the sensation traveled down her spine.

Reagan swallowed and buried his hands in his pockets. "It's no problem," he finally said. "I'm having just as much fun as Aiden is."

Walking off the field, she wondered if Reagan really meant what he'd said. Did he really enjoy playing with Aiden? This all would be a mistake if Reagan ended up disappointing her fatherless son. But when she watched him lift Aiden and drape him over one shoulder, she knew he was sincere. And she couldn't have been more delighted.

****

They decided to drive their own cars to the restaurant. When they entered, the reaction Reagan received amazed her. The scene looked like the parting of the Red Sea. Everyone made way for the popular football player and his guests.

"You can let Mr. Harrison get a table ahead of us," a short, balding man said to the hostess. "After last season, he deserves it!" The group with him nodded their approval.

With a few handshakes and high-fives, they were led to a booth. Reagan was popular because he strived for excellence. How hard did he have to work in order to maintain that standard? Did the pressure ever get too much?

The TV mounted on the wall was currently tuned to a news show. The screen flashed footage of pre-season training camp. Stopping, she watched the video clip of a man catching the football, only to be taken down by a much-larger man. Was that Reagan? She looked over and saw his proud smile. *Wow*. She never wanted to be on the receiving end of one of those tackles.

Julie slid onto her seat, scooting over to make room for Aiden. Wonderstruck, she watched Aiden get seated across from her, next to Reagan.

A young waitress rushed over with their menus, ogling Reagan.

He reacted calmly to the unwanted attention and excitement his presence incited. Motioning to Julie, he requested the waitress take her drink order first.

"My son will have a root beer, and I'll take an ice tea with lemon," Julie said.

Reagan ordered an ice water, and the eager server went to fill their order.

"You get this kind of reception everywhere you go?" Julie questioned. "Does this ever get old? All the hero worship and people falling all over themselves to impress you?"

He looked amused by her puzzled expression. "The attention does get tiring. Since Timber Lake is on the small side for a city that has a pro football team, there are not many places I can go unrecognized. Luckily, the town is used to seeing us players out and about."

"I'll never understand why people idolize athletes," she said, and then let out a laugh. "Here I go again. My husband thought the Warriors team walked on water. So who am I to judge?"

Reagan turned to the boy sitting right next to him. "So, Aiden, what's your favorite part of Warriors Stadium?"

At the sound of his name, Aiden straightened in attention. He'd been eyeing the wall of video games. "I thought the locker room was neat. Do you really have to wash in the big shower? I would wait until I got home to take a bath."

Reagan laughed. "Yes, we all shower in that big room. We get very smelly by the end of a game."

Their drinks arrived, and the waitress asked Reagan if he was ready to order. He again motioned to Julie. The girl blew out a breath before turning her attention to Julie. After taking Julie and Aiden's meal order with a trembling hand, she finally turned her attention to Reagan.

While she listened to Reagan order a seemingly endless amount of food, Julie's jaw dropped. How could any one person eat so much?

"What? I take it you've never eaten a meal with a football player during pre-season training."

"I'm glad I don't have to pay your grocery bills. I only cook for Aiden and myself, so we don't go through a lot of food. But when John was home, I would make huge meals. He was always so happy to eat real food after months of crummy Army provisions."

"My daddy fought in the Army," Aiden said with a quiet voice. "But he died. We moved here to be closer to Grandma."

"Your dad was a very brave man, and you should be proud of him." Reagan then turned to Julie. "I'm sorry for your loss. I know that phrase sounds like hollow sympathy, but I really mean it. The men and women fighting in our military are the real warriors."

"Thank you." Sincere compassion shone in his eyes. Since she'd gotten to know Reagan, she'd thrown out the 'dumb jock' tag. There were many layers to him, and she liked what she found once she started to peel them back.

Their food soon arrived, and the waitress had enough sense to serve Julie and Aiden first, which earned her a smile from Reagan.

"Mom, can I go play video games?" Aiden asked.

"After you finish your meal." She pointed to his plate, filled with a cheeseburger and fries.

"I'm glad I don't have to eat all the food Reagan got." Aiden looked wide-eyed at the spread.

"Someday, maybe in high school, this won't look like so much. If you're still playing football, you'll need to eat a lot to stay big and strong." Reagan flexed his arm.

Oh, my. The arc of his huge bicep, which should be given its own zip code, practically made Julie swoon.

"I can see my food budget going up, even as we speak." She popped a salty fry in her mouth. To think of Aiden as a teenager was hard to imagine. Since he was only seven-years-old, that day seemed far away. In between Aiden's chatter, she asked about Reagan's football season—when it started and how many games they played during a season.

"We play four pre-season games during training camp," Reagan explained. "Then, the regular season starts in September, which is thirteen games long. Maybe more if we make the playoffs."

Aiden piped in. "My football team plays ten games. We've won two games and lost four. How many do we have left, Mom?"

Julie reached over to grab a napkin from the dispenser on the table, and then handed it to Aiden. She motioned for him to wipe off his ketchup-covered mouth. "You have four more. The next one's this Sunday. You'll be playing Michael's team."

"I play wide-receiver. I have to catch the ball, run to the end-zone, and try not to get caught or drop the ball. I drop the ball sometimes," Aiden informed him.

"I have this Sunday off with no practice. Would it be all right if I come and watch your game?" Reagan asked Aiden.

The boy bounced on the booth and let out a shout. "That would be so cool! My friends didn't believe me when I said I met you. Will you really come?"

"Only if it's okay with your mom." The arch of Reagan's eyebrows rose higher over his bright, blue eyes.

Both of them looked across the table at Julie, expectation all over Aiden's face. Julie wanted to say no. She didn't want her son too attached to Reagan. He was a popular, hard-hitting, and very attractive football player. And she was a single mother of an impressionable son. This situation could go wrong in so many ways.

"All right." Finally agreeing against her better judgment. "You're a saint to spend your free time watching a youth football game. Maybe I can take the opportunity to learn something about the game, if you wouldn't mind giving me a lesson from the sidelines."

"Sure, you'll be an expert before you know it."

I highly doubt that. "I'll give you the time and directions before we leave."

"This is going to be the best game ever!" Aiden said. "Can I go play some video games? I'm done with my food."

Reagan handed him several quarters, and Aiden was off and running.

Their waitress came back to see if they needed anything else, and then laid the bill on the table.

Julie opened her mouth to offer to pay her portion of the bill.

Reagan shook his head before a word left her lips. "This was my idea and my treat." He pulled out his wallet and grabbed two fifty-dollar bills.

Their lucky waitress had just earned herself a huge tip.

With his wallet put away, Reagan took a pack of gum out of his pocket and put a piece in his mouth. He then offered her a piece, which she accepted.

Peppermint gum. A good scent on him.

Reagan's cell rang, and he picked it off the table.

The name *Brynn* was clearly displayed on the screen, and she shifted her gaze toward Aiden, who was now gripping the steering wheel on a racing video game.

He hit the ignore button and set the phone face down.

Looking back at him, she caught a quick flash of uncertainty cross his face, like he wanted to take the call but didn't want to be rude. "Thanks for everything." She grabbed her purse to get ready to leave. "You really went out of your way to make Aiden feel special. I don't know how I'll ever be able to thank you for your kindness. But don't worry, it can be our secret." She gave him a teasing smile. "Wouldn't want to spoil your bad boy reputation."

Breaking eye contact, he shrugged his broad shoulders and his gaze dropped to his lap. "No need to thank me, plus my reputation could use a little sprucing up." He shifted his gaze back to her and leaned forward, his hands resting on the table between them.

He now held something in his right hand. The mystery item was hidden in his fist, which lay face up on the table. As he opened his hand, one finger at a time, several quarters were exposed. Motioning his head toward the video-game machines, he gave her a challenging grin. "Ready to play, or are you chicken?"

She sent him a wary look. He was very charming and seemed to be an expert at using it to get his way. Sliding out of the booth, she lifted her head to stare him straight in his blue eyes. "Let's go," she said, pinching her lips tight to cover her growing amusement. "You better bring your A game, because I play to win."

Chapter Five

Three days later, Mary sat with her daughter at the kitchen table, deep in conversation. They both looked to see Aiden stumbling down the stairs, heading over to the sofa and his favorite cartoons.

"Mommy, can you get me something to eat?" he asked in a raspy voice.

"Sure, what would you like sweetie?" Julie asked the little boy who was sporting a severe case of bed head.

"I want a bowl of Fruity Flakes…and toast with peanut butter…and scrambled eggs…and orange juice, oh and a big glass of milk."

"I don't think all that will fit in your tummy. How about eggs and juice?"

Aiden nodded, and Julie went to prepare his breakfast.

Mary moved into the family room to say good morning to her grandson. She snuggled next to his little body on the sofa and gave him a kiss on the cheek. "Morning, sunshine."

"Hi, Grandma," he said, leaning into her. "Reagan said when you play football you need to eat a lot. I'm going to eat a lot today so I can play good. Grandma, did you know Reagan is coming to watch my game today? He's picking us up in his fancy car."

"Your mom told me, you're a lucky boy."

Reagan's kindness meant so much to her grandson. He craved the attention of a male role model, someone who took an interest in his achievements, a man in the stands to cheer him on.

"Reagan's really tall and strong." Aiden flexed his lanky arms. "He showed me this place in the stadium called the weight room, and he lifts these heavy weights to get stronger. I want to do that, too, but Mom said I have to wait 'til I get older."

"Your mom's right. Did you have fun at Warriors Stadium?"

"Yes." As he shook his head, his hair flopped over his eyes. "It was great, and I got to run on the field. Reagan even played football with me. Grandma, what if he thinks Mom's pretty? He's always looking at her and smiling."

"Well, your mom is very pretty, and I wouldn't be surprised if Reagan thinks so, too." Mary watched her daughter bring over Aiden's breakfast plate. She had no doubt any man who spent time with Julie would find her attractive. Maybe, she hoped, Reagan's friendship would be a blessing for not only Aiden, but Julie as well.

Once Aiden had his food, Julie and Mary went back to the kitchen table to continue their discussion.

Julie twirled her coffee mug between her palms. "I don't understand the secrecy. What could have possibly happened in Afghanistan that the Army is trying so hard to cover up? John was my husband. I have a right to know how and why he died. Heath Carter, John's closest friend, hasn't spoken to me since the funeral. All my emails to him have gone unanswered. I don't know what else to do."

Mary put her arm around Julie's shoulder and kneaded out her tense muscles. "Julie, you are dealing with the US Army and very sensitive operations in a war zone. You spent enough time at Fort Bragg to understand how they operate."

"I won't stop until they give me answers. I need to know what they're hiding. While John was over in Afghanistan, his life was constantly in danger. But something was different about his final mission. In his last letter, I think there was something he wanted me to know, in case he never came back."

"Did you ever hear back from the senator's office? A government official may be the only avenue for information."

Julie shook her head. "Nothing but a condolence letter signed by our esteemed Senator. When I finally got a hold of someone in the office, I was told there's nothing the senator could do. John's just another dead soldier." She brushed away a tear with the back of her hand. "I'm thinking of hiring a lawyer."

"Don't give up. I'm sure someday you'll get the information you're looking for. While you're waiting for answers, don't forget to move forward with your life."

"What life?" Julie mumbled and looked away.

"The life you're building in Timber Lake. Last Thursday, for example, taking Aiden to meet Reagan Harrison was fun, right? Aiden really took a liking to him."

Julie smiled. "That might be the understatement of the year. Aiden can't stop talking about him. I thought he would lose his mind when Reagan offered to come watch him play."

Mary slid back her chair and stood. Obviously, Julie was also very pleased Reagan had come into their lives. But for now, her observation would stay unspoken. "I should get home and get ready for church. Can I catch a ride with you and Aiden?"

"Sure, we'll leave in an hour." Julie turned toward the family room. "You hear that buddy? We're leaving for church in one hour."

Aiden mumbled his response.

Mary left the house to make the short walk back home, praying her resilient daughter could once again find meaning and happiness in her life.

****

Reagan drove his luxury SUV toward a small but well-maintained home. After considering Aiden might have liked to ride in his sports car, he decided the two-seater was too small for the three of them. Maybe next time he could bring the sports car and take the kid for a spin. Catching himself, he realized there may not be a 'next time.'

Twice now, he'd found an excuse to see Julie again, each time he'd been left scratching his head over his own impulsiveness. He needed to regain his self-control and stop being led astray by the auburn haired beauty. Then he remembered the party he was throwing for his sister. Maybe he should invite Julie? Or maybe he should let today be the end. No more invitations. Just say goodbye after the game and walk away.

As he parked the car, he tried to calm his growing anticipation. He was so hyped, like he was ready to run on to the playing field. Maybe he shouldn't have had that third cup of coffee.

A climbing vine of white flowers wove its way up

the south facing brick. Small beds of colorful flowers greeted him as he walked on the path.

He rang the doorbell, and Julie quickly appeared.

"Come on in." She motioned a sweeping gesture with her hand.

Reagan stepped inside a home that was cheery and bright. The space was filled with comfortable furniture and beautiful artwork, open windows let in a light summer breeze. Within the ease of her home, Julie looked radiant and relaxed. He noticed her glowing smile and a laidback look with a ponytail resting at the base of her neck. Holy smokes, she looked hotter than ever.

He had dressed casual today, in an attempt to avoid detection. His loose gray shorts and yellow Nirvana T-shirt should make him look like any other guy sitting at the park, watching a kid's football game. A baseball cap and sunglasses topped off his disguise. The last thing he wanted was to divert attention from Aiden and the other kids playing today. "You have a beautiful house." He looked around the family room. "And you have good taste in art. Renoir is one of my favorite painters."

Julie's eyebrows rose.

A jock who loved art—always stunning. "I know… I'm just full of surprises." He winked. "When I travel to another city for a game, I make a point to visit its art museum. Last fall, I saw this painting at the Detroit Institute of Art." He pointed to a green landscape reproduction hanging above her sofa. "It's the *Clearing in the Woods*."

"Impressive. This one is my favorite. I bet the real painting is beautiful. It reminds me of someplace special called Cottonwood Field."

When she turned back to him, her eyes looked distant, lost in the past. "So, thanks for driving us to the game. Aiden couldn't be any more thrilled. I need to get a few things together, and then we can get going."

"My pleasure. Been looking forward to seeing him play. You still up for football school?"

Julie's smile lit up the room. "You bet, and maybe after today I'll understand what's going on. I might even start to watch Warriors games on TV with Aiden."

"Our first pre-season game is this Friday. We play in Los Angeles, but it will be televised here." He couldn't wait to get back on the field. Prove to the skeptics in the media he hadn't lost his edge.

"I'm excited to watch someone I know play." Julie stepped over to the staircase. "Aiden, time to go. Grab your bag and come downstairs. Reagan's here."

Not five seconds later, Aiden flew down the stairs with his black-and-red duffle bag, which overflowed with football paraphernalia. "Look at my jersey." Aiden jumped over to Reagan and held up his pint-sized football jersey. "I have so many grass stains that Mom can't get them all out! I am number twelve, but next year I want to be number fifty-four, just like you."

"Nice jersey, kid," Reagan said as Aiden beamed with pride. He was actually glad to see the kid, which surprised him. Aiden, with his candid and trusting nature, had started to wiggle his way into Reagan's heart.

"Do you have everything you need?" Julie asked Aiden. "We're not coming back because you forgot something."

Aiden bobbed his head while he waited by the

door.

"I have two lawn chairs I need to grab from the back entry. Why don't you two head out to the car. I'll lock up and be right there."

Reagan took Aiden's duffle bag and the cooler sitting on the coffee table, and then walked with Aiden to his car.

Moments later, Julie approached, carrying the lawn chairs and Aiden's booster seat.

"Let me help you with that." Reagan ran to her, tucked the chairs under one large arm, and grabbed the booster seat with his free hand. Once everything was secured in the back of the SUV, he dashed to the front passenger side door, just in time to open it for Julie.

He got into the driver's seat and saw Aiden securely buckled in behind them. The sight of the booster seat in the back seat of his car stole his breath, and he instantly broke out into a cold sweat. But seeing the kid's mother sitting next to him made up for any discomfort. Starting the engine, he put the vehicle in reverse and began to back out of the driveway. As was his habit, he twisted around to see behind him and laid his hand on the passenger seat. It brushed up against Julie's bare shoulder, and his stomach did a small leap. The conflicting texture, his rough hand against her smooth skin, was an enticing sensation, like sand on the shore briefly kissed by a gentle wave. If only his hand could have lingered a little while longer.

"I can't wait for those guys to finally see me with Reagan," Aiden declared from the back seat. "They called me a liar for saying you're my friend."

"I'd like you to wait until after the game to introduce me to your friends," Reagan said, still shaking away the memory of the feel of Julie's skin. "Once people recognize me, they'll want to talk and get autographs and pictures. I want to watch your whole game. Your mom and I will sit away from the crowd, and then afterward, I'll come over and introduce myself to your team. How does that sound?"

"Yeah, I guess that's fine." Aiden squirmed in his booster seat. "I hope Mrs. Wilson brings those orange popsicles again." After that, he turned quiet and stared out the window.

A Luke Bryan song came on the radio, and Reagan reached over to turn up the volume. "Do you like country music?"

"You bet. In North Carolina, listening to country music is mandatory. Back in college, my friend Chrissy and I went to an outdoor, three-day concert. The first night, a storm hit, so the next day the whole place was a giant mud puddle. When we weren't listening to the performers on stage, we slid down the huge muddy hill at the end of the park. I was filthy by the end of the weekend, but I've never had so much fun."

"Sounds like a blast." He pictured her creamy, fair skin covered in mud—a very provocative image. He drove into the park and headed toward the athletic fields. "Which one is Aiden playing on?"

"He's on Field B." She pointed to a grassy area.

The field had bleachers set on one side and a line of trees on the other.

Once parked, Aiden was released from his seat and he grabbed his bag, before running off in the direction of his team. Reagan and Julie took their time, meandering over to the field. A warm breeze carried the smell of fresh cut grass. Julie led him away from the bleachers, where a crowd had started to assemble.

She pointed toward the other side. "How about we sit over there?"

They unfolded their chairs and relaxed in the shade of the oak trees standing watch behind them.

Aiden looked over and waved, and they both waved back.

Reagan stole a glance at Julie. The constant voice in his head, cautioning him not to get too comfortable with either Julie or Aiden, was slowly going mute.

****

Between plays, Reagan educated Julie on the game of football.

She conceded the rules weren't as complicated as she'd thought. Being so passionate about the sport, he made a good teacher. "Football is finally making sense now. Aiden's a receiver, right? They don't throw the ball to him very often."

"He needs to work on shaking off his coverage." Reagan pointed to the erratic action on the field. "See how that defender from the other team blocks him from getting a clear shot at the ball? His quarterback needs to see him open before he'll throw him the ball."

She nodded and watched the scenario unfold before her. Aiden seemed to be making friends with the boy defending him instead of getting free to catch the ball. Sliding off her sandals, she brushed the soft grass with her bare feet. If only John were here. He would have loved to watch their son play. That pleasure had been denied him, along with so many other joys.

After Aiden dropped the football again, Reagan scrunched up his face. Then the corners of his wide mouth tilted up with a playful smile. "Once he starts gaining confidence on the field, he'll be an unstoppable force. I've seen the kid run."

She noticed his gaze drop down to her hot pink toenails, which stood out against the dark green grass. "I ran track and cross country in high school. John was a runner, too, so I guess Aiden comes by his cheetah speed naturally. I've started distance running again, but my legs are so out of shape."

His gaze meandered over her legs. "Your legs look perfect to me."

She turned her attention back to the game but not before catching his preoccupied smile. Heat flushed her face. Her brain hit the panic button. Matt Taylor, Chrissy's husband, had warned her Reagan had a reputation as a cad. He was often seen with a beautiful woman on his arm, even Hollywood starlets, but none of them stayed there for very long.

But Reagan was only here because of Aiden. No way did he want anything with her; she wasn't at all his type. Absolutely nothing to worry about. Reagan would soon be satisfied with his good deed and move on, well before she was in danger of liking him too much.

"Sorry." Reagan went back to watching the game. "That was a dumb guy thing to say." He shifted in his seat then stretched out his long legs and hooked his hands behind his head. "Maybe Aiden should be playing defense. I bet he could keep up with the receivers and disrupt their passing game. I'll talk to his coaches after the game."

"This is a youth football team, and Aiden's coaches are a couple of volunteer dads. Getting football advice from you might be a little intimidating." She couldn't stop staring at his flexed biceps. *What would having those arms wrapped around me feel like?* When was the last time she'd had any type of intimacy with a man? Too long. Of course, that kind of a drought would lead anyone to seriously inappropriate thoughts.

"Yeah, you're probably right."

"Have you thought about coaching someday?"

"Actually, that's the plan. In college, I double majored in education and math. Once my professional career is over, I hope to teach high school and coach football."

"You'll make a great coach. You've been so good with Aiden, extremely patient."

A moment later, the referee blew his whistle, signaling the end of the game. Little boys in large jerseys ran over to the sidelines and encircled their coaches. Then they lined up to shake hands with the opposing team.

Reagan picked up their water bottles and packed them back in the cooler. "I'm having a party at my house a week from this Saturday." He peeked over at her while lifting their lawn chairs. "And I was hoping you would come. Bring a few friends if you want. The more the merrier. The guests will be mostly guys from the team and their significant others." He flashed an easy, confident smile.

"You're inviting me to a party at your house?" She had to do a double take. "Why would you want me there?"

"Why not?" He raised a brow. "You're allowed to have some fun, right?"

Uncertainty pulsed through her as she tried to read in between the lines of his invitation. "You've been very kind to take an interest in Aiden, but please don't feel obligated to either of us." She began to walk away. No way did she want to become somebody's charity case. But that's what they'd become. His good deed for a few weeks—a way to get some positive PR.

"Why do you think I feel obligated?" Catching up to her, Reagan gently took hold of her arm and turned her to face him. "You should know something about me. I don't do anything I don't want to. Give yourself more credit, Julie. I like spending time with you. I can be myself when I'm around you." He relaxed his hold.

But for Julie, the searing heat of his touch lingered. A burning electricity still arced between them.

"You treat me like a normal person, not some unfeeling football star. I thought we were friends."

Her heart beat wildly as she fought to act calm. When she stepped back, he released his grasp, finally seeming to understand her reluctance.

"My sister, Kelsey, is coming to stay with me for a few days before she heads off to college. She's the one who insisted on the party, wanting one last hurrah. I couldn't say no. I thought you'd make her feel more comfortable, since most of the people there will be associated with the team. You're someone who's easy to talk to."

He'd change the tone of his voice, from strong confidence to calm and soothing.

"Oh," was all she could reply, flustered by her foolishness for overreacting. *Maybe going to the party wouldn't be so bad.* She could help him out for a change. "I don't have Aiden that weekend. He's staying with John's parents. And I don't have other plans, so I guess you can count me in. I would love to come and meet your sister."

"Great." Reagan flashed a wide smile. He led her toward the bleachers, where the players were enjoying lemonade and popsicles.

"Would it be all right if I brought my friend Chrissy and her husband, Matt? They're huge Warriors fans and would never forgive me if I attended without them." The prospect of going to his house for a party didn't seem as scary if she had friends by her side.

"Sure, you're welcome to bring anyone you want."

As they walked along side by side, their hands brushed together every so often. The contact gave her a quick shock, each time taking her by surprise.

Approaching the bleachers, Julie noticed a hush fell over the crowd. Their attention was now fully centered on Reagan.

Aiden came running over. "Mom, Reagan, wasn't it a great game?"

Seconds later, Reagan was converged on by a swarm of sweaty boys.

Julie stepped out of the way, not wanting to get run over in the excitement. Seeing him surrounded by the crowd made her realize how hard living your life in the spotlight must be. People not really wanting to know the real you, only the version they see on TV on any given Sunday. She remembered what he had said earlier—*I thought we were friends.* To call him a friend—that would be nice.

"Oh my gawd, are you dating Reagan Harrison?" a female voice drawled.

The woman was impeccably overdressed for an afternoon football game and her high heels punched through the sod as she approached. "I'm not dating anyone," Julie responded. *Who does this lady think she is, asking a question like that?* "Reagan came to see Aiden play. He's just a friend." The word flowed naturally off her tongue.

"Don't tell me Reagan Harrison is only here to watch a bunch of seven-year-olds play flag football." The other woman leaned forward to whisper. "I saw the way you two looked at each other, very intimate. You're not fooling me."

Time to walk away, before she lost her redhead infused temper. "I'm not trying to fool anyone." She went to stand next to Aiden, who seemed ten feet tall.

He directed the other children, yelling, "Don't crowd Mr. Harrison" and "You'll have to wait your turn."

"This is crazy." She ruffled his damp hair.

"Reagan is so cool to come and watch me play and meet my team. I wish he could come to every game." Aiden watched Reagan with hero worship written all over his sweaty face.

When Reagan glanced over, Julie gave him the thumbs-up sign. He winked in reply.

"That would be nice, but you know Reagan's a busy guy. His season starts soon. We can watch him play Friday night, okay? Will you help me cheer him on?"

"Yeah!" Aiden's smile split his face from ear to ear. "But we need jerseys, number fifty-four ones with Harrison on the back. We can wear them for the game."

She took hold of Aiden's hand and moved into the crowd. "Sounds like a plan. Now let's go rescue Reagan from all these people. He looks ready to be saved."

Chapter Six

For a weeknight, The Garage was packed. Reagan
grabbed his pool stick and stared at the table in front of
him, plotting a way out of the trap DeMarcus had set
for him. Stalking around the table one last time, he
aimed and fired, accidentally hitting the wrong ball into
the pocket. "I really hate this game," he grumbled
before taking a drink out of his whisky glass. He set it
back down on the ledge and watched as DeMarcus
finished off the eight-ball.

"Looks like you owe me a drink." DeMarcus stole
the stick out of Reagan's hand then returned it to the
rack. "Come on, loser, Angie looks lonely."

They walked through the crowd and back to their
table. The clack of pool balls sounded as loud and
constant as the pouring rain outside. Along with many
of their teammates, the place was filled with locals
rubbing shoulders with football players. Good-looking
girls appeared like rabbits pulled out of a magician's
hat. Over the past hour, Reagan had been given no less
than fifteen phone numbers. He'd throw away the
scraps of paper later. Picking up girls at a bar was
something he would have done a few years ago, but
thankfully, he'd grown older and wiser.

DeMarcus dropped onto the booth seat and put his
arm around his girlfriend.

Reagan took a spot in the empty booth across from

them and motioned to the waitress to bring him another drink.

"So, who won?" Angie asked with an expression as innocent as a kitten.

"Who do you think?" Reagan took a peanut out of the bowl and flicked it over at DeMarcus. "I swear he cheats."

"I don't have to cheat, you just suck that bad." DeMarcus laughed while cracking open a peanut shell.

"Maybe Reagan's just setting you up for a big fall." Angie nudged her boyfriend in the ribs. "He'll get you to make a huge bet and then clean you out."

Reagan laughed while accepting his drink from a very cute waitress. "DeMarcus is right. I'm awful at pool, but I can't seem to stop playing. There's always hope he'll have an off game, and I'll finally beat him."

Angie grabbed a handful of peanuts and started cracking their shells. "I hear you're seeing that woman you met at the banquet a few weeks ago. I thought you're still with Brynn."

Reagan gave DeMarcus the evil eye before delving into that mud puddle. "I have no romantic interest in Julie. We've gotten together a few times, but always with her son. And Brynn and I aren't what you'd call in a stable relationship. You know me. I like to keep my options open."

Angie poured another glass of beer from the pitcher sitting on the table. "I remember seeing Julie at the banquet. She seemed sweet and really nice."

"Reagan needs to learn to appreciate the benefits of the long-term relationship...because I love my girl." DeMarcus kissed Angie on the cheek. "Julie's the type of woman you should be dating. Someone real, not the

Hollywood version you always end up with."

They were right. But a real relationship right now was out of the question. Since joining the pros, he'd drifted along the rivers of his accomplishments, enjoying all the benefits they offered. But in the last few weeks, he sensed an internal shift—an ever-present restlessness. Things were changing in his life, and he had a good idea why.

"She's still in love with her husband. And I'm pretty sure I'm not the kind of man she would want to date. I think we're both happy getting to know each other as friends." He saw a waitress come over with a fresh drink.

She leaned over to set his drink on the table, smiled, and then walked away.

On the napkin tucked underneath the glass was a series of numbers written with now smudged red ink. He could still make out a phone number encircled with a heart.

DeMarcus noticed the attempted flirtation and laughed. "Trust me, man, you'd be so much better off being with one lady."

Reagan couldn't help but think of Julie, and the way she'd looked at Aiden's football game. The day had been perfect, watching the kid play, and giving his mother football lessons on the sidelines. After the game, they'd stopped for ice cream. She was deliciously gorgeous, sitting at their outdoor table, enjoying her ice cream cone. Listening to her talk, he grew distracted by the tendrils of red hair that broke free of her ponytail. Her face was flushed after spending the afternoon in the summer heat. She created a pretty picture, natural and pure.

Angie tugged on DeMarcus' shirt sleeve. "Looks like the rain's letting up. We should probably get going." She reached over to pat Reagan's hand, which rested on the table. "Reagan Harrison, you're a good man. You deserve someone who will really appreciate you. Just because Julie's a widow doesn't mean she doesn't want to fall in love again." She followed her boyfriend out of the booth then reached over to grab her purse. "I hope you keep seeing her."

"She's coming to the party at my house next Saturday," he told Angie, who then gave him a thumbs-up.

"Now I'm really disappointed I can't come. I'll have to talk to Arnie's wife. She can be my spy."

Reagan shook his head and laughed. "See you two matchmakers later." They didn't understand what he already knew. Anything between Julie and him would only end in heartache. And he wouldn't risk that, for both their sakes.

"See ya," DeMarcus said as the couple walked away.

Reagan finished his whiskey and noticed an empty pool table. Another game would mean the loss of a few more bucks. *What the hell, it was only money.* He walked over to a group of his teammates at the bar and held out a pool stick. "Who's up for another game?"

****

Reagan spent most of the next morning lying on the sofa. Tomorrow was the first game of the preseason, and he had a wicked hangover from the night before. Hopefully, he'd start feeling better soon. He had only two more hours before boarding a plane to LA.

Practice had been relentless, and the August heat

drained any leftover energy. He loved football with a passion, but training camp was always his least favorite time of the year. The recent draft picks and walk-on rookies were all proving their abilities, which made his job that much harder. As a veteran player, his duty was to put those overconfident boys back in their place and remind them they were no longer in college. The pros were a whole different beast. Hard hits for caught balls, picking apart the offensive line to bring the quarterback down, payback for missed tackles—all part of the process of turning boys into men.

Seven years ago, he'd been a newly drafted rookie. Learning the ropes was tough, and the other players pushed him without mercy. But in the end, that pressure had made him the player he was today. During his first season, he'd made a name for himself. People had taken notice of the new inside linebacker who couldn't be stopped. They'd started to call him "The Dragon," and on the football field, he felt like a predator. Last season, he'd won Defensive Player of the Year, and the trophy sat proudly on the bookcase in his study, alongside the many others he'd collected over the years. But that wasn't enough. His career was on the fast track, with no sign of slowing. Ever since he'd first stepped onto the football field, all he wanted was to make a career of playing ball. He would never be happy with only being good. He needed to be the best.

Reagan sat and enjoyed the silence. *What would my quiet bachelor pad sound like once filled with my own family? The wife and children I might have someday.* Maybe in the distant future, he'd finally feel like settling down.

Grabbing the remote, Reagan turned off the TV.

"Better start packing," he said to himself, his voice echoing through the room. The team left for Los Angeles in a few hours. He was ready to get back on the field.

His cell phone buzzed, and he glanced at the text.

Hey, cutie, see you're coming out to LA. You want to get together?

Reagan let out a deep sigh. Brynn was stunningly beautiful, with long platinum-blonde hair, flawless skin, and a dazzling smile. They'd met at a fundraiser and had enjoyed each other's company for the rest of the night. She wanted a sports celebrity on her arm, and he'd been all too happy to fill the role.

Tomorrow, he would be playing a short distance from her home.

—*I'll hit you up when I get there*—

While packing for the few days away, Reagan let his thoughts wander to Julie—a woman as different from Brynn as apple pie was to caviar. He decided to call Julie tomorrow to see what she thought of the game. Reagan had classified their relationship as friends, but the word felt inadequate. Julie was like a warm ember—inviting, comfortable, and easy to be close to. In the past, his relationships with women were more like fireworks, hot and bright but over quickly.

He'd been burned once. His trust shattered after finding the woman he loved was unfaithful. In college, Sarah Collins had been the center of his world, the woman he was going to marry. He'd be drafted to play professional football and she would be his adoring wife. Their picture-perfect life had all been a pipe dream.

After that heartbreak, he promised himself never to be so vulnerable again. He'd successfully avoided any serious relationships up to this point and enjoyed the status as one of the most eligible bachelors in the country. Finding a beautiful woman was never a problem. Finding one he wanted to stay with, well— that was never really a concern.

But that was before Julie Ellis came into his life.

Closing his suitcase, Reagan carried it, along with his garment bag, downstairs. He set them on the floor to go grab his cell phone and the book he had been reading. The view of the lake, and the many boats dotting the glassy water, temporarily distracted him from his mission to get out the door. For a few minutes, he imagined enjoying a beautiful day on the lake. Save that thought for another day. Fishing would have to wait.

The second he stepped into the garage, his phone buzzed. Tempted not to look at the text, he hesitated before pulling out his phone. What he saw brought a huge smile to his face.

**Good luck tomorrow! Aiden and I will be cheering you on! **

—*Thanks. I'll call you after the game to get your review of my performance.*—

Can't wait...

That simple expression of desire and anticipation awoke feelings that had remained dormant for too long.

****

Friday night, Julie's living room turned into a noisy party as they watched the Warriors football game. Julie and Aiden wore their new jerseys, with the name HARRISON boldly displayed on the back. Mary arrived sporting her new red-and-silver Warriors T-shirt. Aiden insisted on having pizza, while Chrissy and

Matt brought chicken wings and chips. They may have been a small crowd but made up for the size with plenty of enthusiasm.

Even a pre-season game turned exciting when Julie and Aiden were friends with one of the players. When the team walked out onto the field for the first time, Julie had an easy time picking Reagan out of the crowd. She'd recognize his trademark swagger anywhere.

During the first half of the game, they cheered loudly when Reagan was credited for several big plays. Aiden studied the TV screen with intensity, giving play-by-play commentary. After halftime, most of the starters, including Reagan, were pulled to allow the rookies and second-string players to prove their skills. Once his buddy had been sent to sit on the sidelines, Aiden wandered off to the kitchen to get another slice of pizza. By the end of the third quarter, he had run outside to play with a few of the neighbor boys.

Chrissy plopped down on the sofa next to Julie. "So spill, Jules. What's going on between you and number fifty-four?"

No surprise. Chrissy was always the group busybody. "Ummm...nothing. Reagan's been kind to Aiden, and Aiden worships the ground he walks on. That's the whole story."

"I don't think there's any confusion about Aiden's feelings toward Reagan or that Reagan is kind to your son." Matt took a napkin and wiped chicken wing sauce off his hands. "We're all concerned about you, we don't want to see you get hurt. News travels fast in Timber Lake and that Reagan Harrison runs with a fast crowd is common knowledge. He doesn't exactly have a stellar dating record, either. Seems to enjoy a quick turnaround."

"First of all, why would you worry about me getting hurt? I'm not dating him, nor do I want to." Julie would give those rumors the credit they deserved—none. Even if Matt's concern might be valid. Her opinion of Reagan would stay based on facts. Like the way he made her feel like the most important woman in the world when they were together. "Second." She forced her voice to remain steady and calm. "Your judgments about him are totally based on gossip. But I can tell you that when he's with Aiden and me, he's down-to-earth and funny. He's just a normal guy."

At that moment, an image of Reagan flashed on the screen. He stood on the sidelines, helmet in hand, laughing with one of the other players, and looking devilishly handsome. How did just the sight of him make her pulse race? *Just an innocent physical attraction. A normal female reaction to his body, which was stacked with hard muscle. Nothing more.* She forced herself to take her gaze off the TV.

Chrissy turned to her and wrapped an arm around Julie's shoulder. "He's not just a normal guy, Jules."

Julie took a deep breath and looked around. She didn't need their concern. "You know I'm still grieving for John. He was the love of my life. I don't have room in my heart for anyone else."

Mary grabbed her daughter's hand. "We trust you'll make the right decisions for your life. I hope he knows what a wonderful woman he has for a friend."

"That's right." Chrissy wrapped her arm around Julie's shoulder and gave her an energetic squeeze. "I'll be scouting Reagan at his party, so he better be on his best behavior."

"Oh, no." Julie laughed. "Don't make me regret inviting you."

"We only agreed to go as a favor to you," Matt said, his lips twitching into a smirk.

"Right," Julie said. "Because I really had to twist your arm. Don't be too hard on the guy. He was nice enough to invite us to his house. I'm actually excited to go, and I can't tell you the last time I felt excited about anything."

"Well, I'm glad to hear that!" Chrissy exclaimed, talking with the speed of a machine gun. "Because I'm planning to have a blast. This is a once-in-a-lifetime opportunity. We'll be rubbing elbows with the rich and famous. I can't wait."

"Don't forget, Chrissy, we have to spend some time with Reagan's little sister. That's the reason I agreed to go in the first place."

"Yeah, yeah." She waved off Julie. "That's your job. I'm talking to as many football players as possible." Chrissy then began her endless list of people she planned on meeting.

"I want to meet him, too." Mary quietly interrupted the long oration. "I want to meet the man who's been spending time with my daughter and grandson. Invite him over for dinner, Julie. Pick a time that works for both of you, and I'll make sure to be here." She clasped her hands together. Case closed.

"I guess I could ask." Julie wanted to outright say no. *Reagan, eating dinner at her kitchen table, with her mother—yikes!* "But I'm sure he'll decline."

"He'll be grateful to have one of your home-cooked meals. I am confident he'll want to come."

Julie wasn't so confident, but what more could she say? She'd ask. He'd say no thanks. End of story.

Before she knew it, the game was over. The Warriors won by fourteen points, and Julie turned off the TV. While putting away the leftover food, she heard her cell phone ring and she ran over to answer the call.

Three pairs of eyes followed her with curiosity.

Reagan Harrison's name glowed on the screen. He'd actually taken the time to call her.

Julie stepped outside, onto the deck, for some privacy. She took a deep breath before answering.

"So, how did I do?" Reagan asked from the other end of the line.

"What a great game." Her skin tingled at the sound of his deep voice.

"Thanks," Reagan said over loud banging and muffled laughter. "I'm waiting outside the locker room. Sorry for all the background noise."

"No problem. I'm glad you called. Thanks to you, I understood what was going on during the game."

He laughed. "You're a quick study."

"I was very impressed with how well you played, but everyone's so aggressive. How can you stand the constant pushing, shoving, and falling down?"

"That falling down is called a tackle." The tone of his voice held unabashed amusement.

"Well, you did that tackling thing very well." Her mind scrambled for a safer topic. "Aiden talked me into getting a Harrison jersey for both of us. Your biggest cheering section was in my family room."

"Great. I can't wait to see you wearing my last name."

A burst of activity sounded over Reagan's voice.

"Sorry, but I've got to go. Tell Aiden I said hi, and thanks for rooting for me. Nice to know someone's in my corner."

"Have a safe trip home. See you next Saturday."

"See you soon," he said, before ending the call.

Julie sucked in her breath like she'd been hit in the stomach. *See you soon.* She'd heard that sentiment before. That was how John always signed off in his letters.

Chapter Seven

Saturday afternoon, Reagan looked around his backyard and concluded it was ready for the invasion to come. The bartenders were in position under the gazebo by the pool, fully stocked with every type of drink. In the outdoor kitchen, the catering staff was busy preparing food. Several of his teammates had arrived a little early and had set up shop over on the paved basketball court. They played a little three-on-three ball, while their female companions had seated themselves on the patio, under the shade of a bright red umbrella.

His sister, Kelsey, walked his way, after a stroll along the beach. Her colorful skirt blew in the breeze and a long, blonde braid swung down her back. Kelsey was the youngest of the four Harrison children, and the most indulged. Reagan being especially guilty of that offense, and in return, she was his biggest supporter.

"Reagan," Kelsey said as she approached, "I saw a beautiful white stork standing in the marsh." She pointed across the yard, toward the lake, to a patch of cattails and lily pads that ran adjacent to his property. "It stood so still, I thought it was a statue. Then all of a sudden, the bird took off into the air. It was amazing!"

"He's a frequent guest around here...likes to stop by after I've been out fishing to look for treats. He seems partial to fish guts."

"*Eww.*" She scrunched her freckled nose. "So when are your other guests coming? I'm looking forward to meeting Julie. I need to find out if she's good enough for my big brother."

"You realize Julie's just a friend, right? Nothing's going on between us." His chest tightened with apprehension. "I wouldn't want you to make her feel uncomfortable with an interrogation. Be a good girl and try not to scare her away."

"Whatever." She gave a dismissive wave. "I'll judge for myself what's going on between the two of you. I've never known you to be just friends with a single woman. Tell me when she gets here. Okay?" Kelsey gave him a wink and walked around to the French doors, going into the house.

"Great," he muttered. The whole time Kelsey had been staying with him, he'd been careful not to say too much about Julie. If she got suspicious, there'd be no stopping the little busybody. But even with his tight lip, she still had a pretty good read on the situation. *Am I really that transparent?*

Over the past week, he'd come to terms with his growing feelings for Julie. Along with the realization came the truth of where they would lead. Their relationship would never develop into anything more than friendship. She still grieved for her husband, and he respected her need to heal. And when she was ready to move on, she would want a man who could fully commit to herself and her son. At this point in his life, the game of football alone earned his total dedication.

Walking over to the stereo system, he turned on the satellite radio. A deep bass sound flowed through the outdoor speaker system and scattered throughout the backyard. A few more guests had arrived—one of the trainers and his wife, a guy from special teams, and the Defensive Coordinator with his wife.

As people made themselves comfortable, Reagan weaved his way through the growing crowd, which had assembled on the large deck. He stopped and talked with several clusters of guests, thanking them for coming and directing them to the bar. The air filled with the sounds of music, talking, and laughter. A few people had changed into their swimsuits and jumped into the coolness of the pool.

Even with all the activity, something was missing, or actually, someone. The party wouldn't really start until Julie arrived. Pulling his phone out of his pocket, he checked if she'd texted. Nope. Had she changed her mind and decided not to come?

At that moment, Julie rounded the corner of the house and stepped onto the patio. Dressed in a vivid yellow sundress that brushed the top of her tan knees, she appeared out of the shadows like a ray of sunshine. Her light auburn hair was wrapped in a low ponytail, which rested over her right shoulder.

She looked around, biting her lower lip.

The sight of her made his pulse accelerate to the point he was afraid he'd drop of a heart attack, right at her feet. "Julie," Reagan said over the noise of the crowd. Each long step brought him closer. "I'm glad you came." He finally reached his destination, never lifting his gaze off her lovely face. As he stood by her side, he realized two people were right behind her—a short, slender woman with a head of brown curls and a solidly built man who held a wide-eyed expression. "Welcome, I'm Reagan." He smiled warmly and shook the man's hand.

"Hi, Reagan. Thanks for inviting us." Julie turned to her friends, who stared with open mouths. "These are my friends, Matt and Chrissy Taylor. Chrissy and I have been best friends since high school."

"Nice to meet you. Follow me, and let's get you something to drink." Reagan led them through the crowd of rubberneckers. Approaching the bar, he turned to Julie. "I made sure they had Riesling. That's what you drank at the banquet, right?"

"Yes, my favorite, thanks." She accepted the glass from the bartender with a smile. "I can't believe you remembered."

A little while later, with drinks in hand, Reagan took them around and introduced them to the other partygoers. Julie had met many of these same people a few weeks ago at the country club, and her eyes widened every time someone said they remembered her. But he knew why Julie had made such an impact at the banquet. She was breathtakingly beautiful and had been in his company for the whole night. The Warriors team could gossip as well as they played football, and Reagan's love life was usually their favorite topic. They were as bad as a group of old church ladies, clutching yellow purses and whispering behind Sunday bulletins. The image brought a smile to his face.

The breeze carried the smell of grilled meat. Soon, hamburgers and brats were served. Matt started making his way over to the food, before getting sidetracked into a conversation with the Offensive Line Coach. Which left Reagan standing with Chrissy and Julie on the pool deck.

"The food smells so good!" Chrissy said. "You two

have fun. I'm getting something to eat." She moved in the direction of her husband, who now stood in the buffet line. "Catch you later!" She shouted, looking over her shoulder.

Reagan watched as Chrissy filled her plate with food and joined a table. She had them all laughing within a few seconds.

"My friend is quite amazing." Julie grinned. "She's the biggest extrovert you'll ever meet. I, on the other hand, am not so talented."

"That's fine with me. I enjoy having your full attention." Her cheeks, already tinted pink from the heat of the day, blushed a bright crimson.

Julie turned away to look back up the hill. "You have a beautiful house. The view from the deck is stunning."

"Thanks." He mentally kicked himself. Yet again, his flirty behavior made her uncomfortable. The last thing he wanted. "Come on, let's head toward the water. The view is even better from the dock."

They strolled along the path that led to the lake. Julie leaned against a huge oak tree. She looked out at the water, at the birds flying above, at the grass below her feet.

Anywhere but at him.

Finally, her gaze found his face and she took a deep breath. "I want to repay you for all your kindness, for all the nice things you've done for Aiden. Would you like to come over to my house for dinner? I'll understand if you don't…"

Reagan didn't let her continue. "I'd love to." She wrung her hands so hard, he was afraid she'd hurt herself. "When were you thinking?"

Julie's eyes grew wide, resembling a pair of sparkling aquamarines. "Well, we're free most evenings. What works for you?"

"I only have a half-day practice this Thursday. Would that be okay?"

"Yes, that's perfect." She unclenched her hands in order to brush back a few windblown strands of hair. "I'll be glad to cook for someone besides just Aiden and myself, and he'll be excited to see you again. Let me know what time to expect you."

Standing next to her, all other activity around them faded away. The noise of the party dimmed to a hum, background music to the sound of her sweet voice. He watched her as she talked. A prism of expressions played across her delicate face, highlighting an unassuming smile. Almost in a daze, he began to reach for her hand, when out of the corner of his eye he saw his sister approaching. Reagan quickly snapped back to reality.

Kelsey strode over, linking her arm through Reagan's. She set her sights on Julie, with one blonde eyebrow cocked. Then her tight set mouth broke out into a huge smile. "Hi there, I'm Kelsey, Reagan's sister. You must be Julie."

"Hi. Reagan told me you are staying with him for a while before you start college. Where will you be attending?"

"Indiana Central, just like my big bro." She nudged him in the ribs with her elbow. "I move into the dorms next week. Reagan's been really cool to let me crash at his place. My mom's driving me nuts. I think she's going through some empty nest thing."

When he'd left for college, his mom had breathed a

sigh of relief over the reduction in the family's food bill. But he knew both his parents loved him, despite his huge appetite. He hoped Julie recognized how important family was to him. Even if he wasn't in a rush to have one of his own. "Our mother is panicking because she's losing her baby. Kelsey's quite a bit younger than the rest of us, and she's been spoiled rotten by our parents."

"Mom'll just have to find a hobby." Kelsey turned to Julie, avoiding eye contact with Reagan. "Would you mind taking a walk to the lake with me? There's a nice breeze coming off the water."

"Sure, sounds nice," Julie said.

She looked blissfully unaware of what was to come.

"Guess I'll catch you later, Reagan."

He watched as the two women headed down the slope of grass, which led to the waterfront. After a minute, they both turned back and giggled. "That's goin' to be nothing but trouble," he mumbled to himself.

"What did you say?" a high-pitched voice asked.

Next to him stood Chrissy Taylor.

She peered up at him with big, brown eyes. "This is a great party. Thanks for having us."

"I'm glad you came with Julie. She's told me a few stories about the two of you in your younger days. Seems that you were quite the little instigator."

She laughed. "Yes, I am little, and yes, I am an instigator. But we sure do have fun together. Julie's the one who makes it fun. She may be quiet, but just remember, the quiet ones will usually surprise you the most."

"I'll make a note of that." He continued to watch Julie, who now stood on the dock.

Chrissy followed his gaze.

"How is she doing with everything that's happened over the past year?" Reagan asked. "I haven't known her for very long, but I can tell she tries really hard to hide her pain. Every so often, she lets down her guard, and I notice a flash of what she really feels."

"I'm glad you care about her." She shaded her eyes with her hand as she looked up at him. "Julie's world was turned around when John died. During their marriage, John was deployed more than he was home. Don't get me wrong, John loved her like crazy and he hated to be away from her, but the military makes for a hard life. She was totally committed to him and hoped someday when he got out, they could start a real life together. That dream ended the day two soldiers appeared at her door."

His own heart squeezed. "She's an amazingly strong woman."

"Julie needs something positive in her life. Something to draw her out of the past and give her hope for a good future. Which brings me to the question I have for you. What are your intentions toward my best friend?"

He studied Chrissy, noticing her stern expression. Although there was over a foot height difference, she did not appear to be intimidated. Not one bit. "I want to be a good friend to Julie. Rarely in my position do I meet such a genuinely kind and honest person, and I value her friendship. At this point, we're just enjoying each other's company." Reagan took a long breath and continued. "Under different circumstances, I'd make an all-out play for her. But I care too much about her and Aiden to be that selfish."

Chrissy's serious face melted into a sweet-as-honey smile.

Sticking his hands in the front pockets of his shorts, Reagan eased out a deep breath. Luckily, he'd avoided the infliction of bodily harm by a very protective best friend—at least for now.

"Good, I'm glad you really care about her. See, Julie's very naïve when it comes to men." Her words tumbled out in rapid succession. "She's only had one boyfriend, John, and other guys steered clear once they found out he was an Army sharpshooter. Julie thought guys didn't find her appealing, when in reality, they were simply afraid for their lives."

"If I would have met her ten years ago, I wouldn't have been deterred by the threat of a bullet." Instead, he would have welcomed the challenge.

"You are a very charming man. Just remember, Julie's different than most women. She may seem sweet and innocent, but deep down she's a fighter. Be patient." She put a hand over his large forearm. "She'll be worth the wait." After that statement, she walked away.

Turning his gaze to the lake, he rested his gaze on Julie. Her yellow sundress blew in the breeze. Yes, he already knew she was different than any other woman he'd met before. He'd been sure of that the first time he'd seen her.

****

Julie and Kelsey strolled along the lakefront, absorbed in conversation. Water lapped onto the shore in modest waves, each carrying the scents of algae, damp vegetation, and fish. Thankfully, a nearby honeysuckle bush interjected sweetness to the air, masking some of the less enjoyable aromas.

Julie enjoyed Reagan's sister. She found her funny and charming, just like her brother. However, where Reagan was practical and grounded, Kelsey was a free spirit. She shared with Julie her love of animals and nature, and about her uncertainty regarding her career choice.

"Reagan told me you were a Pediatric Physical Therapist," Kelsey said. "Do you enjoy your job?"

"I love what I do. What made you decide to go into sports medicine?"

"I'd like to help people, and growing up watching Reagan play sports made me want to work with athletes. He didn't always excel at football. He had to work really hard to reach the professional level. If he got hurt, I'd want someone to take good care of him, to make sure he could play again."

"You'll have plenty of time in college to decide if sports medicine is the right profession for you. I changed my major at least four times before I settled on physical therapy. I know Reagan will be proud of you no matter what you decide to do. He told me he'd like to teach once he retires from football."

Kelsey nodded. "In college, he played football like he'd be drafted by the pros, but he studied for his classes like he wouldn't. He's a very dedicated man, and when he commits himself to something, there's no stopping him."

"I hope he made time to have some fun in college. All work and no play...and all."

"Don't get me wrong, he's still a campus legend.

From what I hear, Reagan found plenty of time to party. He also had a serious girlfriend, Sarah. Everyone thought they would get married, because they were the perfect couple. Sarah ended their relationship right before graduation, and Reagan was devastated. I think that's why he's now so noncommittal with women."

"He's dating Brynn Campbell, right? Aren't they serious?"

"Ha!" Kelsey burst out with a laugh. "Brynn's just a placeholder. She's safe because Reagan knows nothing will ever come from their relationship. My brother tries to hide it, but he feels very deeply."

"Reagan's an extraordinary man." Julie sensed how much Kelsey admired her brother and how protective she was. "From the short time I've known him, I've noticed his confidence and determination. He reminds me of my late husband, never willing to back down from a challenge." She turned to see Reagan on the deck, talking with a group of men. He was taller than most of them, but for Julie, his height wasn't the reason he stood out in the crowd.

"Since John's death, I've had a difficult time assimilating back into normal life. Reagan's helped me realize I can't keep closing off myself to new experiences."

"I'm sorry about your husband." Kelsey's hand rested on Julie's arm. "I hate that war brings so much death and destruction."

"Losing someone you love is a hard fact to accept. One I still struggle with every day." Tears burned her eyes, and she blinked to push them away. "I'm lucky to have my son. He's the most important thing in my life. He's the reason I'm still able to go on."

"Reagan told me all about Aiden. He said he's a great kid and is always saying the funniest stuff. Reagan's got a soft spot in his heart for kids. Last year, he visited Timber Lake Hospital to spend time in the children's wing. He was there for hours...talking with the kids, reading stories, and playing video games."

Julie's heart melted at the image of him surrounded by sick children, who were probably overjoyed by his attention. "I'm sure the kids had a blast. I know Aiden thinks the world of Reagan, like he's Superman."

Suddenly, a burst of noise sounded from the pool.

"We should probably head back." Kelsey tipped her head in the direction of the house. "Don't want to miss any of the action. I'm so glad I finally got to meet you. I think you're as good for Reagan as he's been for you. I've noticed a change in him this visit. He seems to be more balanced, and he's definitely happier. Thanks for being his friend, Julie." A slow smile crept across her face. "I understand you are not looking for romance, but sometimes friends turn out to be the most satisfying lovers." She gave Julie a conspiratorial wink.

Julie was left standing speechless as she watched Kelsey rejoin the party. As Julie slowly walked up the hill toward the house, she considered, for a second, the notion of her and Reagan as more than friends. Just as quickly, she dismissed the daydream. Kelsey was obviously just being precocious. A result of a playful sense of humor.

Leisurely strolling back to the house, she stopped to talk to several people, finally ending at the catering station. She filled a plate with food and sat on an empty patio chair. As she surveyed the backyard, she guessed at least seventy-five people were in attendance, all seemed to be having a blast. Reagan sure knew how to throw a party.

Her gaze skimmed through the crowd, until it rested on Reagan, causing her heart to instinctively skip a beat. An electric charge hit her, one she now anticipated every time her body responded to the sight of him.

He'd trimmed his hair recently, but it still looked unruly—a good look on him. She continued to watch as he leaned against the gazebo, talking to several men. He must have sensed her gaze, because he slowly turned to face her. Their gazes connected and the distance between them disappeared.

In a different time or place, she'd be hopelessly attracted to him. Unfortunately, reality was wickedly cruel, often offering glimpses of possibilities that were never meant to be. If she were to ever fall for him, the cost of love unreturned would devastate her tenuous heart. A handsome and famous football star didn't seriously date a single mother/hometown girl like her. His type was Hollywood glamorous, not "pulled out of the dryer" chic.

John's face came to mind and the ache in her chest opened again. Yesterday, she'd sent a check to her lawyer as a retainer, money she really couldn't spare. Maybe he'd have better luck cutting through the government's red tape.

Julie shook her head, bringing herself back to the present. She was at a party, not a funeral. *Smile. Have some fun. Remember how to do that?*

Chrissy came over to sit in the chair beside her. "What a party!" She took a long drink out of her beer bottle. "He has the most beautiful house and grounds.

The great room looks like a magazine cover, and this backyard... I've never seen anything like this place in real life! And to think he lives here all alone and only during part of the year."

Good thing Chrissy's good mood was contagious. "You're right. He does have a nice home." Julie savored a bite of Greek Salad. The strong flavors of the dressing and the feta cheese hummed in her mouth.

"Did you get a look at the pool? The entire bottom is tiled in a white, blue, and green wave pattern."

She shook her head. "I haven't seen the pool, yet. I just got back from talking to Kelsey down by the lake."

"The whole time you were talking with her, Reagan had this anxious look on his face. I think he was afraid of what his sister might say." She talked with her hands as much as her mouth. A potato chip went flying out of her hand and landed on the grass. "Poor guy, I tried to distract him, but he wouldn't let you leave his sight."

"Well, he didn't need to worry. We had a nice conversation. His sister thinks very highly of him. She wanted to make sure I appreciated him as a person, not just a celebrity. I sensed she thinks I'm more significant to Reagan than I actually am."

"Don't underestimate yourself, Jules. You do look super cute in that dress. Good choice by the way."

"Yes, it was." A simple dress she'd pulled out of the back of her closet. She couldn't remember the last time she'd bought herself a new outfit. "So, did you meet all the people on your list?"

"Almost, but most importantly, I got to talk with Reagan, one-on-one. That man is lucky I'm a married woman, because otherwise I couldn't leave him alone.

My gosh, Julie, he's soooo handsome. How can you stand being around him and not want to rip off his shirt? Have you seen him without his shirt? I bet he looks fabulous!"

Julie nearly snorted out her drink in laughter. "Calm down, or you'll give yourself a stroke. A woman would have to be blind not to notice Reagan, but lucky for him, I am not as fanatical as you."

"Keep telling yourself that." Chrissy rolled her eyes.

They continued to talk and joke around. Soon, the women had attracted a group of guys who joined in their conversation. The football players shared stories of their exploits on and off the field. Outdoor lights turned on as the fiery sun doused itself, slipping into the cool of the lake. The night was clear and warm, and a full moon appeared overhead.

"Every running back on our team hates having to practice against Reagan. He goes loco out on the field…like a raging bull, and you, well, you're the sucker with the red flag," the man sitting next to Julie said.

He sported the most impressive set of long, black dreadlocks she'd ever seen.

"The first time I went against him, I tried to use some clever footwork to slip past him. He brought me down so fast and so hard, I was seeing stars. When you see him standing across from you on the line, you better up your game, or you'll be hurting."

"No pain, no gain…that's my motto." Reagan walked up to the group, looking at Julie with a cocky grin. He grabbed a chair and the other men made room for him to sit next to her. "I hope these guys are behaving themselves." He had a basketball in one hand. In the other was a towel, which he used to wipe off his sweaty face.

"Yes." She swallowed hard. Beads of sweat started to break out on her face as well. "They've been very entertaining. I've learned a lot about you tonight."

Reagan scowled at the men, who visibly cringed. "I hope nothing too incriminating."

"Oh, don't worry. I'm just glad I don't have to play against you."

"You're so little you could probably slip right past him," another teammate said. "Or he'd be too distracted by your hotness. Either way, he wouldn't stand a chance."

The group of men hooted in laughter, all except Reagan, who narrowed his eyes and glared at the speaker. He then hurled the basketball at the man, who caught it in the gut.

Julie enjoyed the entertainment as the players teased each other relentlessly. "Is this what having a family of brothers is like?" Julie asked Chrissy.

"Yup, this is exactly what dinner time sounded like at my house when I was growing up. My brothers were always going at it like this. Don't be surprised if, at some point, they throw each other on the ground and wrestle. Boys never seem to outgrow that stage, especially football players."

She listened as Reagan defended his choice of club apparel.

"No, that shirt was not something Justin Bieber would wear." Reagan turned his attention back to Julie. "Do you need anything? Can I get you another glass of wine?"

"No." She desperately tried to control her laughter. This scene was better than any comedy movie. "Thanks, but we need to be leaving soon. Chrissy should probably find Matt."

He leaned over toward Chrissy. "I believe your husband's inside playing pool. Go through the patio doors and follow the noise. He should be downstairs."

Chrissy stood and followed a couple of guys from the team inside the house.

"You're welcome to stay. I could take you home later," he said. "Knowing this crowd, the party will be going on for a while yet."

Julie considered the invitation, but decided it was time to go. Reagan's company had become way too appealing. And quite frankly, the feeling scared her silly. "That's a tempting offer, but I have to work early tomorrow. I have a patient who needs therapy sessions almost every day. We're not normally open on Sundays, but I made an exception for this girl. She's making such great improvements, and I don't want anything to stop her progress."

Chrissy soon came back with a long-faced Matt.

As Julie prepared to say goodbye, she impulsively reached over to give Reagan a hug. His arms wrapped around her until his solid body fit comfortably against hers, so much so, she had a hard time letting go. "Thanks again. This was really great. We had so much fun."

Kelsey came to stand next to her brother. She gave Julie a quick hug. "Thanks for coming. Hopefully, we can get together again soon."

"Good luck in college. Call me next time you're in town, and we can do lunch."

Reagan escorted Julie to the Taylor's car and held open the door as she got in.

As they pulled away, Chrissy turned around to face Julie, who was sitting in the back seat. "There may be hope for you yet," Chrissy whispered.

Chapter Eight

The day started out cheerful enough, with Reagan coming over for dinner later that afternoon. In the morning, Julie made a trip to the grocery store, and then got her hair cut and styled, something she hadn't treated herself to in a long time.

Then, a nondescript envelope arrived in the mail, with no return address. What was inside left her lying in bed crying for the past hour. The contents dealt a debilitating blow to her heart.

The short note included an apology for not sending the picture sooner, and he was sorry for her loss. He hoped the photograph provided her with a small bit of comfort. The letter was signed *Brad Speronis, US Army*. Brad had served with John through several tours. The date on the picture indicated it was taken only a few days before John was killed.

Julie studied the photo again, memorizing every detail—the sharp rise of mountains in the background, the Humvee he stood on top of, his long unkempt hair and beard, the red Warriors ball cap, his spirited smile. *Could he be peering at me through time and space, letting me know everything would be okay? How could life be okay when you're not here?*

Clutching the photograph, she stood on unsteady legs. The room spun, and she held onto the bedpost for support. After a minute, she walked to the bathroom and leaned over the sink. Cool water from the faucet soothed her tender face and parched eyes. She needed to pull herself together soon. Aiden and her mom were coming back shortly. A lot had to get done before Reagan's arrival in a few hours.

Looking at her reflection, she groaned at the sight of her red and puffy eyes. A dab of makeup here and there would hopefully cover most of the evidence of her tears. She ran a brush through her hair and pulled it off her face. "Well," she told herself, "you still look like a hot mess, but it will have to do." She went into the kitchen and secured John's photo to the refrigerator door with a small magnet.

Just then, Aiden ran into the house through the back door, followed by Mary. "Mom, we're back!" He cried out then took off like a roadrunner upstairs to his bedroom.

Mary dropped a few bags on the table and took a seat. "Who knew second graders needed so much stuff? We got crayons, a pair of scissors, pencils, and a lunchbox. He wanted you to help him pick out a backpack."

"Thanks for taking him back-to-school shopping. I needed time alone to compose myself."

"I noticed you put John's picture on the fridge. Are you feeling any better?"

"Seeing John in that picture reminds me of how much his job truly was a calling. He spent his last days on earth doing what he was meant to do."

"He does look like he's the king of the world, standing on top of the vehicle." Mary smiled tenderly at the picture before unpacking the shopping bags. "So, when's your dinner guest arriving? Am I dressed all right for a celebrity?" Mary spun in her tan Bermuda shorts and pink polo shirt.

Mom looked ready to hit the golf course, which she probably would have, if not for their special guest. "You look lovely. I told him to come around five o'clock, which should give me enough time to put the house in order and get dinner started."

Even though this would be Reagan's second time here, she was still self-conscious about having him over to her—well—quaint house. And after seeing Reagan's multimillion dollar digs, she wondered what his opinion was of her home, and of her. Nothing she could do to change where she lived now. *Might as well make the best of it.*

"Well, let's get cracking!" Mary said, flicking an imaginary whip. "I'll pick up and dust the family room. You do what needs to be done in the kitchen."

Julie gave her mom a grateful hug. "We always did make a good team."

****

A deep rumble cut through the quiet of her house as a beautiful red sports car with dark tinted windows pulled into the driveway. A few neighbors in their front yards stopped what they were doing to watch Reagan step out of the vehicle and stroll up the brick paver walkway. The sight of him sent Julie's stomach into gymnast mode—performing a gold medal routine of flips, cartwheels, and leaps. He only had to knock once before she pulled open the door to let him in.

His left hand held a bouquet of yellow roses and white daisies. "For you." He handed her the flowers before stepping inside. "Thanks for the dinner invitation. Sure you're prepared to feed a starving football player?"

"You bet." At the grocery store, the check-out girl had asked Julie if she was having a dinner party for twenty. *Nope. Just one, tall, athletic, hunk of man.* "I've made enough to feed an army. If you leave here hungry, it's your own fault." The bouquet in her hand smelled divine. "Thank you for the beautiful flowers. I'll get a vase from the kitchen and put them in water."

When Julie returned, she saw her mom had taken care of introductions.

"A pleasure to meet you, Mary. I can see where Julie gets her good looks." He wore his trademark charming smile. "I'm happy you'll be joining us for dinner."

Their talk was cut short by Aiden bounding down the stairs. He propelled himself into Reagan's arms.

"Whoa, kid. Easy there. You almost knocked me over." Reagan set Aiden on his feet before ruffling his brown hair. "How've you been?"

"Great." He yanked on the bottom of his shirt. "Look, I am wearing my Harrison jersey for you. Mom has one, too, but she'll only wear it for games."

"You look better than me in that jersey." He knelt so he was at eye level with the child. "Tell me, how's practice going?"

During the exchange, Julie's gaze fixed on the two of them. When had Aiden and Reagan become so close? Letting Aiden become too attached to him might be a mistake. Once Reagan's interest in them came to an end, he'd break both their hearts.

She moved to stand next to her son, putting a protective arm around his shoulder. "Dinner should be ready in less than an hour," Julie tried talking over

Aiden. "Have a seat and make yourself comfortable. Would you like something to drink?"

"A beer would be great." Reagan sat in a brown leather recliner.

John's favorite chair. Her chest squeezed so tightly she could barely take in her next breath. "I'll be right back." She went into the kitchen to pull a beer out of the refrigerator and stared at John's picture on its door. "I never could imagine anyone but you in that chair." Before she walked back to Reagan, she took a few seconds to steel her emotions. When she entered the room, she took in Reagan's larger-than-life presence filling her family room. Surprisingly, he looked natural sitting in John's chair. It fit him perfectly, just as it had her husband.

While the three adults sat in the family room and chatted, Aiden quieted and listened with short interest. He soon squirmed and eventually skipped over to Reagan. "Would you please practice football with me in the backyard? Coach says I need to work on catching the ball."

"Sure, kid." He took one last swig of beer. "Pardon me, ladies, but duty calls." The two guys headed out, grabbing a football on their way through the mud room.

"I'll put the salad together," Julie told Mary and went into the kitchen. "Aiden," she called as he walked outside. "Don't play too hard...it's hot outside. And don't get your clothes sweaty and dirty before dinner."

"Yeah, Mom," Aiden said as he took off running.

Julie stood in front of the kitchen window, which overlooked her backyard. First Reagan, then her son stripped off their shirts in preparation of the effort to come. Her gaze fixed on Reagan. She noticed a tribal-style tattoo covering his ribcage under his right arm. Another tattoo was visible on his left shoulder blade, which looked like an angel. As they threw the ball back and forth, she became even more aware of how powerfully built he was. His well-defined muscles moved with fluid motion and his athletic arm tossed the ball with ease. He was ripped to the core. She'd forgotten how good a man could look with his shirt off.

Her attention shifted to Aiden, who caught a pass against his scrawny bare chest and slipped past Reagan, shouting, "come and get me."

Although she had lost so much, she also gained so many blessings. Aiden was growing to be a wonderful child. Her mother was now a big part of their lives. She had Chrissy and Matt's unwavering loyalty, and Reagan's recent friendship. She realized he was slowly being weaved into the fabric of her life. Every kind word and thoughtful action from him loosened the knot secured over her heart.

"Well, this view is definitely improving."

Mary's appearance gave Julie a small jump of surprise.

"I'm not too old to appreciate a good looking man when I see one." She stood beside Julie and looked out the window with a playful smile.

"I think they're having a good time outside." Julie turned to start mixing the salad. "And Aiden getting some male bonding time, which is a good thing. I'm just worried about him. That he's getting too attached to Reagan. What if—"

"Stop with the *what-ifs*." Her mom shook her head. "I know you want to protect your son but he's fine. Reagan seems to genuinely care about Aiden." Mary took hold of her hand. "Now, do you have everything ready for dinner? Those boys will be coming in soon, and they'll be ready to eat."

A half hour later, they entered the kitchen, with their shirts back on, famished.

Julie had just pulled the lasagna out of the oven.

"Something smells good in here." Reagan licked his lips while looking at the bubbling pasta dish. "Do you need help with anything?"

"Thanks, but we have everything under control. Aiden, please go wash your hands and face for dinner. We're ready to eat."

"I'll follow Aiden and go wash up, too." Reagan winked, before disappearing down the hall.

Good grief. She needed a minute to collect her stray thoughts—from tattoos to muscles to eyes as blue as a summer sky, to everything in between. She needed to focus on dinner, and on Aiden, and her mother. And John.

What Julie really needed was another glass of wine.

****

Reagan hadn't realized he was hungry until he walked into the wonderful smell of Julie's kitchen. His gut clenched and growled, like it hadn't been fed in weeks. Not only did her meal smell delicious, it tasted even better. After four helpings of lasagna, a bowl of salad, and a loaf of garlic bread, his stomach redlined.

They decided to hold off on the pie until after their supper settled.

"You two are a match made in heaven," Mary said, smiling at both Reagan and Julie. "Julie loves to cook, and Reagan loves to eat. They say food is the fastest way to a man's heart."

Reagan couldn't disagree. Julie cooked the best meal he'd eaten in a long time.

As Aiden finished off the remaining food on his plate, Mary and Julie started to clear the table.

"Let me help." Reagan carried several bowls over to the sink. "It's a little-known fact that I'm an expert dish washer. My two older sisters used to gang up on me and force me to do their chores."

Julie tossed him the dish cloth. "The job's all yours." Her phone rang. She looked at the screen and stepped out of the kitchen to answer the call.

Still holding the dishcloth, he noticed a picture on the front of the refrigerator and walked over to get a closer look. The man was positioned on top of a huge Humvee, machine gun in hand. Most men would be intimidated by this real warrior. So, this was the legendary John Ellis.

"You remind me of him." Mary came to stand beside him. "He was brave and strong, but underneath was a gentle, tender man who loved his family and country. I see the same gentleness in you…how you act with Aiden and with Julie."

"He was a much better man than I could ever be, going off to fight an unknown enemy overseas."

Mary turned her gaze toward him and offered an understanding smile. "Yes, John was special. He gave the ultimate sacrifice for his country. Julie has had to fight her own battles. Being married to a Special Forces soldier takes a courageous woman. I hope you appreciate how special she is. She deserves a second chance to make her dreams come true."

Reagan gave her a nod. He understood Julie's

strength wasn't something seen with the naked eye, like an athlete or even a soldier. What she possessed was so much greater—an ability to carry on, day after day, despite fear, pain, and loss.

Julie walked back into the kitchen. "Sorry, that was the mother of one of my patients. She had a question about her son's at-home therapy schedule."

"You mind if I take Aiden for a walk to the park?" Mary asked. "I could use the exercise after all that food." After locating Aiden, she took his hand and herded him out of the house.

That left Julie and Reagan alone in the house.

"Would you like another beer?" Julie rested her hip against the kitchen counter then cocked her head in the direction of the back door. "We can go sit outside on the deck."

"A glass of ice water would be great. And so does going outside. The air's finally starting to cool down."

They took their drinks and went out onto the wooden deck, which was attached to the back of her home. Placed in the center were two patio chairs surrounded by containers of flowers. Hanging baskets of red and white petunias made a colorful display, and a white arbor in the yard dripped with yellow climbing roses.

"Looks like you have a green thumb." Reagan appreciated the vibrant, colorful life around him, being that he was a guy who loved the outdoors.

"The flowers and garden are my mother's achievement. Aiden and I help water and pull weeds, but that's about all. My house at Fort Bragg had several empty flower beds. Well, I guess they weren't empty since they were full of weeds. I tried unsuccessfully to plant flowers for John to enjoy while he was home. In Afghanistan, everything around him was various shades of brown."

"Tell me about John, and your life at Fort Bragg." He craved understanding her, where she came from, and what had shaped her into the person she was today. Happiness, tragedy, the good and the bad. And what it would take to make this beautiful woman fall in love again.

She let out a soft sigh and glanced his way. "The first time I met John…he brought me to tears. John had gotten mad that our cross-country coach assigned me as his training partner. After our run, he reamed me out for slowing him down. The next day, I came to practice ready to go and actually beat him. I loved to remind him of that day." Julie paused to take a breath. "I'm angry at him sometimes, for leaving me."

Her voice shook, as if those simple words took every ounce of her strength to say.

"For all the times he's left me. I've never said that to anyone before."

His heart squeezed in response to her pain. "You're hurting. Anger is part of the grieving process."

"I was lucky. For a short time, I had everything I wanted." She then began unwinding the story of her life. Revealing that in her youth, she hadn't realized how tough military life would be. She shared the details of her impromptu wedding, and then the many days at Fort Bragg without her husband. "I found out I was pregnant shortly before John left again for Afghanistan. My mom flew to North Carolina for the birth." Julie paused to take a drink of water.

He shifted in his chair in order to move closer.

"Having your first child without your husband there for support must have been hard."

"Oh, yes, it was, but that's what active duty military wives do, we carry on. Aiden was two months old when John saw him for the first time. We enjoyed our time as a family as much as possible. We never knew how long we'd have together. Many times, John was recalled without much notice. I'd have no idea when he'd come home. He spoke Pashto, a language widely used by the Afghan people. He was a good soldier, and John's skills in language and weapons were highly valued by his commanders."

"You must have worried a lot about his safety when he was overseas." Hearing her talk about her late husband affected him deeper than he'd expected. He was actually envious of a man who was no longer alive. But John had enjoyed Julie's love, and he still held her devotion. Yes, he was man enough to admit he was jealous.

Julie crossed her legs then uncrossed them. She folded her hands and rested them on her lap. "Worry is a natural product of having a loved one constantly in harm's way, but I tried to stay positive. I never let myself imagine anything bad would happen to John. I wouldn't let myself go down that road. So when I was told he'd been killed in action, I almost couldn't believe his death was true. The fact that he was really gone didn't fully hit me until we started packing our house to move back to Timber Lake."

Tears dripped off her cheeks like raindrops on a rose petal.

"I'm sorry." He took her small hand into a protective clasp. What he really wanted to do was wrap her in his arms, but he stopped that impulse. "No one should have to go through what you did." He wanted to shelter her from any more pain.

"After everything John did for them, the Army still won't tell me how he died. I was cheated from a future with my husband and now I am being deprived of justice. I'm sorry." She inhaled deeply and wiped a tear away with the back of her trembling hand. "I'm having a hard time going on, day after day, and staying strong."

"You amaze me. The fact that you've come through the firestorm and are still standing tall is evidence of your strong spirit. You've provided a good home for Aiden, and he's a great kid. Getting answers may take more time, but those barriers will eventually be knocked over. The truth always has a way of coming out." He considered the fact his fame granted him access to people and information others didn't, and he could use that influence to help Julie. Perhaps he should make a few phone calls later tonight and start knocking down some of those walls.

The gate flew open, and Aiden and Mary arrived home from the park. "Hey, Reagan. Can I get a ride in your car?" Aiden's footsteps pounded as he ran onto the deck. "It looks super cool."

"You bet." He looked over at Julie. "That is, if it's okay?"

"Of course. I'll get his booster seat out of my car." She stepped off the porch and walked over to the detached garage.

Aiden tipped back his head and groaned. "I hate that baby seat."

"Come on, big shot." He took Aiden's hand, and

they walked to his car.

They met Julie, who installed the booster seat, and then buckled Aiden inside. Catching a glimpse of the interior of the car, she let out a long whistle. "Nice ride."

He imagined Julie riding in the seat next to him. His hand moving slowly to take hold of hers. Julie's lips curved in a smile while they drove down some secluded country road. And his pulse raced in anticipation. "We won't be long. I promise to go slow. And don't worry, the passenger side airbag is turned off."

"I trust you." Julie patted his hand.

The act sent heat flickering across his skin. Her touch lit a spark of brightness and warmth inside his chest.

I trust you.

No words could express how much her trust meant. He closed the door, pushed the ignition button, and the engine produced a low rumble. Within a few seconds, the car was at the end of their street. Before they turned the corner, he looked in the rearview mirror and saw a miniature version of Julie, standing at the edge of the driveway, waving and smiling.

Looking back one last time, something stirred deep within him, something that had been quiet for a very long time. He needed to call Brynn and permanently end their on-again, off-again relationship. No use in denying the truth any longer—he'd unintentionally fallen in love with Julie Ellis.

Chapter Nine

DeMarcus jabbed his fist into Reagan's shoulder. "Hey, man, you sleeping?" He sat in the open seat across the aisle. "Got any plans for tomorrow?"

"Why can't I be left alone for ten minutes? Is it a crime for a guy to get some sleep?" Reagan rested in the large, leather airline seat. The muscles in his abs cried out in pain. His whole body had taken a beating during that afternoon's game. But nothing a hot bath and a good night's sleep couldn't cure.

"You're on a team plane carrying over seventy guys who've just won a big game. No rest until you get back into your own bed." DeMarcus reached over and pulled off Reagan's headphones. "We haven't had a chance to hang out for a while. You want to come over tomorrow? I could grill some meat, and we could throw back a few beers."

"I can be there later in the afternoon. I've got a few things I need to take care of in the morning."

"Those 'things' wouldn't have anything to do with Julie, would they?" DeMarcus wiggled his bushy eyebrows.

"Maybe." Reagan refused to yield any more information.

"How's that going with you two? You sure spend a lot of time together. You still sticking to the story she's just a friend?"

Reagan closed his eyes and pondered the direction his life had taken him over the past few months. Julie had come into his life when he'd least expected, unassuming and refreshingly genuine. What had started as an innocent tour of the stadium had developed into a strong connection. Julie continued to steer the direction of their relationship, even when it meant only remaining friends.

"You're right, I'm probably over there way more than I should be." Ever since their first dinner in August, he'd become a regular at Julie's house. Some days, he'd bring over a pizza and a DVD, and the three of them would assemble on the sofa to watch the latest family movie. Or Julie would cook the most amazing meals that had him wondering how he survived on the food he'd eaten before.

DeMarcus laughed. "Do what makes you happy."

Was spending so much time with Julie really a mistake? Every time he convinced himself to pull away, he found himself back at her doorstep. He seemed to be drawn there like Icarus to the sun. Would he end up being destroyed like the Greek mythological man, only because of his own stubborn fascination? "Julie and I have only known each other for three months, and I can honestly say we have a strictly platonic relationship. I don't see that changing." He put on his headphones. No music played, but the headphones were good for blocking out annoying background noises, like the sounds coming out of his friend's mouth.

DeMarcus stood in the aisle and leaned over the back of the chair in front of Reagan. "I'm not buying what you're selling for one minute. I've been telling you for a while, just because you have a girl don't mean you can't be on your game. You can have both."

The plane started its descent toward Timber Lake Airport. DeMarcus took his seat several rows ahead. Reagan grabbed his duffel bag and put away his hunting magazine.

How could you fall in love with someone you've never held in your arms or tasted her lips? His past relationships had been predominantly physical, with very little emotional connection. Maybe that's what made Julie so special. Even Sarah, his college girlfriend, hadn't possessed so much power over him. Over the years, he'd worked hard to protect his heart. Now, he'd opened it to a woman who loved another man.

The private plane landed in Timber Lake well after dark. The team disembarked, grabbed their luggage, and made their way to the parking lot. Reagan slid into his SUV, glad to be heading home. He checked his phone and noticed a text and several voice messages waiting. He opened the text from Julie first.

**Great game! Especially enjoyed you throwing your helmet at the bench. **

He laughed out loud. That exhibition of temper was the result of some miscommunication from the defensive coordinator. Unfortunately, the cameraman had been right there to catch the whole rage-filled display.

—Thanks…it was a good game. Heading to your mom's tomorrow to play Mr. Fix It. See you there?—

Nope, got to work. Have fun!

Probably for the best, since his home repairs skills were very rusty, and Julie would definitely be a distraction. He began listening to his voice mails—the first was from Brynn and was quickly deleted. He hadn't spoken to her since he'd broken off their relationship, and he wanted to keep it that way. The second was from Greg Jackson, a reporter he'd contacted a few weeks ago. He was an investigative journalist who worked in Washington. While listening to the message, he grabbed a pen, took a few notes, and then saved the message. The reporter's response was exactly what he'd hoped for.

Greg agreed to help uncover the mystery surrounding John Ellis's death, and Reagan decided not to tell Julie. No point in getting her hopes up, just in case this effort led to another dead end.

****

On Monday morning, Mary stood at her front door, waiting, with a cup of coffee and a bagel extended in her hands.

"Just what the doctor ordered." He stepped inside before reaching for the coffee. The smell started recharging his sluggish morning brain.

"You had a tough game yesterday. Are you sure you want to be here working on my house? These projects can wait."

"Sitting around isn't good for sore muscles. Plus I promised to come over soon, and I don't have many days off."

"I appreciate you being willing to help me out. It's nice to have a man around." Mary led him into the kitchen, where she'd laid out her small collection of tools. "Julie, Aiden, and I watched the game together. You played well. Whenever you made a tackle, Aiden cheered, and Julie would cringe. I think she was afraid you'd get hurt."

He already knew Julie cared about his wellbeing. But did she care about him as more than a friend? He doubted her affection went that deep. "Well, luckily I've walked off the field after every play of my career." Reagan downed his coffee. The caffeine slowly forced the synapses and neurons in his brain to flicker to life. "So, what would you like me to work on first?"

Four hours later, he had fixed the leak in Mary's bathroom faucet, changed the light fixture in her kitchen, hung several curtain rods, and quieted a squeaky door. Mary compensated him for his time by making lunch. Set before him on the table was a wonderfully large sandwich full of turkey, cheese, tomato, and lettuce. In addition, she made potato salad and fresh-squeezed lemonade. Being a good guy had its perks, and all this food was at the top of the list. He ate with fervor, not leaving even a crumb on his plate. "Everything was delicious. You're too good to me." He leaned over to give her a peck on the cheek.

Mary blushed. "Aiden told me you're coming to his birthday party next week. Are you really subjecting yourself to a houseful of children?"

"How bad could a kid's birthday party possibly be?" He looked over to see the amused smile on Mary's face. "That bad, huh?"

"You've played against three-hundred-pound linemen. I'm sure you can handle a few second-graders." She shrugged before picking up his empty plate.

"If they're anything like Aiden, we'll have our work cut out for us." He noticed the time and stood. "I probably should be going, thanks for lunch."

"Thank you, Reagan." Mary reached over to touch

his arm. "Not only for helping me today, but for everything you've done for Julie and Aiden. I don't know what's going on between you and my daughter, and it's none of my business. I do know you mean a lot to her, whether she's said the words or not." She walked him to the door. "Have a good week, dear, and try not to hurt anybody." She stood smiling and waving goodbye.

He breathed in deeply the crisp, autumn air. "Now what fun would that be?"

****

A week later, Mary stepped out the front door and raised her face to the sun. What a beautiful October day—the kind that made her forget the Wisconsin winter was just around the corner. The sound of Julie and Aiden coming down the sidewalk shook her out of her daydreaming.

Julie wore a Warriors jersey, slim-cut jeans, and low brown boots, ready to attend her first Warriors game. But instead of appearing excited at the prospect of going with Reagan's family, Julie's lips were set in a firm line and her face seemed pale.

Aiden darted up and gave her a fervent hug. "Hi, Grandma. I wish I could go with Mom to the game to see Reagan play."

She wrapped her arms around her little grandson and squeezed him tight. "I know, sweetheart. But we'll have fun watching the game together on TV. I got those mozzarella sticks you like."

He waved a piece of paper in the air. "Look what I made!"

Mary took it from Aiden's open hand. On one side was a child's drawing of a family—crayon stick figures representing Mom, Aiden, and Dad. The picture was titled: My Family. This drawing showed Aiden held memories of his father, which should put a smile on Julie's face instead of a frown.

Aiden pointed to the figure that was taller than the other two. "That's Reagan. He's holding Mom's hand. I told Mom I want him to be my dad."

Julie came up behind him and sighed. "Aiden, remember what I just told you."

"Huh?" Aiden answered, distracted by his picture. "Oh yeah, but Joe's mom has a boyfriend and now they're getting married. Joe said he'll have two dads, and I don't even have one."

"Dad loved you very much, but now he's in heaven." While Julie stroked his hair, she used her other hand to swipe away a tear in the corner of her eye. "Reagan is not my boyfriend, and we're not getting married. We're friends, just like you're friends with Penny from across the street."

"Whatever." He kicked at the sidewalk. "But I still want Reagan as my dad." Aiden's shoulders sank as he walked around to the backyard.

"I don't know how to make him understand." Julie pinched the bridge of her nose. "He's got a one-track mind...everything in his small world revolves around Reagan."

Mary wasn't surprised by Aiden's insistence. He was more perceptive than Julie gave him credit for. Time for Julie to hear the truth, whether she wanted to or not. "Honey, both of you are single, attractive adults who obviously enjoy spending time together. Even Aiden can see that Reagan adores you."

"Don't go misconstruing kindness for a romantic

interest. I'm not really his type. I'm nobody special." Julie's cheeks burned red.

A sure sign her feelings ran deeper than she'd admit. "You're wrong. You are special, and Reagan would be the first to agree with me. A man with his responsibilities doesn't spend so much of his free time with a woman, unless he's fallen for her. He even spent his day off helping me with repairs around here." She pointed to her house. "Reagan may be nice, but nobody's that nice unless love is involved."

"You know how unprepared I am." Her voice cracked. Julie kicked a small stone on the sidewalk, sending it skipping into the grass. "I can't imagine loving anyone else but John. He was my one true love. No one is lucky enough to find that twice in a lifetime."

"You had a wonderful life with John, and Aiden's evidence of that. But John's gone, and you deserve to be loved again. And Aiden…think about how much he would benefit from a father figure in his life. If you were honest with yourself, you'd admit your feelings for Reagan have grown. I can see you really care." She opened her arms.

The moment Julie entered her mom's embrace, she began to cry.

Mary absorbed the emotional turmoil her daughter released with every tear.

"Why is life so hard?" Julie took a deep breath then exhaled. "I do care about Reagan. But his life is so different than mine. We're friends, yes…but that's all we'll ever be."

Mary wished her daughter would open her eyes to the simple truth. Julie could find love again, but first, she'd have to unlock her heart. "I think Reagan's been waiting for you to be ready, just don't keep him waiting too long."

"Thanks for always being here for me." Julie dabbed at the corner of her eyes and made her way down the front steps. "I should probably get going. Wish me luck!"

****

Julie's stomach churned as she parked her Jeep in front of Reagan's house to meet his family. As she exited her vehicle, a squirrel darted across her path, most likely on a single focused mission to find as many acorns as possible before winter.

Not even the bright sunshine calmed her nerves. After what had happened earlier with Aiden, she worried about their judgment of her relationship with Reagan. The last thing she wanted was for any more misunderstandings. But when they answered the door, all her misgivings evaporated.

Bob and Eileen were the first to greet her, followed by Kelsey, who gave her a massive hug. Reagan's father was exactly as she'd imagined—tall, with wide shoulders and the same strong features as his son. Eileen's petite height took Julie by surprise. How had this small woman produced big Reagan?

She was then introduced to Reagan's older sisters, Stacy and Maggie, and their husbands, Tony and Derek, along with their combined five children. Stacy and Maggie were so similar in looks, they could pass as twins. Both were tall and thin, with light brown hair and hazel eyes. Stacy's husband, Tony, sported a dark, bushy beard. That, combined with his plaid shirt, made him resemble a lumberjack. Derek, on the other hand, looked like a lawyer or engineer. Julie learned he was the former and had a successful law practice in Indianapolis.

Reagan had arranged for a babysitter to stay home with the kids so the adults could go and enjoy the game.

Arriving at the stadium parking lot, the group flipped open the tailgates of their three vehicles and kicked off the party. As they unloaded coolers, numerous food containers, lawn chairs, and the grill, Julie unfortunately found herself the focus of Reagan's sisters.

"So, you've been seeing Reagan for what...three months now?" Stacy raised a single, perfectly shaped brow.

"I've known him for that long," she answered while pulling out an icy beer from the cooler.

"When you say 'known,' you mean date." Maggie piped up with a grin. "Now, I know my brother, and his eyes light up every time he talks about you."

"I'm glad he stopped seeing Brynn," Stacy said. "She's dumber than a box of rocks. I did a happy dance when he gave her the boot. Reagan's much better off dating you."

"But we're not dating," Julie insisted. This was going downhill—fast.

"Don't interrogate her." Kelsey put a protective arm around her. "What feelings she has for our brother are none of our business. We don't need to know all the hot, steamy details."

"Oh, yes we do," Stacy and Maggie said in unison.

Julie's eyes bugged out and her drink caught in her throat. She coughed and sputtered while Kelsey patted her on the back.

"Everything Reagan does is our business." Stacy

clinked beer bottles with Maggie.

"That's just because you want to use the information to tease him." Kelsey poked Maggie's arm several times. "Just like when he was little."

Maggie laughed and turned to Julie. "Reagan is two years younger than me and three years younger than Stacy. The poor boy had it rough growing up. We would dress him in our clothes and parade him around the house. Ah, those were the days."

"That's why he grew up to be so rough and tough." Kelsey flexed her bicep, which was significantly smaller than her brother's. "He had to learn how to protect himself from these two."

Stacy and Maggie must have been a formidable duo against a young Reagan. Julie almost felt bad for the guy. Almost.

Now that Julie was no longer the topic of discussion, she enjoyed the ongoing exchange. Maggie had just finished telling Julie a story, which included Reagan and their mom's nail polish, when Bob Harrison walked over to the cluster of giggling females. "All right, let my son keep a shred of dignity." Bob winked at Julie. "Dear, let me save you from this trio of trouble. Would you mind coming over and help me get the food ready?"

"Sure." She gladly followed Bob around to the front of the car where a small charcoal grill sat. She noticed he walked with a slight limp, maybe a leftover from his own days playing sports. The air was filled with the aroma of brats, hamburgers, and the smoke from countless tailgate grills surrounding them.

Bob sat on a plastic folding chair and pointed to an empty one next to him. "My daughters can be pretty relentless, and you've definitely piqued their interest."

Julie gave him a grateful smile. "Thanks, but I'm really not that exciting. I'm sure they would've gotten bored with me eventually."

"Don't count on it." He stood to flip over the hamburgers and brats cooking nearby.

Bob Harrison was quiet, but carried an inner strength that was hard to miss. With his tall frame and strong build, she could tell where Reagan got his athletic talent from. His hair was the same sandy color as his son's, with an added touch of gray.

Reagan's mother soon joined them. Eileen possessed the charming personality that was also evident in Reagan and Kelsey. She was very small in comparison to her husband, with shoulder-length blonde hair and bright blue eyes.

By the time she made her way into the stadium with Reagan's family, the game had already started. She wove her way through throngs of people dressed in Warriors gear, trying not to stare opened mouthed at several men with large, red Ws painted on their beer bellies. The crowd was loud and rambunctious, and the smell of beer and hot dogs permeated the air. The seats Reagan arranged were ten rows behind the home team's bench, at midfield. The group of eight filed into their row, with Julie situated between Kelsey and Maggie.

"Julie." Kelsey patted her arm to get her attention then pointed to the sidelines. "Do you see number eight standing over by the water cooler? He asked me for my phone number at the party and wants to get together next time I visit. Reagan overheard him and threatened to toss him into the next county. I was so bummed, because he's super cute."

How endearing of Reagan to try to guard his sister's heart, along with the rest of her body. Julie caught sight of the offending player and laughed. "Seems your big brother is slightly overprotective."

"Oh! Reagan's running on the field." Kelsey bounced up and down, clapping.

"He said you've been feeding him well," Maggie said. "I seriously don't know how he survived on takeout and microwave meals for all these years. When he was in high school, my mom couldn't make enough food to fill his stomach."

Reagan broke through the offensive line to take down the quarterback, and the noise level in the stadium erupted. Julie, along with the whole Harrison family, jumped to their feet and cheered. What a rush to see him play in person!

Eileen leaned around to get Julie's attention. "I'm so glad you came with us today. Reagan's always so much fun to watch. I wish we could be here more often."

Julie tore her gaze away from Reagan and turned her head toward his mother. "This is my first Warriors game. I was totally oblivious to football before I met Reagan. My son, Aiden, started playing on a team this summer."

Eileen smiled. "Just wait, if your son continues to play football, you'll become an expert." She returned her attention to the action on the field.

Julie's mind wandered to an imagined future, where she sat in the stands watching Aiden play high school football, with Reagan still by her side. The thought made her take a deep breath and smile. Maybe the idea of a relationship with Reagan wasn't so crazy.

But could she put her heart on the line, knowing he may not feel as strongly? His idea of a committed relationship may be very different. Could she endure any more heartache in her life?

Shouts of "Dragon" snapped her out of her daydream, and she looked over to see Reagan standing on the sidelines. He took off his helmet and grabbed a water bottle, before squirting water into his mouth. Then he turned to face her in the stands. As their gazes met, a slight smile crossed his lips. Her heart fluttered in response.

With a quick nod, he slowly turned to face the playing field.

Reagan Harrison, with his confident attitude and sweet smile, might be the one man worth the risk.

Chapter Ten

On the day of Aiden's birthday party, the thermometer outside Julie's kitchen window read fifty degrees. A striking contrast to the sunny day a week ago when she'd attended the Warriors game. Aiden had wanted a costume birthday party a few days before Halloween. He and Grandma were out shopping for gifts to put into the party bags.

On this busy day, going out for a run didn't make much sense, but here she was, lacing up her shoes. She walked out the door, wearing an old sweatshirt, running tights, hat, and gloves. There was someplace she needed to go before she saw Reagan again. Over the past months, she'd been running regularly, and the activity now felt natural. Not as easy as in high school, when her legs were young and she had very few other responsibilities, but still familiar and freeing.

She took deep, cleansing breaths, causing cool air to flood her lungs. The activity of her body unclouded her mind. Julie turned the corner onto Maple Street, and a narrow path came into view. A familiar trail led to a little opening in the tree line, which continued to Cottonwood Field. She hesitated for several seconds before heading through the wall of trees. She entered the woods through an arch of tree branches, and memory took control of her steps. Suddenly, the air became quiet and still, the sounds of cars faded away.

The only sounds were from her own heavy breathing, the crunch of gravel under her feet, and the song of a lone bird.

Turn left at the grove of birch trees. Head right where the large boulder divided the path. She ran a mile farther and took a left turn, and instead of following it to the right, she quickly found herself stepping into the clearing. The fall leaves were bright orange and red, many still clung to tree branches. Even more were scattered on the ground, providing a disguise for the brown grass. The air smelled of rain and earth, the undeniable scent of autumn.

She visually absorbed the landscape. Ten years had passed since her last visit, but the scenery was the same. She could picture John sitting on the fallen tree next to the creek, with a book in hand, absorbed in his own thoughts. Back then, neither of them had a clue what the future would hold. They were idealistic and full of their own ambitions, ready to take on the world.

They had discovered Cottonwood Field on a hot day in July, covered in tall grass and prismatic wildflowers. A slow-moving creek meandered through the middle, weaving back and forth like a shimmering snake.

She'd named the field for the large Cottonwood tree, which stood guard in the middle of the field. In summer, the tree released an abundance of white fluffy Cottonwood seeds. They had floated through the air like summer snowflakes. The soft puffs filled the sky and stuck to her and John's sweaty skin. They laughed and swung their arms in a failed attempt to avoid becoming covered in the cotton.

John leaned in close to pull off a seed stuck to her

lower lip and their lips met in a shy, first kiss. Throughout their high school years, they visited Cottonwood Field again and again. Their special field offered a place to slowly fall in love—a way to escape the rest of the world.

Julie remembered the conversations about the number of children they wanted to have and where they would live once John retired from the Army. They'd been different people then, and she realized how much she'd changed, especially during the trials of the past year and a half.

Strolling through the field, Julie came to terms with certain facts of her life. She was a widow, and no amount of heartache would bring back John. Every day was as unpredictable as the Wisconsin weather. Instead of fearing the future, she needed to start embracing the gift of life. Which led her straight to Reagan and how he'd altered her life.

Up to this point, their relationship had been strictly platonic. She always assumed Reagan only saw her as a friend. Was that belief just a protective measure to guard her heart? Looking at the situation now with clear eyes, as the fog finally lifted, she saw the truth. Reagan's unwavering loyalty, the way he looked after her well being, and his affection for Aiden—those were responses to feelings much stronger than friendship. The signs had been there all along.

What she felt for Reagan had strengthened over the past three months. The warning voices in her head needed to be quieted. Eighteen months ago, her heart had been cut down and nearly destroyed. Now, every day she became a little bit stronger. Thanks to Reagan, she felt whole again, instead of someone broken.

Walking over to the creek, she noticed a patch of purple Prairie Thistles holding strong against the changing of the season. *No matter how hard I resist, change will come regardless, always of its own accord.* Carefully, she picked a flower as a reminder of what she discovered within herself that day.

Instead of hiding away, she needed to step out onto the ledge and take a chance. Jump, and have faith Reagan's strong arms would be there at the bottom to catch her. Trusting him—a playboy football star with a shady dating record—would definitely be a risk. She'd learned over the past year that risk proved a double-edged sword. Hopefully, she'd be on the winning side this time.

The morning turned to noon, and she headed toward the path that led home. The rain from earlier left the earth with a glossy sheen. Birds came out of their shelters, taking flight into the brightening sky. As she ran, she deliberated on how to tell Reagan what was in her heart. A new anticipation grew with each step home.

****

That night, with Aiden's party scheduled to start in less than an hour, Julie opened her front door to the object of her nervous excitement. What she saw caused her breath to come to a screeching halt. Standing before her was a scrumptious-looking pirate. If fantasies came true, he'd kidnap her and take her to some deserted, tropical island, where they could swim in turquoise water and stuff themselves with coconut and shrimp.

Back to reality, girl. Save the fantasizing for another day.

He shrugged off his coat and hung it in the closet

before she could offer. "Aiden, a pirate's here to see you," she called out. "And he said the birthday boy needs to walk the plank."

Aiden came running. "Reagan!" he yelled and gave him a big hug.

"No fooling you, kid." Reagan, still in Aiden's grasp, looked over at Julie and closed his one exposed eye in an attempt at a wink. "Didn't the eye patch help my disguise?"

"Don't worry. I'm sure no one will figure out who you are. You do make an absolutely terrifying pirate. The children will be shaking with fear." She walked into the family room dressed in her new fairy costume, sparkling wings fluttering behind. She'd spent hours searching for the right costume, with Reagan in mind. The one she'd ended up choosing was short, but not too skimpy, and hugged her curves in all the right places.

"How come I don't believe you? Speaking of children, when are the kids arriving?"

Julie let out a deep exhale, realizing she was quickly running out of time. "Very soon. Would you mind helping me set up some of the games? I could use your help hanging doughnuts from the kitchen ceiling."

"Sure thing." He followed her into the kitchen.

Julie pointed to the supplies on the table. "Here are the doughnuts, string, and tape. Hang the doughnuts at a height so the kids can reach them with their mouths. They eat them without using their hands."

He gave her a crooked smile. "Sounds like fun."

Julie's knees nearly buckled. *Focus. You have a party to run.* But Reagan's lips were way too distracting. "The game is harder than it sounds," she stated, before hustling out of the room to tackle the next task. Distraction was the name of the game, and the only way she would get through this party without doing something foolish.

"Aiden, time to put on your costume. It's hanging in your closet," Julie instructed while putting up the Pin the Nose on the Pumpkin game. Taking a break, she stole a glance at Reagan, who was busy taping string to her ceiling. He looked extremely dashing as a pirate, with his shirt open just enough to offer a peek of his well-defined chest. Julie became so lost in admiration, she let her gaze linger a little too long.

Reagan suddenly turned his attention from the ceiling to her.

Seeming to read her mind, he grinned as mischievously as the Cheshire cat. Her face warmed over being caught, and she quickly looked away. As she sprinted up the stairs, the heat of Reagan's stare followed her like a missile.

She kept Aiden still long enough to get him changed into his superhero costume.

The second he was dressed, Aiden ran down the stairs. "Yippee! Let's get this party started."

Julie followed, and her heart stopped as she watched him jump off the last three stairs.

Not missing a beat, Aiden went straight over to his tall friend. "Look, Reagan, isn't this costume the best?"

"You look super cool." He ruffled the kid's shaggy hair.

Reagan had such a loving heart hidden under his muscular chest. Her own heart squeezed in reaction to the way he cared for Aiden. A quiet knock sounded, and she went to answer the door .

A small witch stood on the front porch. "Hi, Mrs.

Ellis. I'm here for Aiden's party."

"Come on in, Penny." She waved to Penny's dad, who'd walked her over from their house.

"Arrh, small Penny, don't you look lovely," Reagan greeted the girl with his imitation pirate voice. "Welcome aboard."

"Hi, Mr. Reagan." Penny shyly gave him a quick hug and then darted over to Aiden.

"Doesn't anyone believe I'm a real pirate?" Reagan raised his arms and looked around.

Julie only giggled in response.

Before long, the house was full of children in various costumes and parents reluctant to leave with Reagan Harrison in attendance. Finally, after half an hour had passed and all the parents were still there, she started politely shooing them out the front door. The festivities finally began when the last parent exited, and Julie organized the children into small groups. Julie, Mary, and Reagan each took charge of a group and led them through all the activities. Her home was a scene of organized chaos.

The party lasted for two hours. Once the last child left, her living room looked like a bomb had gone off, but Julie was too tired to care. The grownups rested in the family room with their feet up and a drink in their hands. Aiden was still going strong, playing with the new building block set he had gotten as a birthday gift.

"That was the craziest thing I have ever experienced." Reagan took another drink from his bottle of beer. "I thought football fans made a lot of noise, but they got nothin' on a house full of second-graders at a birthday party."

Pirate Reagan had been the hit of the party, and not

a second passed when he didn't have a child attached to him. He had a natural way with kids, and they responded by giving him constant attention. He'd make a great father—someday. "Thanks for your help. You being here meant a lot to Aiden. Plus, I sure appreciated having an extra pair of hands to keep things running smoothly." Julie picked up her wine glass and took a sip, and then rested her head on the sofa. "I'm glad he doesn't have a birthday again for another year."

Mary finished her drink and set the empty wine glass on the coffee table. "I should get going. My head is pounding, and I could use a nice long bath."

"Oh." Julie exhaled. "Sounds wonderful…slipping into a warm bubble bath." She noticed Reagan close his eyes and take a deep breath. *Was he not feeling well?* She rose to walk her mother to the door. "See you tomorrow." Julie gave her mom a kiss on the cheek.

Mary said goodbye to Aiden and Reagan before exiting to make the short walk home.

Julie sat on the sofa next to Reagan, curled her legs under her, and smiled. *Now or never.* She took deep breaths, working up her nerve. The words were right there, stuck to the tip of her tongue.

"I should be going, too." Reagan wiped his palms on the front of his pant legs and stood. Taking a step back, he crossed his thick arms over his body. "I have a defensive team meeting before the game. We need to report earlier than normal."

"I forgot you have a game tomorrow." Her heart sank at his rush to leave. "I'll go get your coat." She walked past him to the closet. When she opened the door, the aroma of peppermint and spicy cologne captured her attention, as always. The coat carried his unmistakable scent.

"Here you go." She handed him the jacket. "Have a good game tomorrow."

Reagan walked over to where Aiden was playing. "Bye, kid. You had a fun party. Thanks for inviting me."

Aiden stopped what he was doing and encircled Reagan's waist with his small arms, leaning into his side. "Thank you for the new football. Can I come over to your house sometime and play catch?"

"We'll see," was all Reagan answered then he walked with Julie over to the front door. "I had fun today. Wild, but fun. Take it easy tomorrow, you've earned it." He opened the door then hesitated. Slowly, he turned to face her.

She noticed he'd lost his usually carefree expression, now replaced with a tense stare.

"You make a beautiful fairy." His voice was low and uneven, the tips of his fingers reached out to stroke her soft cheek. "Goodbye, Julie."

Julie stood on her tiptoes and kissed his cheek.

Before she knew it, he was walking toward his car. "Don't go," she whispered, but the words came too late. As she watched him drive away, uncertainty and doubt crept into her once-confident thinking. How could she have been so wrong? Instead of the beginning of a relationship with Reagan, today might be the end.

****

Reagan and his brother-in-law, Tony, walked through the woods to the tree stand, set two miles away from Reagan's house. The duo was clothed in thick camouflage and carried along their hunting supplies plus food and drinks for the day's pursuit. The

November wind whipped through the trees, stirring dead leaves and tossing around the occasional snowflake. Their hike so far had been quiet. Reagan was still half asleep, a result of waking before dawn. As they approached the tree stand, Reagan set down his gear to take a short break before he started climbing. "Hand me the thermos. I need some coffee before we get set up." His voice sounded hoarse from the cold.

"Here you go." Tony tossed him the red plaid container. "You think we'll have better luck today?"

"I hope so, because your time's running out. Maggie gave you one week for this hunting trip, and not a day more."

"You don't think she'd give me a pass and let me stay a few more days?" Tony's breath was visible in the air. "We haven't seen a deer all week."

"No way. Maggie said she had an appointment at the spa on Monday, and I better have you back home in time to watch the kids. I value my life way too much. Tomorrow, you're getting in the car and driving home, deer or no deer." Reagan put the thermos on the ground and picked up his new compound bow, turning it over in his hands. The bow had been custom-made, with a high draw strength and length. They'd also promised it was fast. Not that he really needed the extra speed, but it might come in handy someday when he was faced with a jittery buck.

"Are you still coming home next weekend?" Tony scraped the sole of his boot on a rock, cleaning off several dirt clumps.

"Yeah, it's the bye week, and we just have a few light practices. I'll catch a flight to Indy on Thursday. Maybe we can head out to Dad's hunting spot. I'll bring my gear."

Tony rested his back against the tree. "Sounds great. Is Julie coming? You haven't talked much about her."

Reagan removed an arrow from the case on the ground and examined the tip. His mind drifted to Julie and soon, he forgot about the hunting equipment in his hand. "I haven't seen Julie in two weeks. The last time we were together... I don't know." He hesitated. "I'm having a hard time hanging with her and acting like I'm cool with just being friends. She's been clear that her heart is still with her late husband. I need to start dating again."

What he didn't say was the last time he'd seen her at Aiden's birthday party, he'd almost lost control. Julie had looked unbelievably attractive in her short, green fairy costume. She'd unintentionally made herself the most desirable creature he'd ever seen. By the end of the party, she'd taken off her shoes, walking around in light green tights. Her sparkling dress and wings were slightly askew, and her red hair, which started in a tidy bun, stuck out wildly in all directions. Her face grew flushed with the activity of the party, causing the small freckles on her nose to turn a shade darker.

That night, after everyone left, he wanted to grab Julie and indulge in the taste of her lips. His hands itched to run through her messy hair and caress a path down her back. If it hadn't been for Aiden playing nearby, he might have let himself give into the desire.

Tony smiled at his brother-in -law. "You've gone and fallen in love with her. Man, I thought you were immune to that bug." He let loose a round of hearty laughter.

"If I tell her how I feel, she may never want to see me again. If I don't, then I continue to drive myself crazy. The relationship's a rollercoaster ride, and I need to get off."

"Do you remember when I started seeing Maggie?" Tony pointed a gloved finger.

Reagan grinned at the memory.

"Your sister only went out with me for the first time because she'd lost a bet. Then I had to practically beg to get a second date. She made playing hard to get an Olympic sport, but I was crazy about her and wasn't giving up without a fight."

The snow fell harder, and Reagan and Tony took hold of their gear, preparing to climb to their stand.

Tony put his free hand on Reagan's shoulder. "I know how scary it can be, when you care about someone so much, you don't want to lose what you have. You become too paralyzed to take the next step. Julie seems like a really nice girl, but she's been through a lot. She may take more time to come to terms with her feelings, but don't let that stop you from being honest. I've never known you to walk away from a challenge."

"Thanks, man." Reagan hunched his shoulders. "I'd call, but after two weeks of ignoring her, I'll probably get hung up on." He'd really dug himself into a deep hole with Julie. But right now, during the middle of the season, his focus needed to stay on football. Not a wounded heart. A few young guns were nipping at his heels. One big mistake and the coaches would have no qualms about substituting in a new, fresh linebacker. "I can't become distracted. I've waited too long for a Super Bowl ring."

Tony climbed the metal pegs placed in the trunk of the tree. "Live with no regrets." Getting to the top, he moved off to the side to allow space for Reagan on the metal stand.

"I'm feeling lucky." Reagan set his equipment on the stand, and then prepared his bow. His gaze scanned the ground below, looking for any sign of fresh deer tracks. "I'm not leaving until I get what I came for."

****

Reagan ended the week without seeing a deer. Guess he could chalk up hunting to another hobby he loved but sucked at. Even without a deer to take home as a trophy, he was grateful for the sage advice of his sister's husband. Tony had been married for eight years, with three kids to show for his dedication. If Reagan trusted anyone for relationship advice, it was Tony.

Now, Tony was on his way home.

And Reagan left early for Warriors Stadium. Today, they played against the Houston Wildcats. He parked his car, and then entered the stadium. After stopping by the locker room to drop off his duffel bag, he walked through the tunnel and onto the field. This was his game day routine. A way to focus on the contest to come. When he stepped onto the field, everything inside him synced. All the hard work and all the sacrifice became laser-focused on winning today's game.

Once done with his meditation, he made his way to the auditorium for the team meeting. The room was a good-sized space filled with large comfortable chairs. Reagan stopped to talk to a few teammates before taking a seat toward the back of the room. An oversized projection screen came down, and the head coach stood behind the podium, ready to run through his expectations for the day's game.

The Warriors were having an excellent season, and the coach stressed the importance of not letting down their guard, especially with a winning record. The season was over halfway done, and they looked forward to a playoff run in less than two months. With a bye next week, the team would be getting some well deserved rest. But all the coaches were clear they wanted another win before the team left on break.

After a forty-five minute lecture with film, the team was released to change into their uniforms and to start warming up. Men filed out of the meeting room and headed straight to the locker room.

"Reagan," DeMarcus called out, jogging to catch up. "These guys will fight us the whole way. The Wildcats have the number-one-rated offense in the league. They'll be hard to contain."

"I know. Their right tackle, Paulsen, will be tough. He's a mind reader. It'll be a good contest."

They continued to the locker room before stepping into a large circular room. On the center of the floor was a large red-and-silver letter W. Rows of benches stood in front of open wooden lockers, which curved around the wall. Uniforms and gear hung, cleaned and organized. A red helmet, polished to a shine, lay on the top shelf of each locker.

DeMarcus sat in front of his locker and removed his dress shoes. "A bunch of us are going to The Garage after the game to play some pool. You want in?"

"Sure, sounds like fun." *Wonder what Julie would be doing today?* Since he'd had no contact with her in the past two weeks, he wasn't even sure she'd watch the game today.

"Cool. Been awhile since you've joined us. Still remember how to play?"

"Hell, yeah." He reached in his locker for his uniform and pads. "I'll even bring the cash to prove it."

"That's what I want to hear." DeMarcus whistled, and then raised his hands to bracket his mouth. "Gentleman, watch your wallets, my man Reagan's back in the game."

An hour later, the Warriors team took the field to a sellout crowd. The air was electric and, at times, the crowd's energy made all the difference to the home team. Reagan stood on the sidelines and absorbed the atmosphere. All around him, fans cheered and music played from the sound system. He was a bull trapped in a holding corral, locked in and ready to go.

The game began with the usual kickoff. Each team fought hard, minute-by-minute and yard-by-yard. The lead alternated during the first half. Reagan had his hands full defending his side of the field. The Wildcats' star quarterback possessed an outstanding ability to elude defenders.

The third quarter came to an end, with the Warriors ahead by three points. At the whistle, Reagan ran to the sideline. He removed his helmet before shaking the sweat off his hair. Needing to rehydrate, he squirted a stream of water into his dry mouth. "You see how Paulsen gets the jump on us?" he asked a large defensive lineman.

"Sorry, Reagan. I can't hold him off long enough to make a clear running lane for you," the man huffed. "If I could get some help containing him, then you'll have a straight shot at the quarterback. He needs that cocky smile wiped off his face, preferably by you shoving it into the ground."

Reagan couldn't agree more. He pulled over the Assistant Defensive Coordinator to update their strategy for the fourth quarter.

The referee blew the whistle, signaling the resume of play. Eleven Warriors players ran onto the field and got in position on their side of the line of scrimmage.

For Reagan, everything went still before the snap of the ball. His senses heightened, he blocked out all sounds but the voice of the quarterback yelling the play call. His vision lasered in on the football in the opposing team's center's grasp. Once the ball was released into the quarterback's waiting hands, he sprung into action, running like an unstoppable train.

Out of the corner of his eye, he noticed their two defensive tackles blocking the other team's right tackle. That gave Reagan an opportunity to slip past the protective offensive line. He was on a blitz run, moving full force straight at the quarterback, who still held the ball, desperately looking for an open receiver. He reached out to grab the quarterback, and a solid force hit his body and threw it to the ground. A searing pain burst from his left shoulder, followed by a blissful void.

Chapter Eleven

On Sunday, Julie's house was as quiet as a theme park on a rainy day. Aiden was staying with his Grandpa and Grandma Ellis for the weekend and wouldn't be home until after dinner. The Warriors game was being broadcast, but she didn't have the heart to watch the game alone. So she'd moped around the house for most of the morning.

After getting comfy on the sofa, she opened a book that she'd wanted to read for a while. Minutes later, she realized she'd been staring at the same page and didn't remember anything about the book. She couldn't focus her mind on anything other than Reagan. Julie set her book on the coffee table and closed her eyes in an attempt to nap.

The antique clock on the wall ticked, ticked, ticked. Bass boomed from a passing car, rattling the windows in her house.

Nope. Sleep was as evasive as her concentration.

On the night of Aiden's party, Reagan had walked out of her house and apparently out of her life. She'd waited two weeks for him to call or text, afraid to make the first move—but nothing. For all she knew, the man had been abducted by aliens. What had she done wrong?

Had he started dating someone new? Maybe a sexy supermodel or another movie star. The image riled every nerve in her body. He might have gotten back together with Brynn, no longer interested in spending time with a widow and her son. She tried to understand. Really, she had, but the pain in her heart wouldn't listen to the logic in her head.

Julie finally gave up the fight to find relaxation and went out to run a few errands. She was now shopping at an almost-deserted grocery store. The whole town of Timber Lake shut down for the Warriors game, she wouldn't be the least bit surprised. At this moment, most residents, with the exception of her, must be at home, sitting in front of the TV, cheering on their team. Guilt stabbed at her heart. Aiden would be disappointed in her when he found out. Maybe she should have stayed home and turned on the game. She opened her mouth to give the woman standing behind the deli counter her order, when her cell phone rang. "Hi, Chrissy." She stepped away from the counter.

"Are you watching the Warriors game right now?"

"No, I'm at the grocery store. Why?"

"This game is crazy! Matt and his brother have been yelling at the TV for the past hour. Reagan's having a hard time against the Wildcats' offensive line."

"Sounds like I'm missing a good one. Give me a call when it's over and let me know who won." If she hadn't been acting so pouty, she would be watching the game herself.

"I can't believe you're not watching. Reagan will be disappointed," Chrissy said.

"I haven't talked to him in awhile." Julie strained to keep her voice upbeat. "I don't think he would care." Her heart hurt saying those words. And if Reagan truly didn't care, her heart would feel something greater than pain.

"Wasn't he traveling last weekend? The team played in Seattle. I'm sure he's busy, with the season in high gear." Chrissy's voice came spurting out of Julie's phone

"He's probably found someone new to occupy his time." She tried not to sound like she was sulking.

"Reagan's not dating anyone. I'd bet my favorite pair of heels he only has eyes for you."

"How do you know?" Julie gripped the phone tighter. Should she dare hope that Chrissy's assurances were true?

"Give him a call. You'll see. Anyway, the real reason I called was Matt's mom told me about a 5K run that's happening at the high school. The money raised goes toward training service dogs for veterans with PTSD. Would you be interested in running with me? It's the Saturday before Thanksgiving."

Anything for veterans was a worthy cause, and she knew how valuable service dogs were to struggling veterans. "Yeah, I would love to. Email me the link, and I'll sign up." Julie heard yelling in the background at Chrissy's house.

"Oh, wow...the Wildcats just scored a touchdown. I got to go and try to calm my husband. I'll talk to you later."

"Bye." Julie tried to push the Warriors game to the back of her mind and went to finish her grocery shopping. An hour later, she carried the last shopping bag into the house when her phone rang. She set a loaf of bread on the counter and picked up her cell to see an unfamiliar number on the screen. Hesitating for a few seconds, she finally decided to answer the call. "Hello."

"Is this Julie Ellis?" the caller asked.

"Yes, this is Julie." *Better not be another telemarketer call.* She'd put her number on the do-not-call list several months ago.

"This is Doctor Miller from Timber Lake General Hospital."

Her first thoughts went to Aiden. Panic rose from her stomach and settled in her throat.

"Reagan Harrison was injured during today's football game. He's been admitted to the hospital, and he asked me to call you. Can you come as soon as possible?"

The flood of relief about her son was quickly replaced with concern about Reagan. She placed her hand over her fluttering heart. "Is he okay?"

"We can explain everything once you get here. Reagan's been hurt, but not seriously. Check-in at the front desk when you arrive. Security will escort you to his room."

"I'll be right there." Her voice shook in the attempt to control her emotions. "Tell him I'm coming."

"I will, Mrs. Ellis. See you soon."

When the call ended, Julie tossed a few items in the refrigerator then grabbed her keys and purse, and she hustled out to the Jeep. Before she pulled out of the driveway, she texted her mom and asked if she would meet Aiden when he was dropped off at home later on.

Traffic was heavy due to the recently ended Warriors game. The drive to the hospital seemed to take forever. Once she arrived, she parked in the hospital parking structure. Inside, she found the front desk. "I'm here to see Reagan Harrison. His doctor is expecting me."

The woman grabbed her hand-held radio and spoke in rapid bursts, informing security of Julie's arrival. "Someone will be here shortly to take you to Mr. Harrison's room." She pointed to a row of chairs.

Julie was too anxious to sit. Instead, she paced around the busy lobby until a tall, burly security guard approached.

"Please follow me," he said in a deep voice.

He strongly resembled Lurch, from the Addams Family, and she tried to suppress a giggle. *Now is not a good time for your nervous laughter compulsion.*

They rode the elevator to the fifth floor, and then exited into a brightly lit hall. Julie followed the guard down a long, quiet corridor, and then stopped when they reached the end of the hall. The room number said 560, but the nameplate was left blank.

She opened the door and quietly stepped into a spacious hospital room. Before her was Reagan's large form reclined on a too-small bed. *Poor baby.* His left arm was in a sling and his eyes were closed, but she thought he looked peaceful. A doctor and two nurses were reviewing medical charts. On the other side of the room, a man in a red Warriors polo shirt studied a series of X-rays on the light board.

"What happened to him?" she asked to no one in particular.

Four heads snapped up, but Reagan stayed still and didn't stir.

A dark-haired man in a white lab coat approached. "Hi, Julie. I'm Doctor Miller, Reagan's attending physician. He gave me permission to discuss his medical condition with you. He was on the receiving end of a hard hit during a play in the fourth quarter of the game and lost consciousness for about a minute. In addition, as a result of the impact, his left shoulder separated. His MRI was clean, no damage to his brain, but he is showing signs of a pretty nasty concussion. We reset his shoulder, and it should heal quickly."

Julie breathed a sigh of relief. "So, he'll be all right?"

"Yes," Dr. Miller patted her arm. "It's nothing a little rest won't fix. He'll need to take it easy for the week."

"Julie, is that you?" Reagan asked with slurred speech.

"Hey, stranger." She walked to the edge of his bed and placed her small hand over his. "Looks like you got into some trouble today. How are you feeling?"

"My head and shoulder hurt like hell, but otherwise I'm fine. Would you hand me the cup of water from the table?"

She gently placed the cup in his hands.

He took a long drink then handed it back.

One of the nurses came to stand next to her. "Mr. Harrison's on some pretty powerful pain relievers so don't be surprised if he isn't too talkative."

As if on cue, Reagan turned away and reached for a plastic bowl on the bedside table. With a low moan, he emptied his stomach. While his back was facing her, the small slit in the back of his hospital gown opened, revealing a muscular back. Even a strong man like Reagan looked vulnerable in a hospital gown.

The gaze of one of the nurses flitted over to Julie, and her lips quirked up in a smile. The other nurse grabbed the full bowl and hustled it into the bathroom.

Reagan turned his head to rest it on the pillow and groaned.

Julie brushed his hair off his forehead. She gave him a tender kiss, as she did for Aiden when he was feeling sick.

"I'm sorry you had to see that," Reagan finally said.

That little bit of throw-up is nothing. "You forget that I'm a mom and a medical professional. Trust me, I've seen a lot worse."

The team trainer came to the bedside. "Reagan, you're on the injury report for the next two weeks. After that, we'll see about getting you cleared to play. You let your body recover, and make sure not to do anything to aggravate your condition."

Reagan's deep, raspy voice muttered something inarticulate.

Dr. Miller stepped over to stand next to Reagan's bed. "He can't be released from the hospital until I know who will be caring for him at home. He'll require observation for the next forty-eight hours to watch for concussion symptoms. And tonight, he'll have to be checked on every few hours to make sure he's responsive."

Everyone in the room looked to Julie. She finally understood what the doctor was implying. "I can't stay with him." Her gaze oscillated between Reagan, the team trainer, and Dr. Miller. "I have a school-age son, and I can't be away from home overnight."

"That's fine," Reagan spoke up. "I understand. I can hire a nurse for the next few days."

The idea left Julie with a nauseous feeling in her stomach. How could she deny him care, when he looked so helpless? Reagan needed her. "Well, I do have a spare bedroom. Reagan could stay with me. My mother lives close by, and she's a nurse. Between the two of us, we could watch him at my house. What do you think about that?" His smile appeared loopy but sincere.

"That would be great." His eyelids drifted closed, once again.

"All right then." Dr. Miller slapped his hands together. He grabbed the clipboard sitting on the counter and scanned over the paperwork. "Let's get those discharge papers filled out. Looks like you've got yourself a patient."

****

Julie pulled into the driveway a little after ten pm. The house was dark, except for a lamp, which glowed from the family room. Julie parked her Jeep and walked around to open the passenger side door.

Mary came outside to give her assistance with Reagan, since he was a big guy and not too steady on his feet.

The two women assisted him into the house, one on each side for balance. Julie took his injured side, avoiding bumping into his sling. Their progress halted at the foot of the steps. Because of the combination of pain pills, Reagan acted like a zombie. Julie wanted to make sure he understood where he was going before they conquered the stairs. As they steered him with each step, Julie and Mary glanced at each other, which started an uncontrollable fit of giggles.

"You shouldn't laugh at a helpless man," Reagan mumbled.

"Sorry." Julie attempted unsuccessfully to suppress

more laughter.

They led him into the spare bedroom and toward the bed.

"Here, have a seat." She patted the orange and yellow comforter.

He eased himself onto the bed and groaned.

Julie swung up his feet and propped a few pillows against the headboard.

Sighing, he closed his eyes.

The trip must have spent the last of his remaining energy.

Mary went out to the car to get Reagan's bag, which contained clean clothes and some personal items. Returning to the room, she set the bag on the dresser. Coming over to Julie, who stood at the foot of the bed, she hugged her tightly.

"Thanks, Mom, for helping me with Reagan, and for staying with Aiden. Can you come over tomorrow morning at eight to stay with our patient while I take Aiden to school?"

"Sure, my shift doesn't start until later in the morning. I'm going home now, see you tomorrow," Mary said, and then turned to Reagan. "Feel better." Not getting a response, she left the room to go downstairs.

A minute later, Julie heard the door close. "What am I to do with you?" she asked, not really expecting a response. She looked at him, sprawled over the bed, dozing as innocent as a child. He'd dressed himself at the hospital, but now he was too drowsy to undress. She stood for a minute, deciding on what to do.

"I just can't leave you like this." Lightly tapping him on his good shoulder, she spoke loud enough to cut through the lethargy. "Reagan, let's get you ready for bed. I'll take off your shoes, but you'll have to help me with the rest."

"Okay," he muttered, half opening his eyes. "I knew you couldn't resist undressing me." He let out a pained noise, which sounded like the bark of a seal.

Julie rolled her eyes, unlaced his shoes, and then slid them off his feet. She helped him sit up and unbuttoned his shirt, removing it without disturbing the sling. As the shirt came off, his broad chest revealed the battering his body had taken that day.

"Don't forget my pants," he whispered. In his attempt to wink, his face contorted, and he closed both eyes.

Did he really think he could flirt when he couldn't even walk without help? "Take it easy. You're in no position to play Casanova tonight. Stand up." She took hold of his good arm and yanked. He was wobbly but stayed upright. Sighing, she understood what she'd have to do. She was a medical professional, after all. And not like this would be the first time she'd undressed a man.

Julie undid his jeans' top button and slid his pants down over his hips. Thankfully, he wore a layer underneath, black boxer briefs. He was being no help at all, and she wondered if he was intentionally letting her complete this task without his assistance. In her kneeling position, she glanced up to see the seductive curve of his lips. "Stop fooling around." She stood and gave his chest a slight push, putting him into to a sitting position on the bed. She slid his pants off one leg at a time, and then went to place them on the chair in the corner of the room. Pulling back the covers, she watched him lift his legs and lay his head on the pillows. His large frame looked strong, but vulnerable at the same time.

"I put a bowl over here, on the nightstand." She pointed to the plastic purple bowl. "In case you have to throw up again. I'll be right down the hall if you need me. Is there anything else I can get you?"

"A kiss would be nice." His eyelids fluttered to a close. "Julie, you're an angel, that's why I love you." He gave a short pause. "I love you."

"You have a brain injury, so declarations of love don't count," she teased, but those words still touched her heart. A lump caught in her throat. "Sleep tight, I'll check on you again in a few hours."

At some point, Reagan had fallen asleep, quietly snoring. She pulled the blankets over his legs but stopped to get a closer look at the tattoo covering his rib cage. The ink design looked Aztec-inspired—a large circular pattern about eight inches in diameter. An intricate outer ring surrounded small rings, which enclosed a round medallion. The middle contained a face with a protruding tongue. She reached out and gently ran her fingers around the edge of the tattoo, feeling warm skin, muscle, and the bone underneath. The tattoo's meaning would have to be discovered some other time.

She covered his body with the blankets, fighting the urge to crawl into bed next to him, curling up next to his warm body. Julie missed the feeling of peace and security she got while sleeping next to a man. Her body yearned for the simple, physical contact of being held. How much time had passed since she'd last kissed John goodnight in their shared bed? As she counted back the months, tightness pressed across her chest. Gathering her willpower, she exited the room but looked back at him one last time before closing the door.

Chapter Twelve

Julie took trips all night long down the hall to Reagan's room—making sure he was okay, and then crawling back into bed. Only to do it all over again on the hour, every hour. She checked on him more often than was needed. But Reagan was her patient, and her worry had kept her awake most of the night.

In the morning, she peeked in on Reagan and found him fast asleep. His snores were a perfect imitation of a bellowing camel.

Next, she went to Aiden's room to wake him for school. She was in the kitchen when he shuffled downstairs a few minutes later. "Grandma said you were at the hospital with Reagan," he said, rubbing the sleep out of his brown eyes. "Is he okay?"

Luckily, Aiden was a very sound sleeper and hadn't even stirred last night when she'd brought Reagan home. "Reagan was hurt yesterday during the game, but he'll be fine. The doctor said he can't be home by himself, so he'll be staying with us for a few days. We'll take care of him until he feels better."

Aiden's eyes grew wide as they searched the space around them. "Where is he? I have to see him."

She pressed the brew button on the coffee maker and inhaled the wonderful smell of coffee. "He's sleeping, so you'll have to wait until after school. Now eat your breakfast, or we'll be late."

Mary came over a few minutes before Julie and Aiden had to leave. "How did our patient do last night?"

"Good, I checked on him a few minutes ago. He's sleeping like a baby."

"I'll keep him out of mischief until you get home. Aiden, have a good day at school."

Aiden grabbed his backpack and lunchbox. "Bye, Grandma," he said before leaving with Julie.

When Julie returned, the smell of coffee and bacon hit her nose, even before she opened the door. As she entered the house, she saw Reagan sitting at the kitchen table with a large plate of food placed in front of him. Thankfully, he had dressed himself, wearing athletic pants and another button-up shirt.

"Looks like someone's feeling better." Julie tossed her purse on the counter.

Reagan smiled while cutting into the large stack of pancakes on his plate. "Thanks for leaving me with the world's best babysitter." With his good arm, he shoved another large fork full of food into his grinning mouth.

Mary stood by the stove, cooking more pancakes. "He was famished when he came down. His stomach was empty after yesterday. The man needed to eat."

Reagan nodded his head. Then, between bites he asked, "Why didn't you watch the game yesterday? The doctor said you didn't know I was hurt."

His frown reminded her of a neglected child, and she suddenly felt awful for missing the game. "I'm sorry. Aiden was gone, and I decided to get some shopping done." She took a seat at the table and happily accepted a plate of pancakes and bacon. "Thanks, Mom."

He waved his empty fork. "You're telling me that shopping took precedence over a Warriors game. You should be kicked out of the state of Wisconsin."

Julie laughed and waved her hands. "Please don't banish me. I promise to watch the next one. Scout's honor." She reached over for the syrup and poured it over her pancakes. "Reagan, I'm glad you asked them to call me when you were in the hospital, but"—she paused—"how do I put this? Why me?"

"I hate to break it to you, but you're my go-to gal. I knew I could count on you to take good care of me. And here I am, sitting in your kitchen eating this delicious breakfast." He took another large bite. Cleaning off his plate, he leaned back with a satisfied groan. "Now, I have a question for you." He pointed at Julie. "How did I get undressed last night?"

Her cheeks warmed under the heat of his gaze. So, he was going…there. "Don't you remember?"

"Well." He cleared his throat. "I remember getting to your house and walking up the stairs, but that's all. The next thing I know I'm waking up in a strange bed in nothing but my skivvies."

A devilish smile played on his lips and mischievous humor lit his eyes.

Mary laughed and set another three strips of bacon on his plate.

"*Ummm.*" Julie stammered. "You were being absolutely no help last night. And I didn't want you to sleep in your clothes. I was only helping make you comfortable."

Reagan's lips twitched with a smile, and he bent over to whisper. "Did you take advantage of me?"

Mary, standing over by the sink, chuckled.

Julie put her head in her hands, attempting not to laugh. Finally, she glanced over. "You're incorrigible! I'm not that kind of girl." Her voice dripped with fake offense. Although last night, the thought of taking advantage of him had crossed her mind.

"Well, that's too bad." He popped a piece of bacon in his grinning mouth.

Julie's face burned with a deep blush. "I see you managed to get yourself dressed this morning." She pressed her lips together to suppress more laughter. "And you have your sense of humor back. You'll be good as new in no time."

"I hope so. As much as I enjoy this pampering, I want to get back to playing football ASAP."

She stood and shuffled to the coffee maker for a refill. "I heard the Warriors won by three points yesterday. The game and your injury were all the other parents at school were talking about. I couldn't take two steps without someone asking me how you are."

Mary washed and dried the last of the dishes. "My shift starts soon." She grabbed her coat. "You two have a good day."

"Bye, thanks for breakfast," they both said in unison.

Once Mary left, they sat in silence, drinking their coffee.

Julie's mind drifted to her son, and how Reagan's unexplained absence had confused Aiden. Ever since Reagan came into their lives, she feared seeing more hurt in her son's eyes. When John left to go on deployment, one of the worst parts was explaining to Aiden why his dad was no longer with them.

Finally, she steeled her nerves and asked the

question that had weighed on her for the last two weeks. "I haven't seen you since Aiden's party, and I got the feeling you've been avoiding me. Aiden's been asking about you, and I, uh...did I do something wrong?"

His brows rose over wide, blue eyes. "Absolutely not. Please don't think that. I'm sorry if I haven't been a good friend lately. I've been dealing with a few issues that have kept me elsewhere."

She could see the conflict in his eyes and wondered how much of the truth he was hiding. For the past two weeks, she'd lived with the same insecurity as she'd experienced when John had left her to go to war. With both John and Reagan, she'd watched a man she cared for walk away, not knowing if he'd ever return. "I hope it's not serious."

"Nothing a little deer hunting couldn't handle." He leaned his body toward her.

"Good. I'm glad we're still okay." She stood and grabbed their empty plates and coffee mugs, and then she rinsed them off. Mundane work to keep her from going over and curling up in his lap. "Aiden really missed you. I hated to see him upset. I'm worried you might hurt him."

Reagan followed, carrying the syrup bottle to return to the fridge. "I'm sorry, Julie. I acted like a self-centered jerk. The last thing I'd ever what to do is hurt Aiden. You've been kind enough to let me be a part of your life. I don't want to do anything to screw that up."

She wanted to believe him, without reservation. He did seem sincere. "I could've tried harder to get a hold of you, and I didn't. It's not all your fault."

Reagan closed the refrigerator door. "Yes, it is

totally my fault. You have every right to be upset, so thanks for giving me another chance." He glanced over at a stack of mail that was tied together with a yellow ribbon then picked up the stone bird sitting on top. "Where did you get this?" He balanced the bird on his large palm.

As she tried to answer, her voice caught in her throat. She pushed down the sorrow that threatened to rise. "John gave me the bird as a gift when he returned for the first time from Afghanistan. He was good at developing relationships with many of the locals, and they loved to trade with him. This little gem he got for a can of soda."

"It's beautiful." He placed the stone back on the pile of letters. "I forget you'd rather not talk about certain things with me."

"I find it hard to talk about a lot of things, but that doesn't mean I don't want to share them with you. I'm glad I can." She went to stand next to him, and her heart melted at his concern. With most people, she kept her personal grief private. Reagan was one of the few she could talk to freely about John. He truly listened, and that was a rare thing.

He faced away, gazing out the window. "Will it ever get better?"

Julie wiped a tear from her eye. "Every day, the sun shines a bit brighter, music sounds more joyful, and happiness begins to overpower sadness. I hope at some point, I'll be free to fully experience life again. That I'll live entirely in the light." They were standing so close together, and her gaze drifted to his mouth. Something awoken inside—burning desire pulsed through her veins. She forced herself to look into his eyes.

"I promise to be here for you, whenever you need me." Reagan held her gaze. Reaching out, he brushed a loose strand of hair and tucked it behind her ear. The action caused him to lose his balance.

Julie grasped his arm to steady him. "Let's get you to the sofa. You look ready to pass out." Step by cautious step, she led him into the family room. "Come on, lie down, and I'll get you a blanket." When she returned downstairs, she found him with his eyes closed and breathing deeply. She gently covered him and whispered, "Rest awhile, my guardian dragon."

He stirred in his sleep and grabbed her hand that held the blanket. His soft kiss brushed the top of her hand. A moment later, he drifted off again.

Julie spent the hours he slept going through paperwork and paying bills. Even after a year and a half, the Army still sent her forms regarding her survivor benefits. A lawyer had helped her during the initial process after John's death, but now she was navigating the web of bureaucracy by herself. Money was always tight, just like when John had been alive. Some days, she struggled to make all those loose ends meet.

While sitting at the table, she grew tired, so she went to curl up in John's recliner. She threw a blanket over herself and watched Reagan as he slept. He'd come to her when he needed help, and the thought soothed her insecurity. She watched him, lying on her sofa, and her body warmed with the connection they shared.

His injury had revealed how much she cared. And at the moment, she couldn't imagine her life without him. Her mind drifted until her eyes became languid with fatigue, finally she lulled into a peaceful sleep. She'd been dreaming of Reagan when his stirring roused her from sleep. Opening her eyes, she saw him sitting on the sofa. "Hey, feeling any better?" she asked with a yawn.

"Yeah. You look like you were just as tired as me. Do you mind if I go take a shower?"

"I put out a fresh towel and washcloth in the bathroom. Let me know if you need anything else."

Listening with care as he made his way upstairs, Julie followed the sounds of Reagan's footsteps and the creaking of floor boards. Soon, the sound of running water drifted downstairs, along with a stream of curse words. Julie grimaced. His shoulder must still be very painful.

A short time later, Reagan came into the room wearing a clean shirt, jeans, and damp hair.

The man was more attractive than anyone had a right to be.

Standing uncomfortably on the other side of the family room, Julie was unsure of how to voice all the emotions stirring just under the surface. She took a step forward, but then hesitated. Her heart pounded so hard she was afraid it would burst.

She had to release the pressure off her chest. "Reagan, you already know this past year has been very difficult, that I've had a hard time moving on. I've shut myself off to almost everyone, until I met you." She pushed out the words, the release causing courage to seep in and fill the cracks of her former insecurity.

He remained as still as a mountain. Not even a muscle in his face so much as twitched, to give her an indication of what he was feeling.

Julie took another step in his direction, not caring anymore if she sounded silly. "You've been the breath of fresh air I've needed to move me out of the past. Missing you these past two weeks has made me realize how much I need you." She missed their long talks over dinner. How he would call her after a hard practice, and they'd be on the phone well into the night. And she missed the times when she couldn't find the right words, but he just seemed to understand. "You're a good friend, but I want more."

"Oh, Julie." He reached her in three long strides. "Do you know how hard being around you was when all I've wanted is to hold you?" He cradled her face in his large, rough hands. "And kiss you until we both go crazy."

Looking into his eyes, she wanted him with every fiber of her being.

When his lips touched hers, she opened like a flower to the warmth of the sun. His kiss was a tender expression of the pent-up passions that were finally being allowed their freedom. Julie raised her hand and placed it around his neck. Her other hand lay on his chest, feeling muscle ripple under his shirt. His lips moved on hers in an unhurried, rhythmic pattern and a strong arm wrapped around her waist, holding her tightly.

When their lips parted, he continued to hold her close, the palm of his hand resting on her lower back. "I've wanted to do that since the first night I met you at the country club. You make it really hard on a man to keep his self-control," he whispered in her ear. "But, I figured you couldn't resist my charm forever."

She laid her head on his chest, careful to avoid his

injured shoulder, and heard the steady beat of his heart. "We'll need to take this slow, for both our sakes."

"I want to date you, Julie Ellis." He ran kisses along the bare skin of her shoulder. "I want the world to know you're my girlfriend."

She sighed with contentment. "I don't want the world's attention. Only yours."

The warmth of his breath glided over her skin, from her earlobe to the base of her neck. Her body shivered at the sensation. "We have a couple hours before I need to get Aiden from school." She stepped back and tipped her chin to look at him. "What would you like to do?"

He answered the question with a roguish smile before descending on her mouth.

She retreated again, in order to catch her breath. Placing her hand on his chest, she felt the rapid beat of his heart. "Slow...remember? How about a movie? I have a wide selection of chick flicks."

Reagan sighed. "I've successfully avoided chick flicks, up until now, but looks like that streak is coming to an end."

****

They lay wrapped around each other on the sofa, watching *Pride and Prejudice*, which Reagan learned was Julie's favorite movie. Being here felt so right, having Julie close beside him, like everything in the world was as it should be. He'd gotten too comfortable, while trying to make sense of Mr. Darcy's snobbery and Elizabeth Bennet's obvious detest of the man, and fell asleep about halfway through the movie. He awoke to see Elizabeth and Darcy were now married, both looking happily in love. The credits rolled across the screen.

Julie quietly eased herself off the sofa. "You missed a great movie. Lizzy got her Mr. Darcy." She sighed. "I need to get Aiden from school. Will you be okay if I leave you alone for half an hour?"

"Sure, I'll be fine. My head's finally stopped pounding. I think your kiss was magic, better than any medicine."

"Happy to be of service." She leaned down to softly kiss his grinning lips. "Do you need me to get you anything before I leave?"

"Nope, I'm good." He started to stand and became lightheaded. The room spun like a carousel around him. Swaying, he reached out to Julie for support.

"Whoa there." She put an arm around his waist and helped him onto the sofa. "Just stay put until I get home. Doctor's orders."

"Yes, ma'am." He loved when she got bossy. He hadn't meant to be untruthful, but he had no intention of lying around on the sofa while Julie was gone. Reagan only had thirty minutes to complete his mission. Slowly and carefully, he stood and made his way to the staircase. As he entered her bedroom, he noticed personal, feminine touches, along with the sensual smell of roses. The walls were painted a pale, pink. On her dresser, fresh flowers sat in a vase next to a row of glass perfume bottles.

He walked over to her nightstand, picked up the book she'd been reading, and grinned. The cover showed a muscular man embracing a woman. Both appeared to have lost half their clothing. He remembered finding books similar to this around his house growing up, belonging to his mom and sisters.

Looked like his innocent Julie enjoyed reading steamy romance.

Inside her closet, he found the information he'd come for. After jotting down a few notes, he went downstairs to wait for Julie and Aiden to get home.

As he walked to the sofa, Reagan noticed several photo albums sitting on a white bookcase. Picking one, he paged through the record of Julie's life—high school friends, a formal-looking Julie and John dressed for prom, pictures of college fun. He paged ahead and saw several wedding pictures. Julie looked beautiful in a simple white dress, wearing a carefree smile. John stood straight and tall next to her in his Army dress uniform. They looked young, happy, and in love. A few pages later, he saw photos of a glowing pregnant Julie. In the next picture, she was holding a small bundle wrapped in a blue blanket. Aiden's first few years were documented with care, Julie probably not wanting her absent husband to miss any of his important milestones.

In these pictures, she had a sparkle in her eye, and her smile was cheerful and untroubled. The woman Reagan met had lost some of that light and love of life. He was struck by the stark contrast in Julie, from before John's death to now. Rebuilding her spirit became his responsibility. He wanted to provide her with new memories.

He returned the albums to the shelf just as Julie and Aiden pulled into the driveway. By the time they came inside, Reagan had settled back on the sofa.

Aiden threw his backpack on the floor and came darting straight over to the sofa. "Mom said you're staying with us because you're hurt." Aiden's eyes grew wide. His gaze scanned over Reagan's body.

"Why are you wearing that thing on your arm?"

"This is a sling, and it helps keep my arm still. I also hurt my head, but I'm okay, so don't worry."

Aiden reached over and rubbed his small hand through Reagan's hair until he found the bump on the left side of his head. "That feels weird."

"You're telling me, kid." Reagan winced at the starburst of pain that radiated inside his skull. "How was school?"

"Mrs. Viste made me sit on the bench at recess. I didn't have my math sheet done." Aiden's shoulders slumped.

Poor kid. Reagan remembered losing many grade school recesses to incomplete homework. "That's no fun. Recess is the best."

Aiden ran to his backpack and returned holding a colorful sheet of paper. "I have an adding one for today. Will you help me?" He pleaded with big, brown puppy-dog eyes.

"You bet." Reagan stood slowly. "Let's go work on your sheet at the kitchen table."

Julie stood in the doorway to the kitchen, smiling. "Can you handle second grade homework?"

"I'll holler if we need help, but I'm pretty sure I got this."

After they got situated, he talked Aiden through the worksheet while Julie was nearby, making dinner. Sitting in the kitchen, Reagan recognized the larger meaning of these simple actions, like a small pebble hitting the water, sending out rippling waves through the still surface. He was now part of their family, and he'd go to the ends of the earth to protect them. His feelings for Julie made him stronger, not weaker, as he once feared.

Over the years, he'd tried hard to avoid this very thing. But with the right person, he may be able to have it all—a successful career and love. *Could happiness really be this easy?*

After supper, the two adults washed the dishes while Aiden raced upstairs to get a book. Reagan leaned over to kiss Julie, who had her hands elbow deep in the sudsy sink. Aiden, who'd reappeared and now stood by the kitchen table, peered at them with narrowed eyes. Reagan could almost see the gears turning in his head.

"Is my mom your girlfriend?" Aiden asked Reagan. "Because you only kiss someone who's your girlfriend."

Reagan put his arm around Julie's waist. "Yes, she is, kid. Is that okay?"

Aiden's pressed-together lips turned up in a huge grin. "Yeah, it's okay. Just don't kiss all the time 'cause that's gross." With that, he spun on his heel and went to sit on the sofa and read.

Reagan stepped behind Julie and swept aside her ponytail, giving her a kiss on the nape of the neck. She smelled so good. He trailed his finger behind the kiss, and he whispered, "Kissing you would never be gross."

She noticeably shivered at his light touch.

Later that night, Aiden pulled Reagan upstairs to read him bedtime stories. The kid giggled as Reagan's deep voice made silly noises to go along with the story.

Once the books were read and prayers said, Julie tucked her little son into bed, blowing him a kiss and turning off the light.

Reagan went down the hallway to his temporary bedroom and grabbed his cell phone, noticing a barrage of texts and missed calls. Media, teammates, friends, and family were all concerned about his condition. He made a call to his mother, whom Julie had talked to earlier that day, and let her know he was still doing fine. She sounded disappointed he couldn't come home this weekend but didn't hide her excitement that he was with Julie.

The sharp ache in his shoulder was now unbearable again, along with a pounding in his head, and he swallowed two pain relievers to take off the edge. Unfortunately, he knew the pills would make him sleepy, but he hoped to enjoy some time alone with Julie before he started dozing off.

He walked downstairs to find her talking with Mary in the family room. Hiding his disappointment at having company, he smiled at Julie's mom as she came over to give him a gentle hug.

"How are you feeling?" she asked while studying Reagan's face. "His pupils don't look dilated anymore."

"I noticed that, too," Julie said. "I think he's out of the woods with the concussion."

Reagan got comfortable as the women discussed his medical condition. He had to admit, his care was in excellent hands.

"Reagan," Julie called out and snapped her fingers. "Are you still planning to see the team doctor at the stadium tomorrow?"

He slowly opened his eyes. "I've got a Defensive Team meeting at the stadium, which I should attend, and then I'll go see the medical staff. If I get the all-clear, than I can catch a ride back to my house afterward with one of the guys."

"I'll drive you to the stadium tomorrow on my way

to work," Julie said. "I think you should be fine to go home, although we'll miss you around here."

Mary zipped-up her coat. "Glad you're feeling better, Reagan. See you soon." She gave him a quick wink.

"Thanks, Mary. I'm really lucky to have the two most beautiful women watching out for me."

After Mary left, Reagan made a move to pull Julie onto the sofa. She dropped next to him and snuggled into his side, but by now the pain pills had kicked in. In his foggy mind, all his previous intentions evaporated. They sat together and watched TV, his head resting on her lap, while she raked her fingers through his hair. The act relaxed him into almost a hypnotic state.

When Julie told him to go to bed, he didn't resist but held her hand as she led him upstairs. He stood in the doorway of his room and watched as she went into the bathroom to get ready. When she finally exited, his woman was more beautiful than ever.

His body slanted toward the door frame, suddenly needing support. Julie's hair had been let free of its faithful ponytail, auburn waves cascading over her shoulders and down the back of her faded shirt. Standing before him, she was a vision straight from a Renaissance painting.

When she reached him, she lifted herself up on her tiptoes, meeting her soft lips to his.

He became dizzy by her taste and smell, floral and fresh—a drunken man who'd lost all orientation. She was a cocktail of overwhelming sensations.

"Goodnight," she whispered. "I'm glad you came to me when you needed help." Julie twirled around on her bare feet and walked back down the hall.

He refused to move until she had disappeared into

her room. His body begged to follow her, but his respect for her won out over his instincts. "Sleep tight, my beautiful angel," he said quietly as he turned into his own room. "I will never go to anyone but you."

Chapter Thirteen

Julie spent the better part of her Saturday tearing apart her closet, figuring what to wear. "How am I supposed to pick out an outfit when I don't even know where we're going?" she asked herself. *I really, really, really hate surprises.*

Last Tuesday, when she'd dropped off Reagan at Warriors Stadium, he'd left her with very specific instructions. She was to leave Saturday night free because he had a special date planned. The only hint he'd given her was to expect to be out late. She had tried her hardest to get him to spill the beans, but he was as stubborn as a mule and wouldn't budge.

While rummaging through the back of her closet, she found several of John's clothes that, after the move, she had unpacked. Julie slipped an olive-colored twill coat off the hanger and brought it to her nose. Memories flooded her mind, causing a stinging pain in her chest. She slipped her arms into the coat sleeves, and then wrapped them around her chest. "I miss you." With John, everything had fit together so easily. Their relationship had been as comfortable as a favorite pair of fleece pants. The feeling of nervous excitement Reagan aroused was new. Something she'd have to get used to.

She took off the coat and returned it to the closet then walked over to her phone to call in back-up. She needed help, and fast. At this rate, she'd meet Reagan at her door wearing pajamas, which would totally serve him right.

A few minutes later, Chrissy arrived, curling iron and make-up bag in hand. "This is a crisis." Chrissy's brown curls bounced around her face. "How come he hasn't told you where you're going tonight? How does he expect you to know what to wear?"

"I don't know. How about jeans and a T-shirt?"

"I don't think that's such a good idea." Chrissy started rummaging through the closet. "My first date with Matt was at a bowling alley, but I doubt that's Reagan's style. Let's choose something that might be too nice instead of too casual. How about this short green skirt and white blouse? You can show off your legs."

"Mom," Aiden yelled. "Someone's here. He's got a box."

A knock sounded at the front door while Julie descended the stairs. She opened the door to see a delivery man standing on her front porch, holding two white boxes.

"Julie Ellis?" the man asked.

"Yes."

"These packages are for you."

"Please come in." She directed him into the house.

He placed the boxes on the coffee table, and then held out the scanner. "I'll need you to sign the confirmation of delivery."

Julie signed and went to her wallet for cash to give as a tip.

"That's not necessary. The tip has already been covered." The man took back the scanner and made his way to the door. "Have a good day." He left as quickly as he came.

"Oh my gosh!" Chrissy shrieked. "There's a card. Open it!"

"If you insist." She couldn't help but be infected by her friend's enthusiasm. Picking up the cream-colored envelope that rested on top, she inhaled the sweet scent of peppermint. After running her finger underneath the flap to open the envelope, she pulled out a note card made of heavy stock. The front was plain, but inside she saw Reagan's sizeable script.

Dear Julie,

Please accept these gifts in appreciation of your excellent care.

I look forward to seeing you tonight.

Yours,

RH

She opened the larger of the two boxes and gasped when she saw its contents. First, she pulled out a fitted, champagne-colored silk cocktail dress with a beaded sheer neckline and cap sleeves. Never in real life had Julie seen a dress so breathtakingly beautiful. The sound of Chrissy's squealing stopped temporarily, as she stared at the dress, slack jawed.

Next, Julie lifted a white fur bolero jacket and a small jewelry box. She opened the jewelry box to reveal gold drop earrings, adorned with diamonds and emeralds.

"Holy cow," Chrissy squeaked.

A second, smaller box sat on the coffee table. Julie untied the ribbon and removed the lid. Inside were gold heels and a clutch purse, both matched the dress. "I guess we figured out what I'm wearing tonight." Julie gave a small laugh, still stunned by the gifts.

They carried the items upstairs. "I should hang up the dress." Julie went into her closet to retrieve a hanger.

"I don't think you'll be bowling tonight." Chrissy spread out the jacket, shoes, and purse on the bed. "I predict something very fancy and expensive in your future."

"You think?" She burst out in an almost-hysterical laugh. Her palms started sweating, and she forced herself to take a few calming breaths. Years had flown by since her last real date. She'd been a teenage girl with a ten o'clock curfew. And tonight wasn't just an ordinary date. She would be on the arm of a rich, famous, and very handsome man. "I think I'm going to be sick." Julie clutched her middle.

Chrissy reached over and took her by the hand. "When you called me on Tuesday and told me you and Reagan finally got together, I flipped. You deserve to be treated like a princess. Whatever he's planned will be great. Don't get distracted by all this fancy stuff. He's still the same great guy you fell for."

"All right, I hear ya, but I just thought of another problem." She tugged at her ponytail. "What to do with this hair?"

At six o'clock, Julie heard a car pull into her driveway. Her mom had come over earlier to help Chrissy with lookout duty. They both called out Reagan's arrival while Julie put on the finishing touches upstairs.

The sound of Reagan's deep voice kicked up her pulse another notch.

The two women came upstairs to check on Julie.

They rushed into the bathroom, where she was fixing her hair one last time. She'd finally decided to sweep her hair to one side. Her unruly waves had been straightened and then curled into five large, red ringlets, which lay over her shoulder.

"You look beautiful." Mary wrapped an arm around Julie's shoulder. "Your date has arrived."

Chrissy's mouth curved in a huge smile. "You better go before I leave with him. He looks smokin' hot in that suit."

Julie checked herself in the mirror one last time. Her face glowed with excitement, her hair was still behaving, and the gold earrings sparkled against her skin. She thanked her mother and Chrissy before descending the staircase to Reagan. "Sorry for keeping you waiting." He had knelt next to Aiden, talking like a father would to his son.

His head turned at the sound of her approach. Their eyes met.

The tightness in Julie's chest melted at the sight. Reagan was here, for her.

"You look absolutely stunning." He stood to take her hand, giving it a soft kiss.

Inside her small family room, he looked like a fashion model. His face was clean shaven, and he'd even made an attempt at styling his overgrown hair. "You have great taste." She twirled, and the dress glistened as she moved through the late afternoon sunlight.

"Thanks, but I can't take all the credit. My mother and sisters have trained me well. For a grown man, I know way too much about women's fashion."

Aiden came beside her and placed his small hand

in her own. "Mom, why are you two all dressed up? Where are you going?"

"I can't tell you, it's a surprise." Reagan winked before returning his attention to Aiden. "But doesn't your mom look beautiful?"

"Aiden." Julie gave him a kiss on the cheek. "I'll see you in the morning. Don't forget to take along your overnight bag to Grandma's."

"Yeah, I won't. Love you, Mommy, see you tomorrow." He went back to play with his train, obviously bored with the goings-on of the adults.

Reagan wrapped her hand inside his own and escorted her to the waiting car, which was one of those luxury brands with deeply tinted windows.

The driver opened the back passenger door for her, and she slid onto the butter-soft black leather.

Closing the door behind her, he moved around to the other side.

"This car is gorgeous."

"Tonight was too cold for Cinderella's carriage, so I opted for the next best thing." Reagan wrapped his arm around her shoulder, bringing her in close to his warm body. "Thank you for agreeing to come tonight. You look exquisite."

Reagan made a perfect Prince Charming. She hoped this magic wouldn't disappear at midnight. "The dress you got me fits like a glove. How did you know what size I wear?"

"I have a confession, and don't get mad, but on Monday when you went to get Aiden from school, I snuck into your closet."

She wagged a finger at him and frowned. "That was clearly a violation of nurse's orders. I remember telling you to stay on the sofa. What else were you up to while I was gone?"

Reagan laughed out loud at her scolding. "It was worth risking your anger to see you in this dress."

After an hour's drive, they arrived in downtown Chicago. When the car stopped in front of a nondescript building, a doorman hurried over to open the door for Julie. She stepped onto the sidewalk with Reagan exiting right behind her.

He took her elbow, leading her under a brick archway and into a small, elegant restaurant. Inside, the entrance was painted with beautiful frescos of country landscapes. The maître d' approached them, wearing a wide smile. He was a short, balding man who spoke with a thick Italian accent. "Mr. Harrison, Ms. Ellis, welcome to Mestiere. Please follow me to your table."

They were taken to the rear corner of the restaurant and seated at an intimate table for two. Reagan pulled out a chair for Julie and waited until she was seated, before settling himself across from her.

"Your waiter will be with you shortly." The maître d went back to his post at the front of the restaurant.

Julie took a minute to appreciate her surroundings. The restaurant, which was decorated in a modern style, still retained the old world charm of the building. Contemporary paintings hung on exposed brick walls, and the rustic wooden tables created a cozy space. Overhead lighting was kept low, with candles and wall sconces providing illumination.

Their waiter arrived with a wine list and dinner menus.

Reagan ordered a bottle of Riesling, Julie's favorite wine, and the waiter left to fill the request.

"I thought you didn't like wine." She stared across the table at her handsome date. The sight of him made her heart skip a beat. Waves of electrical energy danced over her skin.

"I'll make an exception for tonight." He watched her with half-mooned lids.

Julie opened the menu, needing to take her gaze off him. *Breathe. Don't forget to breathe.* "This is all in Italian. I can't read anything on the menu."

"Mestiere is the top Italian restaurant in the Midwest." He grinned. "They make the best marinara sauce on the planet. I think they keep a little Italian grandmother in the kitchen."

"Yum. Pasta sounds delicious. Will you order for me?"

"I'd be happy to." He reached across the table to hold her hand.

They stayed that way, connected by sight and touch, until the waiter returned with their wine. He poured them each a glass, and then Reagan ordered their dinners.

The nervous butterflies, which had fluttered inside her stomach, had now morphed into a hum of excitement. Tonight was different than any date she'd ever been on. Being wined and dined with Reagan felt perfectly right. He'd taken her into his world, and she had to admit, it was pretty darn nice.

"I'm glad you don't need your sling anymore." She glanced at his injured arm.

"I feel good. Hopefully, I'll get cleared to play in next week's game."

Their first course arrived, consisting of a salad of baby greens with a tasty homemade dressing and small bites of garlic toast. Reagan raised his wine glass. "To the most beautiful woman in the world. You've made me a very happy man."

She smiled as their glasses clinked, and then took a sip of the delicately flavored wine.

As they dined, their conversation traveled through many topics but many revolved around stories about their childhoods and families. Reagan told tales about his older sisters and the trouble they had caused him. About the special bond he and his dad had. How they would go fishing and hunting to escape a house full of females.

Julie told him about her father—how he'd left the family when she was two years old. She hadn't heard from him since and didn't want to. He'd given her the red hair, but that was all. Everything else she owed to her mother.

The food was delicious, just as Reagan had promised. Definitely haute cuisine, but with a taste that could only be described as 'homemade with love'. When they finished their meal, Reagan paid the bill and stood to take Julie's hand, pulling her to him.

A perfect gentleman.

He kissed her softly before a waiter brought her coat, and he helped her slide it on. They stepped out of the warm restaurant into the cool, November air, to the waiting car.

"How did the driver know when to pick us up? I didn't see you make a call."

"If you pay people enough money, they become very good at reading your mind." He chuckled and opened the car door, letting her get seated. He slid in next to her and pulled her close, moving his hand to her chin and stroking it gently.

The driver pulled away from the curb.

Julie gave no thought to their destination. She tipped her head forward, meeting her lips to his, and gave into the deluge of sensation. The kiss was slow and intense, as if he was savoring a delicious meal.

She couldn't help but recall John's kisses, which always possessed a sense of urgency. When he'd come home after deployments, their coming together had been fast and fervent. Her time with John always had a caveat—she never knew when those stolen moments would disappear.

Coming back to the present, she pushed the comparisons out of her mind. Tonight was Reagan's night. He deserved her whole attention.

"What are you thinking?"

He stared into her eyes, which must have hinted at her distracted thoughts. "Nothing." She willed herself to enjoy and appreciate the here and now. "So, are we heading home?"

He laughed and wrapped his arm around her shoulder. "Not yet, I have another surprise planned."

****

A short time later, at Reagan's direction, they arrived in front of a seemingly abandoned building. A neon sign reading Club Remix hung crookedly above the entrance. Outside stood a long line of people, which snaked down the sidewalk. But he wasn't concerned about getting inside. Not when he was good friends with the owners.

Reagan exited the car and opened the car door for Julie. She took his hand, and he helped her step out over the curb. The loud, thumping beat of music emanated from every gap in the facade. As they approached, a large bouncer immediately lifted a thick, red velvet rope. Reagan motioned for Julie to pass through ahead of him.

"Welcome, Mr. Harrison," the bouncer said, while another man opened a large metal door, inviting them in.

The sounds of the girls calling out his name were immediately cut off when they stepped inside. All he heard was music over the hum of a multitude of voices. The building looked like a warehouse in another life, with its three-story ceiling and large open space. A long glass-topped bar filled one side of the room. Behind the bar hung shelves, displaying hundreds of bottles. The DJ booth and dance floor took up the middle section, and vibrantly colored tables filled the first floor. Above was the second level, which ran the perimeter. A catwalk overlooked the dance floor.

Normally, a night at the club was no big deal, just a way to get together with friends and blow off some steam. But Julie was on his arm, and he felt like a king. He couldn't wait to be seen with her. She looked stunning with her dress hugging every delicious curve.

A woman with waist-length black-and-purple hair arrived to escort them to a roped-off staircase. She removed the barrier, which led them upstairs to the VIP section. From there, they followed her to a booth, which was already occupied by another couple—Reagan's good friends.

Nick stood and held out a hand for him to shake. "Reagan, man, good to see you."

Leah gave Reagan a hug and kiss on the cheek. "I'm glad you're here. It's been way too long."

His chest swelling with pride, Reagan put his arm around Julie's small waist. "Nick and Leah, I'd like to introduce you to my girlfriend, Julie Ellis. These two are very good friends of mine, Nick and Leah Breyer."

"Hi, Julie," Leah said. "Thanks for joining us."

Wide-eyed, Julie looked at both of them and gasped. "It's so nice to meet you."

Nick Breyer was the star of the latest round of Batman movies. His wife, Leah, was a tall, raven-haired model. When he'd planned to meet up with them at the club, he hadn't taken into account Julie might be intimidated when thrust into the world of celebrities. Hopefully, she'd soon realize Nick and Leah were very nice people. For a Hollywood couple, they were very unpretentious.

The group of four seated themselves around the booth. Reagan held Julie's hand, stroking her palm with his thumb in reassurance.

Nick leaned over to Julie and spoke above the noise of the music. "What I want to know, Julie, is why such a pretty girl like you is dating this ugly beast?" He pointed to Reagan's annoyed face.

Julie laughed and gently patted Reagan's cheek. "He's not so bad."

"I'm just lucky she can look past my lousy friend," he shot back.

Leah elbowed Nick in the side, "You boys be nice, we're here to have a good time. Let's get some drinks ordered."

"Do you dance, Reagan?" Julie asked over the music pulsing in the background.

"Not very well, but I've been known to make an appearance on the dance floor. The scene usually ends with me fleeing for my life. Those ladies can get pretty crazy." He shrugged. The only lady he cared about driving crazy nowadays was Julie.

"Would you mind going with me to dance?" Leah asked Julie. "These guys are no fun. They can stay here and talk football."

"Sure." She gave Reagan a quick kiss before the girls made their way downstairs.

Reagan and Nick went to stand next to the railing, observing the dance floor beneath them. Reagan watched as Julie and Leah moved through the crowd to the center, the techno music vibrated the air. They merged into a sea of moving bodies. Multicolored lights flashed around them. The crowd was electric.

As Julie danced, Reagan noticed the layers of stress falling away. They peeled away to uncover the happy, carefree girl he'd seen in her photo album.

Like she had her own personal spotlight, Julie seemed to shimmer and glow. He couldn't take his gaze off of her. "Thanks for meeting us here," Reagan said to Nick. "I figured Julie would hit it off with Leah. I really want her to have a good time tonight. With work and caring for her son, she doesn't take much time to just go out and have fun."

"Reagan, you surprise me." Nick tipped his head toward Julie. "She's very pretty, but I never pictured you dating a single mom. That's a lot of responsibility, and not really your style. You avoid commitment like the plague."

"She makes me a better person. I'm done playing around." As Reagan continued to watch her from above, all his feelings converge into one truth. "She's the one, Nick."

"I'm happy for you." Nick gave him a slap across his broad back. "But just so you know, I ran into Brynn last week out in LA, and she wasn't very happy with how you ended things. You know, there's no wrath like a woman scorned and all. Anyway, Brynn thinks you'll get bored with your new 'girl next door'—her words, not mine—and you'll be back in her bed very soon. I thought you should know, in case she starts trouble." Nick then motioned to the dance floor. "Looks like our ladies are hot property."

Reagan noticed several men surrounding Julie and Leah. The women attempted to move away from their crowd of admirers, but with no luck. After Leah was grabbed by a sweaty-looking man, she shook her head and pointed up at Reagan and Nick. Reagan let loose an intimidating scowl and headed to the stairs, down to the first level and onto the dance floor. With the imminent threat of bodily harm, the troublemakers escaped into the sea of bodies.

Nick and Reagan wove their way through the crowd. Leah took Nick by the hand and led him in a seductive dance, clearly advertising her claim.

Reagan, having eyes only for Julie, grabbed her around the waist. Together, their bodies moved in unison to the music. He pulled Julie close and lifted her off her feet, holding her with one strong arm. "You're as light as a bird." She was raised to his eye level. With their lips at such close proximity, he was drawn like a magnet to iron. After a long kiss, he slowly lowered her feet to the ground but kept a hand resting securely on the curve of her lower back. The contact burned hot, a mix of pleasure and pain—satisfaction and longing.

"You sure know how to show a girl a good time."

She rested her hands on his shoulders.

"I'm glad you're enjoying yourself."

"This is the most fun I've had in ages."

Warmth filled his body. Nothing made him more content than seeing Julie happy. "Good, because I'm a slave to your pleasure. Putting a smile on your face is my new mission in life."

Around one am, Reagan noticed Julie's eyelids grow heavy. They said goodbye to Nick and Leah, and then left the club. As they started their journey home, smooth jazz serenaded them from the car's speakers, which was a welcome sound after the upbeat techno music of the club. Julie slipped off her shoes to curl up on the seat, resting her head on Reagan's chest. "Thanks for the best first date ever," she sighed in a drowsy voice.

He wrapped his arm protectively around her, nuzzling into her silky, rose-scented hair. "You deserve to be spoiled."

"All I need is you," she said before drifting off to sleep.

He stayed awake for the ride to Timber Lake in order to watch her sleep. He would be content to stay in the backseat of the car all night, never leaving her side. When the driver pulled into the driveway to Julie's house, he didn't have the heart to wake her. Reaching for her purse, he found the house key, smoothly exited the car, and went to unlock the front door. Coming back, he swept her in his arms. He barely felt her weight as he carried her into the house and finally laid her on her bed. Brushing back her hair, he leaned in close. "Julie, honey, we're home."

She opened her eyes a crack, and then closed them.

"What? I must have fallen asleep in the car. Did you carry me up?"

He sat on the edge of her bed, rubbing her hand between his large palms. "I'm heading home now."

With her eyes still closed, she patted around until she found his arm. "Don't go. Stay with me tonight. I don't want to be alone. I'm so tired of being alone."

How could he deny her? He'd never leave her side, if that was her wish. "Ok," he whispered. "I'll be right back." He went outside to tell the driver to leave for the night. Coming inside, he locked the front door and turned off the lights downstairs. He returned to find Julie changed into an oversized T-shirt and snug in her bed, breathing at the slow pace of sleep.

He went to find the shorts and shirt he'd left in her spare room and changed out of his dress clothes. Sliding into bed next to Julie, he drew her in his arms and covered them both with a heavy comforter. She let out a sound that was practically a purr.

For a while, he held onto her, until he was sure she was fully asleep. Then, he carefully slipped out of bed and settled for the chair tucked in the corner of her room. Rest seemed elusive, as he couldn't stop watching her. Eventually, he slipped off into his own peaceful sleep, not bothering to dream, since reality proved to be a better companion.

Chapter Fourteen

Julie peered over to the digital clock on her nightstand and was shocked to see the time. *Ten am*! She never slept so late. Letting her head rest on the pillow, she closed her eyes to relive last night. She'd felt like a fairytale princess, with Reagan playing the role of Prince Charming.

The smell of peppermint infused into her room reminded her of Reagan. She smiled at the memory of his strong arms wrapped around her. For a night, she'd felt protected as she drifted into a perfect sleep. After countless nights alone, enduring dreams that reminded her of everything she'd lost, she was grateful Reagan's presence had chased away those demons.

Noticing he was not in her bedroom, she pulled on a pair of fleece pants and a sweatshirt then went downstairs. She rounded the corner to see Reagan standing in her kitchen, attempting to make breakfast.

"Good morning, sleepy head," he said while pouring her a cup of coffee. He wore athletic shorts and a faded gray T-shirt.

His tousled blond hair looked incredibly sexy. She grabbed the warm cup like a life preserver and took a sip. "That's good, thanks. Why didn't you wake me?"

He went back to the stove and picked up a spatula. "You looked so peaceful. I didn't want to disturb you."

She sat at the table and stifled a giggle as he moved

around her kitchen, a bemused look on his face. "What are you making over there?"

Reagan scraped the contents of a frying pan onto two plates. "Welcome to Café Harrison. Today we are featuring waffles and scrambled eggs. Hope you're hungry."

What a silly guy. And yes, she was starving. "Wow, you're good-looking and can cook. What more could a girl want?"

"Unfortunately, this is the extent of my kitchen skills. I've learned only a few basics to keep from starving." He walked over and set a plate before Julie. Table service, topped off with a kiss on the cheek.

"I could get used to this." She stabbed a piece of waffle with her fork while Reagan came over with his own plate piled high with food. After her first bite, she had to admit his cooking wasn't too bad. He'd added cinnamon to the batter, and the spice gave the waffle a nice savory flavor to balance out the sweet. "Will you need a ride home later?"

"I didn't want to bother you, so I called a car service. They'll be here at noon. I thought it best I wasn't still here when Aiden came home."

"I guess you're right." Why did their time together always end so soon? She hated saying goodbye. "So, what's your schedule like for this week?"

"I have an appointment with the team doctor tomorrow. I hope to be cleared to go to the gym."

Julie stood behind him and took hold of his injured arm. "Rotate your shoulder. I want to feel it move."

He obediently raised his arm.

With one hand over the joint, she moved his arm slowly back and forth. Under her fingers, the ligament moved smoothly. "The swelling's gone down. The ligament's resting in the right place, not getting hung up on any other tissue. I don't think you'll have a problem being cleared."

"I love having you as my own personal physical therapist." Smiling, he grabbed her around the waist and pulled her onto his lap, before running his fingers through her wild mass of hair. "Do you know how adorable you look right now?"

She quickly took a mental inventory of her appearance. Her carefully styled hair from the night before was now sticking out in all directions. The clothes she wore were comfortable but old and faded, bare feet stuck out of oversized pants. "You really think I'm adorable looking like this?"

He answered by drawing her into a deep kiss. She wrapped her arms around his neck, tasting the sweet syrup still on his lips. He pulled her close, his left hand caressing her back while the right was tied up in the waves of her hair. She became swept away in a storm of electric sensation, pulsing with a life of its own. His muscular body pressed to hers, strong arms held her secure. Reagan's hand continued to explore her body, slipping under her sweatshirt. With his fingertips, he stroked the smoothness of her skin, his touch was pure heat. His lips trailed down her neck.

She tipped back her head, and a low moan escaped her lips. That sound of pure longing broke through her trance, leaving her unnerved. John's face materialized behind her closed eyes. Julie tried to block out the little voice that told her she was being unfaithful. An alarm rang in her mind. Even though she'd been a widow for over a year, she still felt guilty about being with another man. Her mind and body were filled with too many sensations and emotions that would not reconcile—one begged to give in to the seduction, the other flashed a warning to stop before she'd gone too far. She pulled away, resting her head on his shoulder.

His breath rasped in and out in ragged spurts. "What's wrong?"

"I'm sorry—" she fumbled, not wanting to tell him what was really in her heart, afraid the truth would cause him pain. "Asking you to stay last night wasn't fair. I imagine you're probably really frustrated with me right now."

As she spoke, he put a quieting finger over her lips. "Don't apologize. All I want is to be close to you. To feel your heartbeat and listen to your cute little snore." With a finger, he lifted her chin.

"Hey, I don't snore."

"Whatever you say, my dear." He pinched her nose. "As long as I know you're mine."

"Thanks for understanding me." She softly kissed his cheek. The rough stubble tickled her lips. "Even when I don't understand myself." She went to sit in her chair to finish her cup of coffee.

At that moment, she noticed the kitchen. *What an unbelievable mess! Who'd actually cook breakfast...a class of rowdy five-year-olds?* She gave Reagan a sideways glance, to see him moving a last piece of waffle around his plate, collecting any remaining egg and syrup. "Did you use every bowl I own?"

He was the messiest cook she'd ever seen. A huge pile of dirty dishes sat on the counter, covered in dried waffle batter and egg. Bits of syrup-laden crumbs dotted the kitchen floor, like a sticky breadcrumb trail.

His smile held no hint of guilt, and he shrugged. "Nobody's perfect."

No, not perfect—but he was pretty darn close.

****

Monday morning, Julie took Aiden to school and then went to work. As she walked through the physical therapy office, she noticed smiles and long glances from her co-workers. When she arrived at her workspace, she discovered the reason. On her desk sat a huge bouquet of red roses. A small, white card stuck up above the flowers, covered with a large letter R.

Not wanting to draw any more attention, she pushed the vase to the corner of her desk. They were beautiful flowers. She only wished Reagan wouldn't have sent them here. While reading over her daily patient files, she heard a high-pitched whistle.

"Pretty flowers," Amy, her PT assistant, said. "Are they from Reagan Harrison?"

Julie pressed her lips together and raised her head, trying to maintain a cool and calm demeanor. "Why in the world would you think they're from him?"

Amy grinned and tossed a copy of the day's morning newspaper on her desk. "Nice try, but the jig's up." She pointed to a large black-and-white picture in the gossip section. The image was a little fuzzy, but it clearly showed Julie and Reagan cuddled together at the club. Beneath was the caption: "Has Reagan Harrison Fallen for the Girl Next Door?"

Julie gripped the paper in stunned silence. She read the short article, which accompanied the picture, and let out a surprised squeak at the sight of her name. *Was this what it's like to date a sports celebrity? With the whole world a silent spectator to your private moments.* "Why would anyone put this story in the newspaper?"

"Reagan Harrison is a hot topic, and anyone he dates is news." Amy sat on the corner of Julie's desk, eyeing the picture one more time. "Way to go, Julie, he's quite a stud."

Julie recognized the playfulness in Amy's tone and smiled. "Okay, the flowers are from Reagan, but that's all you're getting out of me today." She handed Amy a large folder before pointing out an exercise schedule. "Gossip time's over. Let's get to work."

Throughout the day, Julie's cell buzzed with numerous calls from an unknown number. Since she was working, she let them go straight to voicemail. At lunch, she checked her phone to see five missed calls but no voicemails. Her phone vibrated again, another unknown number call. *Who in the world keeps calling?* She tapped the answer key. "Hello, this is Julie Ellis." The tone of her voice was crisp and professional.

"Well, well," came a smooth female voice on the other end. "You've finally decided to answer your phone."

"Who is this?" Julie didn't disguise her growing agitation.

"Brynn Campbell...maybe you've heard of me?"

Her entire body stiffened at the sound of that name. "Sure, I have, but why are you calling me?"

"Because Reagan's mine. You better not get too comfortable with him. He tends to float around with women, but he always comes back to me."

Her voice grew as irritating as the sound of broken glass. The call abruptly ended. Still in shock, Julie placed the phone on her desk with a shaking hand. One thing was for certain—Brynn meant to cause trouble.

But what if she was right? Would Reagan grow tired of Julie's boringly normal life?

By the time she finished her lunch, Julie's thoughts had turned from her love life to work. She focused solely on her next patient, a twelve-year-old girl who had been diagnosed with Muscular Dystrophy. Her therapy plan used exercise to keep her muscles strong and active.

The girl, named Emily, was in the middle of a leg massage when she let out a giggle.

"Did I tickle you?" Julie lightly brushed her fingers over her leg, which made Emily laugh harder.

"No," Emily said, catching her breath. "I think it's funny you're famous."

"What?" Julie remembered her picture in the paper. "I'm not famous. I was just sitting next to a famous person."

"I know." Emily got a dreamy look in her eyes. "He's sooooo cute!"

The fact even twelve-year-old girls found Reagan good looking shouldn't be a surprise. Julie looked at the smitten little girl and chuckled. "You're right. He is super cute."

****

After a brief struggle, Aiden was finally upstairs asleep. Now, after a long day of work and parenting, all Julie wanted to do was unwind.

"Don't skip over any details." Chrissy leaned back on the sofa and propped her bare feet on the coffee table.

She brought in two glasses and a bottle of wine, curled onto the sofa, and told her friend about the luxury car with driver, the restaurant, the club and their movie star companions.

Wine splashed from the glass in Chrissy's wildly gesturing hand when she found out Julie had gone to *Club Remix*. "You have to promise to take me with you next time, Jules. I've been dying to go."

When Julie finished telling her story, she laid her head back on the sofa, and closed her eyes. "I had fun, don't get me wrong, but I'm not used to being fussed upon like that. Reagan went way above and beyond anything I'm used to. I'm not sure I deserve him."

"Of course you do, silly. I think he wants to be worthy of *you*." Chrissy pointed her finger at Julie.

She peered over at Chrissy and raised a brow. "I come with so much baggage, I could have my own department at a store. The Julie Ellis Luggage Collection, which has a nice-looking design yet totally nonfunctional."

Chrissy snorted out a laugh. "So what you're saying is you don't come with those little spinny wheels?"

"Funny. I need a refill." Julie giggled, holding out her empty glass.

"Oh yeah, I forgot to tell you." Chrissy grabbed the almost-empty wine bottle and poured the remainder into Julie's glass. "I saw your picture in the newspaper today."

"That's crazy, right? I was surprised when I saw the article. This whole thing is a lot to get used to." She leaned forward. "Which reminds me, I got an interesting phone call today."

"Yeah? From who?" Chrissy scooted toward Julie.

"From none other than the Brynn Campbell. Get this...she told me not to get too comfortable with

Reagan."

"No way." Chrissy set her glass on the coffee table. "A while back, I remember seeing pictures in some tabloid of her and Reagan attending a movie premiere."

"They were seeing each other when we first met. From what Reagan said, they haven't spoken since he broke off things in August."

The corners of Chrissy's mouth drooped, and she rested her chin on her folded hand. "Do you think she'll try calling again? Maybe you should tell Reagan."

"I don't want to get him involved. He's too busy with the football season to worry about a crazy ex-girlfriend." She straightened her spine. No one, not even a movie star, would get away with bullying her. "I was an Army wife for five years, and I've learned from the best how to put up a fight. This woman doesn't know who she's dealing with."

Pride radiated from Chrissy's smile. "That's the spirit. Good to see the combative spark in your eyes again."

****

When Reagan walked through her door Sunday evening, he found Julie in the middle of a rare tirade.

"When will you learn to pick up after yourself?" Julie tossed a full basket of toys on the shelf. "You need to start learning some responsibility."

"I'm never talking to you again," Aiden yelled and climbed the stairs to his room.

"Honey." Reagan approached, like one would an ornery tiger—with extreme caution. *What was with the sour mood?* "You're this upset over Aiden not picking up his toys?"

Julie took a black band off her wrist then yanked

back her hair to put it in a ponytail. "I'm sorry...you're right." She walked into the kitchen, returning with an official-looking envelope from the Department of War, the United States Pentagon.

He carefully pulled out the sheet of crisp white paper. On the top of the letter was a clear, formal heading. After he spent a minute reading the correspondence, he placed the letter in the envelope. "No wonder you're so upset." He took her hand and guided her over to the sofa.

She rested her head on his broad shoulder. "I contacted an attorney a few months ago, to see if I had any legal right to know the circumstances of John's death. The lawyer said dealing with the government is always uncertain, but he would send them an official letter of inquiry. The letter you just read was their response."

Reagan considered what to say next. This was all new territory. Best tread very lightly. "The letter states his mission details are sensitive and for the safety of others, they need to be kept classified. Do you buy their explanation?"

"I don't know what to think anymore, but I can't help feeling they're covering up something. The Army won't even confirm his rank at time of death—like he disappeared from the ranks of the Special Forces Unit he was serving."

"The medical report states he died from two gunshot wounds." He noticed her face pale even further. Talking about the murder of her husband was difficult, but necessary. Any information could help the reporter uncover the truth. "Did John ever give you any idea about what his missions entailed, especially right before his death?"

She shook her head and reclined into the back of the sofa. "No, he never talked about that. I don't think he could, even if he wanted to. During our last conversation, we talked about things that now seem unimportant. The last letter I received only said that if something happened, I should go to his best friend, Heath, for answers. Heath mailed John's letter to me after the funeral. Since then, I've tried to contact Heath, but he never returned any of my calls or emails. Last I heard he's deployed again overseas."

Reagan took her hand, knowing nothing he could say would make her feel better. Seeing Julie so upset motivated him to do anything to protect her from further pain.

After a moment, Julie started crying. "Some days, I think I'll go mad with frustration. I need to know the truth. I want to keep fighting, but I don't know how much I have left."

His job on the football field was straightforward—to defend the end zone. But defending the heart of the woman he loved was a tougher challenge. He'd never felt as helpless as he did right now, holding Julie while she grieved. "Truth sometimes has a complicated journey, with setbacks and obstacles, but it's a force that can't be stopped."

Her body wilted, and she sobbed into his embrace. "Thank you," she finally said. "You're right, the truth will come out."

"Of course I'm right," he teased, placing a finger under her chin and lifting her face so he could see her small smile. He gave her a soft peck on the tip of her nose. "I'm always right."

He continued to hold her close, enjoying the softness of her body next to his. When she closed her eyes, he set a robin's egg blue box onto her lap.

"What's this?" She wiped the moisture off her face and stared wide-eyed at his gift.

"Something to put a smile on your face. I got a little trinket when I was in New York last week."

She untied the white ribbon with a widening grin and drew open the lid. "Oh," she gasped. "It's beautiful!"

"Let me put it on you." He gently held the bracelet and took her hand. After he set the clasp, he dropped several kisses on the inside of her delicate wrist. Her skin felt warm against his lips. The platinum bracelet looked as beautiful on her as he'd imagined, appearing like a vine winding around her wrist, with tiny delicate leaves adorned with diamonds.

"Thank you. I missed you while you were gone."

"I hate leaving you." He combed his fingers through the loose waves of her hair. "How about I take you to a movie next weekend?" Finally, a genuine smile warmed her face.

"That would be nice. I haven't gone to the movies in a long time."

"Great. You choose a movie and tell me the time. I'll pick you up after the team's work out on Friday."

"I hope you plan on showering first."

"Nah, I thought I'd impress you with my 'dripping with sweat' look."

"Oh no." She inhaled deeply. "I like the freshly showered, yummy smelling Reagan so much better. I better go upstairs and smooth things over with Aiden." Julie gave Reagan a kiss before she disappeared to the

Laurie Winter

second story.

Reagan read the lawyer's letter one more time to search for any information he could share with the reporter working on uncovering the truth. As he tidied the paperwork, he saw a letter sticking out from underneath the pile. He carefully pulled the folded sheet of paper from the worn envelope and started reading John's last love letter to his wife.

May 22, 2012

Dear Julie,

I'm just going to say it... I don't think I can stand being away from you for one more day. As much as I love what I do, the toll it's taken on our marriage is too high. I've missed seeing Aiden's first day of preschool, his Christmas program, and so many other moments I'll never get back. I'm sorry I'm not there for you, to wake up with you every day and be by your side as you take care of our family.

I wish I could tell you what's going on here. What I can say is that things are more dangerous than they've ever been. My team is doing our best to secure the region for the soldiers who will be here soon to replace us. I wanted you to know that if something happens to me, Heath will tell you the truth. He's like a brother to me and will look out for you and Aiden if I no longer can.

Tonight, I'm waiting to see if the Army will give the green light to a mission of utmost importance. If we go, we have no choice but to succeed. This mission means the difference between life and death for so many Afghans, as well as Americans.

As I sign off, I want you to know you have been the best part of my life. Everything I do, I do for you and

Aiden. You deserve so much more than what I've given you. Someday, when I'm out of the Army, I promise to devote my remaining days to your happiness. I love you, Julie. Don't ever forget that.

See you soon,

John

Reagan folded the letter and returned it to the bottom of the pile. By the worn creases, he could tell John's words had been read numerous times. That kind of love, the love John and Julie shared, seemed so sacred. A tightening knot of uneasiness formed in his gut. Tension rolled over his forehead, neck, and back. He suddenly felt like an intruder in their marriage.

He understood why Julie was having such a hard time letting go. Why she struggled to open her heart to a new relationship. Reagan loved her with everything he had. But would that ever be enough?

Chapter Fifteen

Only two more weeks until Christmas Day. The shopping season had shifted from hurried to utterly crazy. And Reagan was ready to step into the madness. He was strangely happy to escort Julie on a one-day shopping blitz. Mary was watching Aiden, so they had the whole day to spend together.

"*Brrrr.*" Julie climbed into the passenger seat of his SUV, bringing with her a blast of icy air.

She leaned over to give him the sweetest kiss, instantly warming the air around them. "Hey there, beautiful."

Julie was so bundled up, only her face was visible—haloed by a purple hat and scarf. "I do miss North Carolina this time of the year."

The snow had started overnight, bringing bone-chilling temps. On the morning news show, the weather lady had predicted five more inches of snow would fall throughout the day. He loved playing football in this kind of weather—but driving through it, not so much.

"How about we plan a trip to someplace warm? Football season will be done at the beginning of February, hopefully with a Super Bowl win, and I'd love to take you and Aiden on vacation. I'm thinking of this resort in Puerto Rico I've been to a few times. The place is beautiful, with white sand beaches and clear turquoise water."

She sighed and gazed out the icy window. "That does sound wonderful. By February, I'll be ready to flee this state."

After a stop for breakfast, they made their way to the first store on Julie's list. With the other shoppers focused on the holiday rush, not many noticed the Warriors linebacker who walked among them. He stopped to sign a few autographs and took pictures with fans, but for the most part, he was left alone to enjoy his time with Julie.

They left the store with Reagan carrying several large bags, which he loaded into the rear of the SUV. "The rate you're going, my car will be filled in no time."

"I hope so." She'd just got seated when the wind blew the passenger door closed with a bang. "And having you here is making Christmas shopping fun. Thanks for coming along."

"Just think of me as your personal shopping assistant. Your wish is my command…carry bags, push the cart, even clear your path of other shoppers."

Julie laughed. "Well, I don't know about tackling the other shoppers, but I'm happy you're here to carry my bags."

Good to know his arm muscles could be used for more than playing football. "I'd like to go to Champion Bike Shop next. I want to get a bike for Aiden. I know he won't get to use it for a few months, but eventually, the snow will melt. Would you help me pick one out?"

She clapped her gloved hands. "Aiden would love a new bike. He told me his bike is a baby one, and he won't ride it anymore."

"Perfect." He drove onto the street.

A snowplow lumbered past them, its metal blade scraping the ice-covered pavement.

As he drove to the bike store, he reflected on the upcoming Christmas. This year's celebration would be one to remember. His family had understood why he wanted to spend the holidays in Timber Lake this year instead of coming home. When he'd been home for Thanksgiving, they'd been direct and relentless in their questioning about his relationship with Julie. His sisters were already planning the wedding. They must be psychic.

He hadn't told them he'd purchased an engagement ring, choosing a three-carat cushion-cut diamond, clear and flawless, set on a platinum band. The ring cost more than his first car, but Julie deserved nothing less. She might not be emotionally prepared to marry him right away, but he would be content just to slip his ring on her finger, proclaiming his dedication. Maybe he'd propose on Christmas, or maybe he'd chicken out and wait until after the holidays. Just thinking about getting down on one knee left him more nervous than the night before his first pro-football game.

When they arrived at the bike shop, the snow was falling harder than before, and they slipped multiple times walking across the parking lot. After an hour with the young store worker, Reagan purchased the perfect bike. He was sure Aiden would love the red bike, which boasted silver flame decals along the frame.

"I will give you a call as soon as the bike is assembled, Mr. Harrison," the shop manager said. "We'll be sure to have it delivered well before Christmas."

"You've been very helpful." Reagan shook the

guy's hand. "Thanks." Leaving the store with Julie, hand in hand, he had a strong desire for a perfect Christmas.

"I don't think even the snow will stop Aiden from riding his new bike," Julie said right before losing her footing.

Reagan grabbed her arm as she started to fall. Drawing her close, he held her securely to his body while brushing her hair off her face. The falling snow faded into the background as he became lost in her blue-green eyes.

"I love you," she said softly against his ear. "I hope you know how much you mean to me."

He'd waited so long to hear her say those words. "I love you, too, Julie. More than you know." His throat constricted, and when he spoke, his voice wavered with emotion.

She kissed him one last time before brushing the snow off her coat and hair, and then climbed into the car.

As he started the ignition, he wanted to pinch himself, to make sure this all wasn't just a dream. Had Julie really said she loved him? And was he now sitting in his car, next to the most beautiful woman in the world, ready to ask her to marry him? He started driving to the next store, only going a few hundred feet, when Julie's phone rang.

"Hi, Mom," she answered cheerfully.

He watched as her formerly happy face turned pale and somber while she listened. Her hand trembled with slight vibrations.

"Oh no," she finally said with a strained voice. "We'll be right there."

She turned to him. Julie's eyes were wide and glistened with tears. "We need to get to Timber Lake Hospital. Mom's waiting in the ER. They've been in a car accident." She hesitated and burst out in a sob. "Aiden's in critical condition, they're taking him into surgery right now."

****

Through her teary haze, Julie saw Reagan grip the steering wheel with tense strength. He wove the vehicle expertly through the city streets. The roads were ice-covered and slick, and she understood how easily a car accident could happen under these conditions.

While they were stopped at a red light, Reagan glanced over.

She was trying so hard to hold it together. An uncontrollable trembling had taken over her body.

"What happened?" He reached to steady her hand.

"Mom and Aiden were driving to the grocery store. They were hit going through an intersection. The other car slid and crashed into where Aiden sat." Pain laced through each word. "He was unconscious when the paramedics arrived. They stabilized him and then took him to the hospital. The doctor told Mom that Aiden was bleeding internally and would need immediate surgery." She started sobbing, her breath releasing in short gasps. "I can't lose him, too," she repeated over like a mantra.

Finally, they arrived at the hospital, and Reagan parked the car by the Emergency Room entrance.

The second the car stopped, Julie jumped out and raced to the hospital doors. Inside, she found her mom sitting alone, sorrow weighing on her features. Julie went to sit beside her, and they held each other close.

"Oh, Mom, I'm so scared. I don't know what I'd do if—" Julie faltered, her throat tight.

"He's a strong boy." Mary placed an arm around Julie's shoulders and squeezed. "And the doctors are taking good care of him."

"Is he still in surgery? Have they given you any updates?" *Please let him be all right.*

"The nurse at the desk will take us to the surgical waiting room. The surgeon will give us an update soon."

Reagan appeared behind her, and they were all escorted upstairs to the waiting room.

Even though the space had been designed to make anxious family members feel more comfortable, Julie couldn't relax. She paced back and forth, around the rows of chairs. Finally stopping in front of a long window, she folded her arms protectively around her body and stared absently outside.

A bird, which didn't seem bothered by the snow and cold, perched in a bare tree a few feet from the window.

Julie watched the tiny sparrow prune its wings, and then it flew away. "Mom, I'm glad you weren't hurt." She turned to face her mom. "The accident wasn't your fault. I know you couldn't have avoided it. I'm relieved you were there for Aiden."

"I should have done more to protect him." Mary gasped and let loose a stream of tears.

Julie walked over and cupped a hand over her mother's hand.

Reagan, sitting next to Mary, put his arm around her shoulder and took hold of Julie's free hand. The three formed a triangle, and Julie drew strength from their bond.

A short time later, a tall doctor entered the room, dressed in blue scrubs with a surgical mask resting around his neck. "Aiden's parents?" he asked, looking from Reagan to Julie.

"I'm Aiden's mother. Tell me, how's my son?" Her stomach churned with nausea in anticipation of the doctor's news. Pressing her lips together, she tried to control the urge to throw up.

"I'm your son's surgeon, Dr. Roberts." His voice was gentle but confident. "Has your mother updated you on Aiden's earlier condition?"

She swayed and felt Reagan's arm slip around her waist, essentially keeping her standing. "Yes, she said Aiden was bleeding internally."

"That's correct. When he was brought in, he was unconscious, and his heartbeat was very weak. The impact pushed the car door into his body. His child booster seat saved him from being totally crushed. Aiden has a broken leg and bruising, and that's the extent of his visible injuries. Most of the damage was done inside his abdomen. Aiden's in the middle of surgery now. We're controlling the internal bleeding. Then, we'll start mending his affected organs, mainly his kidney and liver."

As Julie tried to digest the information the surgeon relayed, her brain froze with shock. "How much longer will his surgery last?" Her voice sounded forced and raspy.

"Hard to say, Mrs. Ellis. I have an excellent team working on your son." Dr. Roberts gave Julie's hand a quick squeeze. "Aiden's strong, and I believe he will pull through this. Your mother did an excellent job at the accident scene. She treated Aiden until the first responders arrived. Her nursing skills and quick thinking make me very optimistic about Aiden's recovery. One of the nurses from the OR will update you again soon." Dr. Roberts gave a reassuring smile and exited the room.

With him went Julie's faith and prayers.

Reagan guided Julie's shaking body to a chair. "You need to sit and rest now. Try to relax, he's in good hands."

"He has to get better." Julie looked through tear-filled eyes at Reagan. "I couldn't survive if he was taken from me."

Minutes passed slowly into hours, and their vigil continued. Every half an hour, a nurse arrived to update them on Aiden's condition. Julie couldn't focus her vision, and her head pounded with nervous tension. She was caught in a horrible nightmare.

Finally, after the longest four hours of her life, the surgeon walked back into the room, looking drained but in good spirits. "We stopped the bleeding," he said. "Aiden's stable but the next twenty-four hours will be critical. He's being taken to the ICU for observation. A nurse will be coming shortly to escort you."

"Thank you," Julie gasped, relief flooding through her body.

Dr. Roberts nodded and left the waiting room.

Reagan stood at her side, stroking her arm. "Aiden will pull through this. He'll be okay."

Their escort arrived a short time later, a middle-aged nurse, who took them up one flight of stairs to the ICU wing. "Sorry," she said, "but I can only allow in parents at this time. Mrs. Ellis, you may follow me to

Aiden's room." The nurse looked at Mary and Reagan. "We have a small lounge for ICU visitors. You can wait in there if you like."

Reagan gave Julie a reassuring kiss on the forehead before she walked away.

She was desperate to see Aiden with her own eyes—to touch him and to let him know she was there. As she walked through the double glass doors, which sectioned off his room, her stomach lurched at the sight of Aiden's small body hooked up to tubes and machines. His face and arms were bruised, and she noticed a bump under the blanket from the temporary cast affixed to his leg. Aside from the occasional beep or hum of the monitors, the room was quiet and still. Aiden, in a medically induced sleep, looked peaceful.

She sat on the small, upholstered chair next to his bed. Leaning forward to brush his small face with her cheek, she breathed in his sweet, little boy scent. "Oh, my baby. You don't know how much I need you. After your dad died, I would have given up if not for you. You have to fight. Come back to me."

She stroked his brown wavy hair. *He needs a haircut*. She smiled, in spite of her worry. His hair grew so fast, just like his father's.

"Your dad always told me how proud he was of you. He said you were so fearless, ready to try anything. He couldn't wait to see you grown up. He'll never get that chance, but I still want to, Aiden. I love you so much." Tears burned in her eyes. The hole in her heart from John's death, which had been in the process of healing, once again tore wide open. One tear escaped and rolled over her cheek, the droplet falling onto Aiden's hair.

****

After Julie went to Aiden, Reagan and Mary found the visitor's lounge. The small alcove was placed away from the main patient area, with a TV set high on the wall and a kitchenette situated in the corner.

Mary walked over to pour herself a cup of coffee. "Do you want anything?" she asked Reagan.

He tried to get comfortable in the undersized plastic chair. "A bottle of water would be great." Folding his hands, he prayed that Aiden would pull through. He loved the kid, and the fact that he was stuck in the waiting room, instead of with Julie and Aiden, made him sick with worry. He was tempted to use his fame to push past the rules and go to them, right now. But Mary needed support, too. So, he'd wait.

Mary reached in the mini fridge and took out a bottle, and then passed it to Reagan. She sat and rested the cup on the small table by her chair. "I feel so guilty about what happened. We never should have been out in that weather. Aiden wanted to make pizza, so we headed to the grocery store to buy the ingredients. He was so excited."

"It was an accident, Mary, and not your fault. You may have saved Aiden's life." He took a long drink. The cool water refreshed his parched throat.

Tears welled in her eyes, which she wiped away with the crumpled tissue in her hand. "Julie can't lose Aiden after everything else she's lost. For the first time in a year, she's actually happy, and you're the reason. Hold on to her tight. She'll need you to get through this."

He glanced over to see cuts and bruises on Mary's wrists and folded hands. She needed medical attention.

"You're hurt. Have you been seen by a doctor yet?"

"No, no." She shook her head. "I'm fine, just a few bumps. I honestly didn't even notice." But as she raised her hand, she winced.

"You need to get that checked out. I don't think your hands are fine. Let me go find someone to take a look." He walked around the corner to the nurse's station. A minute later, he returned. "A nurse will take you to the ER. They'll take good care of you." He noticed the swelling that emerged under the bruises on her wrists.

With Mary gone to the ER, Reagan was left alone with his own worries and thoughts. After thirty minutes, a nurse came to take him to Aiden's room. He walked with long strides into the ICU room. As soon as he came to Julie, he pulled her into a comforting embrace. Seeing Aiden's little body, damaged and still, stunned Reagan. If he was feeling this amount of panic, what must she feel right now?

They held each other close for a long while, her body tense against his. He kissed the top of her head and stroked her back. "What did they tell you about his condition?"

"We have him fully sedated right now. Tomorrow, he'll hopefully wake up." She stepped back to look at him, her eyes shone with tears. "I'm so scared."

"This kid's a fighter," he said, his voice a bit raspy. "He'll get through this, just have faith."

She reached over to clutch his hand, and they huddled together by Aiden's bed, to keep watch over the boy they both dearly loved.

Chapter Sixteen

The next day, Reagan again gained permission to enter the ICU and made his way to Aiden's room.

In the corner, Julie slept in a recliner, looking like a curled-up kitten. A soft blanket covered her body, all the way to her chin. When she opened her eyes, she stretched and let out a long yawn.

"Good morning, love," he said in a hushed voice, so not to wake the sleeping kid. "How's Aiden today? Any better?"

"No change, which is good, I guess. His doctor was just here earlier and said they'll be taking Aiden off the sedative soon. He should wake up later this morning." She caught sight of the bag and drink tray on the counter. "You brought food," she sighed.

"Yeah, I figured you would appreciate some real food and coffee." He handed her a cardboard coffee cup. "Cream, right?"

"You're a lifesaver." She took a lengthy drink. "Maybe after a few more of these, I'll feel human again."

"Bagels and cream cheese are in the bag." He took a seat next to Aiden's bed. "Good news that he'll be waking soon. Your mom will be coming by later. She was pretty tired last night when I took her home. I can't believe she fractured both wrists and never told anyone she was in pain."

"That's my mom for you." Julie spread cream cheese on a bagel. "Always taking care of others first. Thanks for watching out for her…making sure she was cared for yesterday."

"Whatever I can do to help." He rested a hand on the counter and leaned toward Julie, brushing his fingertips across the top of her hand. "I need to leave after lunch to go home and pack. The team plane takes off at three. I'm sorry. I hate having to go." This was the worst time to leave town. But the team had a game tomorrow, and he had to be there.

"I forgot you have a Monday night game." Her gaze fell, returning to her bagel. "You'll be gone for just two days, right?"

He pulled her close and placed a kiss on her downturned mouth. She recoiled ever so slightly. He suspected that Julie, since Aiden's accident, had become withdrawn. Like part of her wanted him by her side, and another part—the part of her heart closed off to him—didn't want anyone but John. "Yes." He forced his voice to stay calm and reassuring, like he wasn't afraid his whole world was in danger of falling apart. "I'll be back by your side very soon."

****

As the day progressed, Julie saw small responses from Aiden. Every so often, he would open his eyes and call her over. With that reassurance, his body would relax and allow sleep to reclaim him.

During one of his wakeful moments, he mumbled, "I miss Daddy."

Hearing his plea left her struggling to breathe. Aiden needed his father. At these moments, she missed her husband with an ache that threatened to tear her apart. John should be here with his son. They both needed him so much.

The next morning, Aiden stayed awake for longer periods of time.

His doctor told Julie that he was hopeful Aiden would be well enough to go home by the end of the week. Julie and Mary spent the day by Aiden's side, making sure someone was always there when he awoke.

That night, for the most part, Aiden stayed alert and focused. He even asked to watch the Warriors game on TV.

Julie didn't pay attention to the game, instead her sole focus stayed on her son. The color had returned to his cheeks and his eyes sparkled. Seeing him brighten before her eyes, she knew Aiden would be okay. He looked once again like her high-spirited boy.

After the game was done, Julie hit the remote and turned off the TV. "Lights out, peanut. Time for bed."

"Wasn't that cool?" Aiden yawned. "I can't wait 'til Reagan comes to see me tomorrow."

"Me, too." She noticed his eyelids were growing heavy. He was drained from all the excitement of the past few hours. As he fought sleep, she lay next to him and cuddled close, feeling the warmth of his fragile, doll-like body. Stroking his back and humming a soothing melody, she helped him drift off to sleep in less than a minute.

Walking close, Mary leaned over to give Aiden a kiss on the forehead. "Goodnight, sweet love." She patted Julie's hand. "You sleep well, too. See you tomorrow."

****

Reagan stepped into Aiden's hospital room to see Julie standing in front of a small mirror, wrangling her auburn mane into a ponytail holder. She was a sight for sore eyes. He'd never known he had a thing for gingers, seemingly this one in particular, until he'd met Julie.

Aiden remained asleep, even with the morning sun shining through the east-facing window.

"Good morning," he whispered.

Julie turned as he stepped toward her. She wrapped herself in his arms, with her ear pressed against his chest.

"I'm so glad to be here." He bent over to kiss her soft lips. He sensed her lack of desire at their kiss, but he chalked up her reaction to stress and being overtired.

"Ewwww, gross," a scratchy voice sounded from the bed.

Their kiss ended in laughter as they turned to see Aiden peeking through half shut eyes.

"I'm happy you're feeling better." Reagan moved toward Aiden. *Good to see the kid hadn't lost his sense of humor.*

"I still hurt," Aiden explained. "My tummy has stitches. You wanna see?" He didn't wait for an answer, quickly tossing aside his blanket and lifting his shirt.

The sight of his little body so bandaged and bruised hurt Reagan's heart. He set a smile on his face in order to lift Aiden's spirits. "Whoa, look at that. You must be pretty tough to have all those stitches. How's your leg feel?"

"It hurts a lot, but look at the cast I got. I got a red one for the Warriors!" Aiden tapped on his leg, which was now encased in a hard shell.

"That's awesome, kid. You're rocking it."

Julie stood back and watched the entertaining exchange. "I don't understand. What's with guys and your fascination with bodily injury?"

"You wouldn't understand, woman," Reagan grunted in a caveman impersonation. "It's all part of being a man."

Aiden let loose a deep belly laugh, which soon turned to tears of pain. "*Oooh*, Mom. That hurts." He moaned and grabbed his stomach.

She moved to his side and ran her fingers through his mop of hair. "Laughing will hurt for a while. Your tummy's very sore. You'll have to be careful and sit still while your stitches heal."

Reagan grabbed the bag he'd brought and handed it to Aiden. "This might help with that."

Aiden peeked inside, and his tears suddenly stopped, replaced with a face-splitting smile. "The new Gamer Remote system," he shrieked. "And look, there's a bunch of games, too. Thanks, Reagan. I love it." Aiden began tearing into the box.

Julie walked behind Reagan and wrapped her arms around his waist. "We watched you play last night. Aiden stayed awake for the entire game."

He turned in her hold, now standing face to face. "I wish you could have been with me...seventy-five degrees and sunny." Reaching behind her, he lightly pulled on her ponytail. As he looked at her, he noticed her green eyes seemed guarded. Like she was hiding something in the very depths of her soul, something she didn't want him to see.

Later that afternoon, Reagan and Julie went for a walk to get fresh air, leaving Mary to sit with Aiden while they were gone. She walked at his side—their hands physically connected. But he felt certain she was mentally somewhere else. He wasn't angered by her quiet mood, understanding the emotional toll of the past few days. But he still needed to see her smile. Maybe a little comedy would lighten the mood. "What do you get when you cross a snowman with a vampire?" He was on his fifth joke and yet to earn a grin. Only groans and looks of pity.

"I don't know, Reagan." She shrugged. "Bloody snow."

"Frostbite." He bumped her hip. "Get it?"

Finally, the faintest of smiles pulled at the corners of her mouth, followed by laughter. "I plead for mercy. No more jokes."

Good, because he had no more. Except for the ones he'd heard in the locker room, and he would never repeat any of those to Julic.

When they returned, Aiden was showing Matt his new video game system. Matt was getting a play-by-play of Aiden's latest quest.

Chrissy, who sat in the recliner, jumped out of the chair when she saw Julie. "I'm sorry we couldn't be here sooner. Aiden looks really good after everything he's gone through." She engulfed Julie in a bear hug.

"Yes, he's doing very well. I know you and Matt couldn't be here earlier, but I'm happy you're here now. I was so scared."

"But he's going to be fine. He'll heal quickly." Chrissy stepped back and gave Julie's arms a squeeze.

She nodded. "That's what the doctors are telling me."

Chrissy clasped her hand and looked over at Reagan. "I'm glad Reagan's here to watch over you. I worry about you less, knowing he's with you."

Her endorsement meant a lot to Reagan. He found a chair next to the bed, and the three guys talked video games. Aiden showed him how many levels he'd completed in the short time he was gone. After twenty minutes of Aiden's tutorials, he needed a break. Reagan decided to make a trip to the cafeteria, and Matt joined him.

"That was the perfect gift," Matt commented when they left the room.

"Thanks. I figured Julie will have a hard time keeping him still while he heals."

After a few wrong turns, the guys found the cafeteria. The large room was brightly lit by a wall of windows. Various medical personal and patient family members filled rows of tables. Reagan and Matt perused the rows of prepackaged food items and bright-colored drinks arranged in tall coolers. Farther down sat a restaurant-style counter, with a food menu hanging above. They purchased the requested items—coffee for Julie and Mary, diet cola and a candy bar for Chrissy, a bottle of water and apple for Reagan.

Matt ordered a grilled cheese sandwich and a bowl of soup.

Since Matt had to wait for his food, Reagan started back to the pediatric floor alone. When he approached Aiden's room, he heard the sound of Julie's and Chrissy's hushed voices, and John's name being spoken. He stopped in the hall and waited, not wanting to interrupt.

"I'm not sure about anything anymore," Julie said "I want to be free to love again. I'm so torn, because I can't let go of the past."

"Aiden's accident pushed you off balance, and now you're questioning your feelings," Chrissy said. "You were terrified he'd been taken from you, too. All the pain of losing John has resurfaced. Don't let it pull you into the darkness. You've come so far over these past few months because of Reagan. Let that be your focus."

"Some days, I wonder what he's doing with me. He deserves so much better than this, hanging around a hospital. He could literally have any woman he wanted, so why does he want me? Someone who might never love him the way he deserves."

"Because he loves you," Chrissy countered. "Stop being so hard on yourself and accept the fact that you deserve to be happy. John would want that for you."

"John's not here for his son…which breaks my heart." Julie sniffled. "I want him here with us."

"Julie," Chrissy said quietly. "Time for you to accept reality…John's gone."

Julie's words landed like a punch to the gut. The ghost of John Ellis was still a third party to their young and fragile relationship. He walked past the nurse's station until he came to a small, empty lounge.

Taking a seat, he inhaled deeply, needing solitude to assess the situation. He pictured Sarah, handing back her engagement ring and breaking his heart. After all this time, he failed to learn from his earlier mistakes. How could he have been so foolish to think proposing to Julie was a good idea? The memory of her husband—the man she loved since high school, the man who died a hero's death, would always be a barrier to their own happily ever after.

He thought of the success he'd worked so hard to achieve. To think this emotional turmoil wouldn't seep onto the playfield would be foolish. He'd have to be careful. The last thing he wanted was to end up with a crushed heart and a broken career. When enough time had passed, he took the drink tray to Aiden's room.

Matt had returned and was in the middle of eating his sandwich.

"Where did you go?" Julie asked. "Matt said you left the cafeteria before him."

Reagan offered her an apologetic grin. "Sorry, I must have taken the long way."

She looked solemnly into his eyes. "You okay?"

He handed her a warm cup of coffee and nodded. "Never better."

****

Miraculously, Aiden was released from the hospital in less than a week after his accident. He came home to an impromptu celebration with cake and balloons. Christmas Day was a week away, and Julie had so much to be grateful for. Aiden's laughter filled her house again, and Reagan would be spending the holiday with both of them.

This past week had been very busy for Reagan, with football practice and other obligations, but he put everything else aside in order to be there for Aiden's homecoming. He was so good to them, always putting her and Aiden's needs ahead of his own.

Julie often wondered if she deserved someone as wonderful as Reagan, when her heart was so hopelessly divided. How could she explain the deep love that remained for John? And would Reagan understand her devotion to her late husband didn't take away the love she felt for him?

Aiden, propped on the sofa, worked tirelessly on

building a skyscraper with his new block set. With Reagan sitting next to him, she went into the kitchen to start dinner.

"Do you need any help?" Reagan called from the family room.

"Only if you are looking for an excuse to escape," she answered.

Reagan's help was a godsend. Aiden needed loads of extra attention since getting home. Something he'd taken advantage of to the extreme.

The sound of Reagan's laughter echoed from the family room. "I'll be right there."

Julie motioned him over with the large knife in her hand. "You can peel potatoes." She pointed to the dirty, brown lumps piled on the counter.

He walked over to her. "I would love to," he said. "Just don't stab me when I do this." He grabbed her from behind and swung her around to face him.

She melted into him. The man was so disarming. As much as she wanted to slow things down with him, she couldn't help but be drawn in. Julie absently set the knife on the counter. She reached up and brushed his cheek with the back of her hand. "You need to shave," she murmured.

He ran kisses over her delicate neck, tickling her with his stubble.

She giggled at the conflicting sensations.

"Do you still think I need to shave?"

"No. I now understand the benefits of facial hair."

He brushed his fingers through her hair, winding a section loosely around his index finger. "You are so beautiful...my sweet addiction."

Meal prep temporarily forgotten, she leaned against

the counter, and he descended on her with a demanding kiss. His arm slipped around her waist, pressing her body against his. Her hands moved along his arms, her fingers massaging the muscles in his neck and pulling through his messy hair. Finally, she gathered enough willpower to pull back and tried to catch her breath. "Dinner will never get finished if we keep this up."

"You're right." He grinned. "But this is more fun."

He looked devilishly handsome, which was so not fighting fair. Blushing, she picked up the knife to resume chopping carrots. Quickly looking over her shoulder, she caught a glance of the picture of John hanging on the refrigerator door. For a moment, she felt lightheaded and grabbed the counter to steady herself. Her guilt surfaced again—a feeling that never fully went away when she was in Reagan's arms.

When they finally sat around the table for dinner, Reagan was uncharacteristically quiet. Somewhere along the way, he'd lost some of his earlier humor. "I was thinking once the football season's over and the weather gets a little nicer, we could go to the Art Museum in Chicago," Julie proposed. "Maybe stop at Navy Pier, too."

"Hey, Reagan, I don't know why you would want to go to an art museum," Aiden piped in. "I told Mom you should go to Pro Wrestling Smackdown instead, but she said no."

"Well, that idea does sound like fun, too." Reagan grinned at the little boy with sauce covering his mouth and chin. "But I like art museums, and I don't think your mom would be happy watching wrestling."

"You're right, no wrestling for me." She watched as Aiden gave Reagan a sympathetic nod of the head.

Like two branches from the same tree. They might not be father and son, but their bond grew deeper with each passing day. She couldn't do anything to ruin her relationship with Reagan.

Reclining back on the chair, Reagan placed his hand on Aiden's shoulder. "Hopefully, the Warriors' season won't finish too soon. We've got a pretty good shot to win the Super Bowl this year. If we win Sunday's game, we'll have home field advantage for the playoffs."

"If you go to the Super Bowl, can I come, too?" Aiden asked. "But, you know, just to watch."

"For sure, kid." Reagan gave Aiden a high five.

Later that night, with Aiden tucked securely in bed, Julie was hoping for some alone time with Reagan. She wanted desperately to push all doubt and insecurity out of her heart. Unfortunately, Aiden had plans of his own. He'd already been caught a few times, peeking around the staircase, afraid he'd miss the action downstairs.

After several trips to Aiden's room, she was now snuggled comfortably with Reagan on the sofa. The room was dark, only illuminated by the tree's colored lights. The soft melody of Christmas music played in the background. She rested her head on his chest. His arms wrapped around her in a protective embrace. Around them was stillness and peace.

But only for a minute. Until out of the corner of her eye, she saw movement at the top of the stairs. *Not again.* "Aiden," she called out. "For the last time, stay in bed and go to sleep." She heard the movement of small feet from above, followed by a door closing. "He's getting good at using those crutches." She shook her head in exasperation. If he didn't get to sleep soon, she'd be dealing with a crabby child tomorrow. "When do you leave for LA?"

"Tomorrow morning. Most of the team is returning on the plane right after the game, but I have to stay a few extra days. My sports agent has lined up some commercials to shoot while I'm out there. Don't worry, I'll be home in time for Christmas."

"Oh, right." Would she ever get used to seeing her boyfriend's face on the TV or in print ads? Probably not. Just like she'd never get used to being at the center of attention whenever she was in public with him. "I forgot I'm dating someone famous."

"Don't be too impressed." He rubbed the small of her back. "My agent does all the hard work. I just go along with it. The extra income puts food on the table."

"I'm sure you'd starve without it."

"I wouldn't starve because I'd live on love," he whispered into her ear and gave her backside a pinch.

"Hey, that hurt," she squealed.

"Mom, I'm thirsty," Aiden called from upstairs.

"I should get going." Reagan attempted to rise.

"Not yet." She kissed him rapidly along his neck, over his chin, and stopping at his waiting mouth. She felt his hand roam over her back, pulling up on her shirt so he pressed against her skin. He rolled her on top of him and wrapped one arm around her to hold her tight. She felt the desperation behind his kiss, and the way he held her…like he was afraid she'd slip away. Their lips pulsed together with gaining intensity.

Lost in overwhelming bliss, her memory slipped backward in time. In her mind, she was laying on the grass, in the middle of Cottonwood Field, with John's mouth moving over hers. "John," she moaned, before

Laurie Winter

snapping back to reality to realize what she had just done.

Reagan instantly pulled away. His blue-eyed gaze pierced into hers.

As he searched her soul for the truth, she shrank away. She'd called out another man's name. Those words, that truth, couldn't be taken back.

He untangled himself from Julie and got off the sofa.

"No," she cried. "I never meant—"

Reagan cut her off with a wave of his hand. "I know you would never hurt me intentionally, but I can't play second string to another man...even if he's dead."

She gasped, her hand fluttering over her heart. How could she make him understand she was constantly at war with guilt and grief?

He grabbed his coat, put it on, and slid his stocking hat onto his head. "Your heart was never mine. I'm not John, and I never will be."

"Reagan, I'm sorry." She saw the grimace on his face. How could she have done something so hurtful? One slip of the tongue in a moment of weakness, and she might have lost the man she loves.

"I'm the one who's sorry." Reagan leaned over to kiss to top of her head. As his lips touched her hair, he inhaled deeply, and then walked out the door.

Chapter Seventeen

Reagan pulled his rented silver luxury car in front of the busy LA nightclub. Opening the car door to get out, he bumped his knee against the door frame. "Ugh," he mumbled. His whole body hurt after yesterday's game. The Warriors had won by only a single field goal, which was too close for his satisfaction.

Reagan's agent and a few friends had insisted on taking him out that night. At first, he resisted the idea, but eventually agreed. The group was meeting at Lex, a popular nightclub in downtown Los Angeles. Lex was packed with trendy LA patrons, looking to let loose and have a good time. Reagan had no trouble moving past the long line and went straight into the club.

They were led to a half-circle table with booth seating and an excellent view of the dance floor. When the five guys were seated, their waitress came over to get their drink orders. Reagan glanced around the club. The dance floor and bar were crowded, even though the time was only ten pm, which meant the party was just getting started.

"How did the commercial shoot go today?" Blake, his agent, asked.

"Fine. I go tomorrow for the stills." He reclined against the back of the booth. The whole product endorsement side of his career wasn't his favorite, but companies paid big money, which made doing forty takes during a commercial shoot bearable.

Blake brushed a hand over his dark, slicked-back hair. "Just give me the word, and I'll keep those deals coming. You're a hot commodity right now. Makes my job easy."

"Sure, I'm happy to help you support your ex-wives," Reagan joked.

Their drinks arrived, and a glass of whiskey was placed before him on the polished metal table.

"Good to see you among the living, Reagan." Jason, his former college teammate, raised his glass. "Cheers!"

Reagan took a refreshing drink. "Glad to be back," he said with a relaxed grin.

"I heard a rumor you've become domesticated in Wisconsin." Jason grinned, and his perfect white teeth gleamed despite the dim lighting of the club. "You finally met a woman who reined you in?"

"What? I don't believe it," Damien, another college teammate, commented. A flashing red strobe light, originating for somewhere by the dance floor, bounced off his shiny, bald head. He extended his muscular arm and gave Reagan a slap on the back. "He's a hero to us married guys. I've been living vicariously through him for the past four years, ever since I said 'I do'."

Reagan found himself thinking of Julie and how he'd felt two nights ago, when his world came crashing down. The pain of hearing her say John's name had been worse than anything he'd ever experienced on the football field. With one word, she'd wiped all the color from his life, leaving behind only a dull gray. "Things didn't work out with the woman I was seeing in Wisconsin. I won't bore you with a long story but I will report that I'm back in the game."

"I'm sorry to hear that." Blake's grin faded. "I saw a picture of you two. She's cute. Maybe I'll take a trip to Wisconsin and soothe her broken heart."

"Not a chance." Reagan gave him a light punch on the arm.

As the hours passed, the friends cracked jokes and told stories. The drinks kept coming, and finally, a couple of the guys went to dance with some girls who'd stopped by their table. Reagan was in no mood for empty flirtations, so he contently stayed at their table and watched the action on the dance floor.

Noticing his empty glass, he looked around for their server. Out of the corner of his eye, he saw a blonde woman slide into the booth next to him.

"Reagan Harrison, am I ever glad to see you," Brynn purred. She wrapped her arm around his shoulder and leaned in close, placing her lips next to his ear. "I heard you'd be here tonight. I've missed you."

Brynn looked great tonight, in a gold, sparkling mini dress. Her long hair tickled his arm. Back when they'd dated, he'd been enchanted by her glamour. Now, he thought she simply looked over-processed. Not like Julie, whose graceful beauty was totally natural. His chest tightened at the memory of the morning after their first date, when he'd made breakfast. Even with messy hair and no make-up, she was more attractive than Brynn would ever be.

He forced himself to stop looking at the past. What he needed was a push forward. "Brynn, you're just what I need right now." He pointed to the dance floor, and she took his hand, pulling him to his feet. He wrapped his arm around her small waist and led her through the crowd.

After a few songs, the music slowed. As they moved to the beat of the music, she didn't feel right in his arms—like jamming the wrong key into a lock. Brynn was too tall, too thin—and not Julie. He cursed himself for being unable to kick the memory of Julie's face, with her lightly freckled nose and strawberry-tinted lips, out of his mind.

"I've missed you." Brynn kissed a spot on his neck, right under his ear. Her finger trailed up the arch of his bicep. "You're so incredibly sexy."

"We always seem to end up together," he said in resignation. "You and I are uncomplicated. We have a good time, and then we go our separate ways. No expectations."

She looked at him and smiled. "I know you, probably better than you know yourself. Other women want too much from you. That's why I've never minded when you went off exploring. You're not made for a long-term relationship."

Was she right? When Julie needed his love and support, he'd let his own hurt come before her needs.

"What are you doing later?" Brynn asked. "How about you come back to my place for a nightcap?"

Reagan's buzz quickly turned into a headache. Too many conflicting emotions clattered around, fighting with the voice in his head. The loudest yelled to walk away. Going with Brynn would only lead to regret.

He looked into Brynn's beautiful eyes. *Would kissing her push away all his doubts?* Tipping his chin, he locked his lips onto hers and drank her in. She eagerly responded, tightening her hold around his shoulders. He wanted to fill his head with Brynn, and forget about the auburn-haired spirit who haunted his mind.

Nothing about their kiss was right. She tasted too bitter, she didn't smell like roses but something unpleasant and spicy, her body felt sharp and bony, not comfortable and soft as she pressed against him. He stepped out of her embrace and began walking off the dance floor.

"Reagan," she called out after him. "Where are you going?"

"Time for me to go. Alone." He returned to his table. "I've had a long day, guys. I'm heading out."

"See you around, man." Jason gave him a pat on the back. "Don't be a stranger."

He walked out the front door of the club. A cool, refreshing breeze hit his face. He gave his valet ticket to the attendant and stood on the sidewalk, waiting for his car. His head pounded as a result of the loud music seeping out of the club.

The kiss he shared with Brynn had proven he could never kiss another woman without comparing her to Julie. A week ago, he'd been ready to start a new chapter and finally settle down. But after putting everything on the line, he still played second string. He could never go back to his old life. His one and only decision was this—how far was he willing to go to keep Julie in his life?

****

Days passed, and the silence continued. Julie still hadn't heard from Reagan. Every one of her calls had gone to voicemail. Sometimes, she'd call and listen to his voicemail greeting, just to hear his voice. By Christmas Eve, she stopped hoping for a phone call or a knock on the door. She and Aiden had gone to Christmas Eve service, and then to Mom's for dinner. They'd opened a few gifts, before Julie took Aiden home to put him to bed.

Now, she lay on the sofa, her dark family room only lit by the glow of her Christmas tree. The stillness around her stood in sharp contrast to the storm raging in her heart. Reagan had left five days ago to travel to LA, and she assumed he was now in Indiana to spend Christmas with his family. The holiday they'd planned to spend together had been called off, and Aiden cried himself to sleep that night, not understanding why Reagan had walked out of their lives.

She could forgive Reagan for not wanting to be with her. She'd hurt him and couldn't deny John was still front and center in her heart. The disappointment they'd both caused Aiden was a tougher pill to swallow. Her conflicted feelings were not fair to either Reagan or Aiden. A decision had to be made, and over the past few days, she realized what she needed to do. She wasn't ready to start a new relationship. Maybe she never would be.

As she snuggled deeper under the soft purple blanket, she wished John would walk through her front door and make everything okay. But that would never happen. She was left to face her future alone.

A sharp knock on the door startled her. Still wrapped in her blanket, she shuffled over and opened the door to see Reagan standing on the other side. The sight of him instantly comforted her aching chest. A reviving hum pulsed through her body.

For several seconds, they stood staring at each other in silence, until Reagan cleared his throat. "I wanted to bring Aiden's bike." He motioned to the red bike with the huge bow sitting on her front walkway.

"Come in." She stepped aside to let him push the bike past her and into the house. His peppermint-infused scent once again filled her home. He leaned the bike against the wall. Bags now hung under his formerly bright, blue eyes. His skin was pale. The expression on his face was troubled and worn, like a man fighting a war.

"I'm sorry for leaving. I was hurt, and I let my pride win over my heart. I still love you, and maybe you still love me. Can we work this out?"

She saw a tear threaten to break free from the corner of his eye, which weakened her conviction. How could she cause him more pain?

He swiftly wiped it away. Standing before him, she tightened her hold onto the blanket wrapped around her like a protective cocoon. "I do love you, Reagan, but to keep dragging you along while I figure out things is not fair. Half of my life was intertwined with John's. I can't remove him without ripping out a part of myself in the process." Inside her chest, she felt a stabbing pain, like a knife slicing through her heart. Her gaze fell on the wedding picture placed up on a bookshelf. Their wedding day had been perfect. Their life together had been a rollercoaster ride. Now, she was left finding her way without John. *Be brave, and do what you need to do.*

"I need you, Julie. I don't want to go back to a life without you." He wrapped her up in his strong arms.

She melted into his embrace, resting her head on his chest.

"I promise to be patient. You and Aiden mean so

much to me."

"We both know this isn't just about you and me. Aiden was devastated when I told him you wouldn't be with us for Christmas. I can't let him get caught in the middle while we work out things." Reluctantly, she stepped away.

He released his hold. Reagan's gaze lowered to the blue stone bird she held in her hand. His shoulders dropped. "I've loved you since the first night I met you. Just know you have my heart, if you ever decide you're ready to move on." Taking her face in his hands, he kissed her.

A kiss that weakened her resolve and shook her to her core. She could no longer restrain the tears, which now flowed freely down her face, falling like raindrops onto the floor. "You are a good and honorable man, Reagan. And I'm better off having had you in my life." She brushed the scruff on his face with the palm of her hand. A sensation that was both familiar and comforting. "You'll find love again, and she'll be a lucky woman."

Reagan opened the door but then hesitated. "Tell Aiden I love him. I never told him."

Something inside her shattered. She used every ounce of willpower to stop herself from running back into his arms. "He knows."

After looking back one last time, he stepped outside and closed the door behind him.

Chapter Eighteen

Spring came to Timber Lake with a sudden outbreak of green. Residents, who had been starved by a long winter indoors, devoured the warm weather with abandon. The piles of snow became a distant memory, replaced with lush grass and green leaves. Along with the change in seasons came rebirth and renewal.

For Julie, spring meant a second chance. "Mom, are you sure it's not too early to plant flowers?" She yanked up a brown, dry weed, scrunched up her nose, and threw the clump to the side before pulling another.

"The threat of frost is past, and these geraniums are hardy. Now is as good a time as any to get them in the ground."

After throwing another weed on the growing pile, Julie continued to work on the neglected flower bed. Dead plants and leaves littered the dirt. She hoped once the flowers were planted, the color in her backyard would lift her spirits. Her mind drifted to Reagan, and her heart filled with the persistent regret over how she'd ended their relationship. She knew that as much as she missed him, she'd done the right thing by setting him free. He deserved to be the center of someone's world, not an addition to an already broken heart.

She often wondered what Reagan's life was like now. Did he have someone new to love? Was he happy? Did he miss her as much as she missed him?

Mary handed her a small trowel. "Did you have fun last night at the concert?"

"Yeah. The lead singer was really good. I'm glad I decided to go." Julie took a geranium and placed it in the freshly dug hole. Then she moved the displaced dirt to fill in around the flower, patting the ground with a few gentle taps. With Aiden visiting John's parents this week, she'd kept busy. Between work and going out with her new friends, she had little time to sit around and sulk.

"Do you have any other plans while Aiden's gone? Maybe we could go to a movie." Mary brushed dirt off her red pants before walking to the gate and grabbing another flat of flowers.

"The girls from work asked if I wanted to go out for drinks tomorrow night. And I have a long run planned with my running group on Wednesday morning. Maybe we could go on Thursday night. Would that work?" Julie took the flat from her mother's hands and set it on the grass.

"Sounds good." Mary smiled and nodded her head. "Let's check and see what movies are playing when we go back in the house."

Julie's knees ached, so she stood to stretch out her legs. The white trellis standing beside her garage was now bare, and she remembered last August when it was full of fragrant blooms. She had taken a picture of Aiden and Reagan in that very spot, and both were wearing their Warriors jerseys. The photo was now framed and placed on Aiden's dresser, next to the picture of his dad.

Aiden's anger over the break-up had gradually faded, but his pain over losing his friend and father figure had left his heart tender. *If only I'd done a better job of protecting my son, who had already suffered so much tragedy.*

That was why, for the past few months, she had pushed herself forward. The heavy weight of her emotional struggle eased with the passing of time. She'd made the decision to start living again. She owed Aiden a stable and happy future. Finally, for the first time since John's death, she'd given herself permission to heal.

After an afternoon of yard work, Julie only had the energy to warm up leftover chicken casserole for dinner. She watched TV while she ate, and after an hour of flipping through channels, she hit the off button on the remote. Yawning, she took her plate into the kitchen sink. The pile of John's letters sat on the counter, going unread for several months. She walked past the letters, brushing her hand over their smooth surface, and went upstairs to get ready for bed. A sense of calm and peace filled her.

Tucked under the covers, she tossed and turned for several minutes before slowly drifting off into a deep sleep. Suddenly, she found herself running down a tree-lined path. A soft summer breeze moved through the green leaves.

Up ahead, John motioned for her to come follow him.

"Wait!" she called out, elated to see him again after so long.

He ran ahead and quickly disappeared into the dense forest.

Julie sprinted forward, but her legs moved heavy and slow. Glimpses of John would appear, and then he'd vanish. "John, stop. I can't keep up." No one was there to hear her plea. She continued running through twists and turns, finally spying a man dressed in Army desert fatigues. His broad back filled the space between the tree branches.

She reached him and wrapped her arms around his waist. An earthy smell washed over her. The same one John always carried after returning home from deployment, reminding her of their coming together after long separations.

"My sweet Julie, I've missed you." He stood at the entrance of Cottonwood Field and caressed her cheek with the palm of his hand.

Eyes burning, she clung to him, crying into his shirt. "Why did you leave me?"

"It was my time. You always knew I might never come home."

"But, I need you." The words rasped from her throat. "Aiden needs you." He'd come back to her, and she was never letting him go. She tightened her hold.

"You're both strong." John took her hand and led her into the field filled with flowers of every color. Birds flew above them in a cloudless cobalt sky. "Remember when I promised you'd be mine forever?"

"Yes." Blinking fast, she memorized his ruggedly handsome face. "You were leaving for boot camp. I was a wreck, and you brought me here, reassuring me that everything would be okay."

He smiled. "That's right, and you'll always be mine. But you need to let me go. I want you to live a wonderful and full life, one without regrets."

"You are my life." She sobbed and buried her face in his coat. How could he talk of leaving her again? "I miss you so much."

He soothed her with a soft caress. "Remember me when you look at our son. He's the best parts of us both. Let the love you feel for me flow into him." John held her face in his hands. His gentle kiss contained a thousand goodbyes. "Let me go, my love, and be free to find the life you deserve."

With those words he was gone, vanishing out her grasp. "John!" she shouted over and over. The only reply was the echo of her tormented voice, and the cry of a distant blue jay. The breeze stirred the tall grass and all was quiet. Nature was in mourning. She was left standing alone, the field suddenly dark and still. A full moon shone overhead. Paralyzing fear washed over her.

Out of the shadows emerged an outline of another figure. He stepped into the beam of moonlight and motioned for her to come. Moving quickly, she ran over to Reagan, who was waiting with open arms. She collapsed into his embrace, immediately feeling safe. That broken piece of her heart was whole again. The part she'd kept empty after John's death now filled with love—love for Reagan. "You came for me."

"Of course," he said. "I'm here to take you home, but the choice is yours. Stay here, or come with me."

Knowing the decision she had to make, she took Reagan's hand and held it tight. "Show me the way home."

When she awoke, the morning sun weakly illuminated her bedroom. Disoriented, she felt her damp pillow, which was stained with tears. What a shock, to wake up and realize the memory was just a dream. John's presence had felt so real. After two years, they'd finally had a chance to say goodbye. As much as her heart ached, it felt lighter than in a long time.

John had told her to let him go, knowing she was still hanging on. He'd sent Reagan. She'd chosen to leave sorrow behind and move on with a love that was real and present.

Julie climbed out of bed, pulled on her robe, and went downstairs. The picture of John still hung on the refrigerator door. Lifting the magnet, she took off the photo and studied it for several minutes. She traced his face and body with the tip of her finger, and noticed the smoothness of the photograph was in stark contrast to the roughness of the real man. Then, with a test of will, she walked upstairs and placed John's last picture in the top drawer of her dresser. She grabbed the blue stone bird laying on her nightstand, set it next to the picture, and then with shaking hands, gently closed the drawer.

Now, she was ready to reach out to Reagan and find out if he still carried any love for her. Maybe he'd moved on, but she needed to know if anything was left to save. She'd call him later that afternoon. With the day off of work, she was in for a long, restless day. She prayed that after all the hurt and time apart, he had not given up on her.

****

Reagan stood outside on his deck, watching the birds swoop over the water in search of their breakfast. He, on the other hand, had no appetite and nursed a cup of coffee. He'd spent the last four months running from Julie's memory. Today, he'd have to face his feelings head on.

Walking away from Julie had been the hardest thing he'd ever done. Accepting defeat was not in his nature, but his pride had forced him to stop trying for something not meant to be. He often wondered if he'd made the right decision. When he'd left her house that cold December night, their relationship might have ended, but his love for her had not.

And neither had he stopped loving Aiden. He missed the kid. Reagan's life seemed empty and dull without the energetic boy. At times, he'd been tempted to reach out to Aiden or send him a gift in the mail. But he'd always stopped himself. The last thing he wanted was to confuse an already hurt child.

Last week, he'd moved back to Timber Lake in preparation for the coming football season. Since being back, he'd dreamed about Julie every night. She haunted him persistently, and he hoped after today, he could make peace and finally move on. His doorbell sounded, and Reagan set his coffee mug on the glass patio table to go answer the door. "Hey, come on in." Reagan motioned to the nervous-looking man standing at the front door. He had a scruffy beard and tattoos covered large sections of his exposed arms.

"Thanks for seeing me earlier than we'd planned. I wanted to speak privately before Greg arrived." Heath Carter shook Reagan's extended hand.

"No problem. Can I get you something to drink? I was just finishing my coffee out on the deck."

"Water, please," Heath replied.

After Reagan handed him a glass of ice water, he led Heath onto the deck.

"You have a beautiful house and yard," Heath said, after taking a drink. "This view is amazing."

"Thanks."

After a moment of silence, Heath cleared his throat and handed Reagan a weathered envelope. "This is for you. After our phone conversations, I knew this letter was meant for you."

Reagan accepted the blank envelope. "What is this?"

"John Ellis was my best friend." Heath turned his gaze toward the lake. "I first met Julie after they got married, when she came to Fort Bragg as a new bride. Those two were my family, and Julie always made me feel welcome. What happened to John in Afghanistan destroyed her, and I wasn't there for her or Aiden." He shoved his hands in the front pockets of his jeans. "I let my own grief prevent me from doing the right thing. Time to stop hiding. That's why I'm here."

Reagan nodded. "What you're sharing with Julie today is a good start."

"Seeing Julie isn't the only reason I came to Timber Lake." He rocked back on his heels. "I had to deliver this to you. John wrote it the night before his final mission."

"I don't understand." Frowning, Reagan glanced at the envelope. Why had Heath given him this?

"That last night, John felt a sense of dread. Every mission is dangerous, but we'd always come back in one piece. Right before we left, he instructed me to keep his letter safe, and only to open it if he didn't make it home." Heath took a drink of water. As he lowered the glass, his hand trembled. "When I finally worked up the courage to open it, I realized what he'd done. The letter was meant for the man who would fall in love with Julie."

Relaxing his jaw, Reagan looked again at the envelope, which became instantly more valuable. "Why are you giving this to me? Julie and I ended our relationship months ago."

"Your love hasn't ended, and your actions tell me your feelings are unselfish and true. Julie deserves that kind of love again." Heath stepped off the deck and walked slowly toward the water.

Reagan now stood alone. What was so important for John to convey to another man, one who may someday fall in love with his wife? He gently opened the envelope and pulled out the yellowed paper inside. The writing looked hurried and unsteady, like John wanted to put these thoughts to paper before he lost his nerve. Reagan began reading.

Dear Sir,

We've probably never met, so let me introduce myself. My name is John Ellis, and I had the privilege of being married to the most amazing woman. Since you're reading this letter, I'm sure you've already realized how special Julie is. As much as thinking I may never come back to her hurts, I have peace knowing a man exists who will help her fall in love again.

Julie put up with a lot being married to me. I haven't been there for her like a good husband should. While I was running around the world, she's stayed behind to keep a home ready for me when I returned. She took care of our son when I wasn't able to and made sure Aiden knew how much I loved him. Her heart is strong and resolute. When she loves, she does it with complete devotion. Knowing Julie, leaving my memory behind and starting a new life with someone else will be hard.

Please be patient and give her time to heal. When she does turn that corner, she'll love you with a commitment that will take your breath away.

I met Julie when I was a junior in high school, too young and full of dreams to fall in love. But I couldn't help but love her. When I enlisted, I hated leaving her behind. My biggest regret is not giving her the life I promised. She deserves to have her dreams come true.

If Heath has given you this letter, I know you are worthy. Thank you for caring for her and Aiden in my absence. Your love for them will be greatly rewarded. You can trust me on that.

Thank you for allowing me to put my faith and trust in you.

In gratitude,
Sergeant John Ellis

Reagan lifted his head and wiped away the tears that had pushed free. His hand shook while he folded the letter and slid it into the envelope. After reading that, how could he say goodbye to Julie again?

Chapter Nineteen

Julie sat on the sofa and tried to focus on the book in her hand—an exercise in futility. Even *Pride and Prejudice* couldn't hold her attention. An unexpected ring of her phone sent her stomach leaping into her throat. Glancing at the screen made her heart skip a beat when she saw Reagan's name. She'd just been ready to call him. *Must be divine intervention.* Inhaling one steadying breath, she answered the call. "Hi, Reagan." She tried to keep the tremor from her voice.

"Hi...hope I'm not calling at a bad time."

She absentmindedly reached up with her free hand to fluff her hair. "Oh no, I'm just hanging out at home. Aiden's gone to his grandparents, and I have the day off."

"Julie," he said then cleared his throat. "I need to see you today."

"Do you want to come over?" Did he want to mend their relationship? The butterflies in her stomach were fluttering wildly. "We can talk here."

"I'll be over in an hour, if that's okay?"

"Sure, whenever. I'm happy to see you again."

"I have some information to share."

His voice sounded detached, like he was talking to a stranger. A chill brushed across her skin. What if his love had been replaced by indifference? "Sure. I'll see you soon." She didn't care about his motivation for reaching out. All she wanted was Reagan back in her life. After ending the call, she ran upstairs to pull herself together before he arrived.

Julie was at the door before Reagan could knock. "Hi," she said in a quiet voice. "Come in."

He leaned in and gave her a quick peck on the cheek.

The heat of his kiss seared Julie's skin. Seeing him again made her heart rise with hope, and her legs went weak with desire. He remained as handsome as she remembered. As Reagan moved inside the house, she noticed the other two men standing behind him. "Heath!" She ran out and threw her arms around him. "What are you doing here?" Her dear friend looked tired and worn, with a scruffy beard and dark bags under his eyes.

He grinned and stepped away. "You're a sight for sore eyes." His deep voice cracked. "I'm here to do something I should've done a long time ago."

The third visitor approached and held out his hand.

He looked to be in his forties, with a small but rugged build. Julie received a firm handshake.

"Hi, I'm Greg Jackson. I work for the *Washington Times* as an investigative reporter."

"Pleasure to meet you, Greg, but I don't understand what's going on." Panic rippled through her core. What was going on? She glanced at Heath, hoping he held the answers.

Heath took Julie by the elbow. "Let's all go inside, Jules. You'll need to sit for this."

She went inside to find Reagan pacing back and forth in her living room. Her worry grew. What was the real reason for Reagan's visit? And how did he know

Heath? Julie guided the group into the kitchen. "Would anyone like something to drink?"

Reagan took her hand and guided her to a chair. "Have a seat." He sat in the chair beside her.

"Julie." Greg rested his folded hands on the table and leaned forward. "Last October, I received a call from an associate at the newspaper. Reagan contacted him in an attempt to uncover the mystery surrounding your husband's death."

Shock numbed Julie's body. She could barely feel Reagan's large hand surrounding hers.

Greg straightened in his chair. "After I had a chance to talk to Reagan, I agreed to do a little digging into the story. As a journalist, I'm trained to sniff out a cover-up, and the story the Army told me stunk to high heaven. Of course, their denials piqued my interest, and I've spent the last six months deeply investigating the circumstances surrounding the death of John Ellis."

Glancing over at Heath, she saw his normal strong form shrink. He'd kept the truth from her. "Tell me." She felt the world shift underneath her. Every muscle in her body tensed with anticipation. After all this time, she was finally getting answers.

"Julie." Heath raised his head to make eye contact. "I'm sorry. While I was on active duty, I had orders not to disclose any aspect of our missions, including the one that killed John. Last month, my enlistment ended, and I returned to civilian life. That's when I got a call from Reagan. He told me about your attempts to find out what happened to John and how much you've struggled. He convinced me to meet with Greg and tell him what I knew. I was surprised to learn Greg was already familiar with many of the mission details."

"I've made several trips to Afghanistan." Greg raised a thick notebook. "Even though the mission was highly classified, I still found some people willing to talk. When this story finally breaks, it will be national news. Be prepared."

"John died a hero." Heath's voice became choked with emotion. "What happened was controversial, but the world should know his bravery."

"John loved you like a brother." Tears welled in her eyes, blurring her vision. "I need to know what he died for."

"First, you should know John and I were part of a Delta Force unit." Heath rubbed a hand over his beard. "John never told you because he didn't want you to worry any more than you already did. As Delta operators, everything we did was highly classified. Technically, 'The Unit' doesn't exist. We received specialized training, in order to take on the most dangerous missions."

Heath shifted in his seat. "In the spring of 2011, a series of deadly bombings in Afghanistan killed many American service members, along with countless citizens. After extensive intelligence gathering, the CIA learned the man behind the bombings was a college-educated US citizen who'd traveled to Afghanistan to join the Taliban. He had the knowledge and the materials to make sophisticated bombs. This guy moved from one safe house to another, and we had a hard time keeping track of him. Finally, we learned he was being housed just over the border, in Pakistan, with minimal security. In a few days, he would be moved deeper into the country."

"I didn't think you were allowed to cross the

border." Julie digested every little detail of Heath's story and compared it to what John had shared.

"We're not," Heath said. "That was one reason everything about the mission was clandestine. No one outside our direct chain of command knew the details. At that time, our twelve-man team was stationed at a Firebase set in the foothills. When we got the final go-ahead for the mission, our team loaded into two choppers, which inserted us under the cover of night, high in the mountains. We walked several miles over supply trails before we crossed the border. Fortunately, the trails were clear that night, and we didn't come under enemy fire."

Julie imagined the many challenges John had experienced during each mission and shuttered. She'd always been impressed by his bravely, and no more so than right now.

"A few hours before dawn, we reached the safe house and situated ourselves to secretly observe the movement around the area. John, being the best shot, had the best vantage point. He could look out over the whole compound and cover the rest of us at the same time. By the time the sun rose, we realized more Taliban were present than what our intelligence brief reported. The place was swarming with activity."

Heath wiped away beads of sweat from across his forehead.

Seeing her friend's distress, Julie poured him a glass of water and set it on the table.

"Thanks." He took a drink, stood, and then started to pace. "This story doesn't get any easier with the passing of time."

"I understand." But in reality, Julie could never

understand the demon's haunting Heath—the man who'd been with John during his last moments.

"Officially." Heath spoke with his hands along with his words. "We were instructed to bring in the target alive. He was an American citizen. But on scene, our commander made a tough call. We couldn't get through all the Taliban fighters to take custody of the bomber. We were commanded to shoot on sight. He was a serious danger to every soldier and citizen in Afghanistan, and he needed to be stopped at all costs. Even in a way that was politically incorrect."

She didn't consider herself naive, not after living around the military for so many years, but Heath's story shocked her. John had never shared so many details about his missions overseas.

"After hours of waiting, a man finally emerged from a tiny, dirt hut," Heath said. "John signaled he had the target in his sights, and our captain gave him the go-ahead. He took him out with one shot, but our cover was blown. Taliban were everywhere, yelling and grabbing their AK47s. We gave them a good fight until Will got shot in the leg. John stepped out to provide cover fire so we could pull Will to safety. That's when John got hit twice, first in the neck, and then in the upper arm."

Heath's straight posture crumpled. He gripped the top rail of an empty kitchen chair until his knuckles turned white. "As the team's medic, I'm trained to provide trauma care in combat situations, and this was my best friend." He looked at her with wide eyes. "Julie, I did my best to wrap his wounds and stop the bleeding. Our captain gave the order to fall back, and I pulled up John to get him on his feet. Then, we raced to the planned extraction point. The enemy fighters were dangerously close, trailing right behind us. I noticed John looked pale and weak, but he kept pace with the team. He used the last of his strength to push back down the mountain, the whole time providing cover fire. I believe he saved our lives, because his shots kept the Taliban from overtaking us."

Bile rose in her throat. The edges of her vision blurred blood red. In her mind's eye, she pictured John continuing to fight, even while he knew he was dying.

Heath took a few deep breaths. "We contacted the Operation Command center and notified them we had two wounded. When we got onto the medivac chopper, John had already lost too much blood. The bullet had nicked his carotid artery. I did everything in my power to save him." Heath's voice wavered. "I pulled out your picture, the one he always carried in his uniform pocket. He stared at it for the longest time, and then told me how much he loved you and Aiden. By the time the chopper returned to the base, he'd already slipped into unconsciousness. At the hospital, the doctors tried to bring him back, but they were too late."

Throat burning, Julie walked to where Heath stood. As he began to sob, she wrapped her arms around him. Waves of emotion washed over her. With painful acceptance, she came to grips with what happened during John's final hours. She held onto Heath, and after several minutes of shared grief, Julie led him to the table.

"The Army doesn't want to acknowledge the fact a US citizen was killed on Pakistani soil." Greg shook his head. "Technically, the man was an enemy combatant, but his death will still trigger questions by the media and civil liberty groups. I believe, since John was the shooter, they wanted to keep his name a secret. They're afraid of retaliation against his surviving family. I would advise you take precautions, Mrs. Ellis, when this story goes public."

"Thank you for giving me the truth." Julie looked deeply into Heath's hazel eyes and sucked in a deep breath. "I've always known John died for something he believed in. He loved his job, and I'm not surprised he gave everything to protect his team."

The chair screeched, and Reagan stood. "I should get going. You and Heath have a lot to talk about."

Her heart lurched, and her hands fluttered to her chest. She had to convince him to stay. So many things needed to be said. First and foremost, that she still loved him.

Greg and Reagan made their way toward the front door.

Julie followed in their wake. "Thank you for your part in this, both of you." She glanced over at Reagan, who seemed only interested in the laces of his shoes.

"Reagan is the one who orchestrated the whole thing. I was just doing my job." Greg gave her a brief handshake before walking to his car.

Heart in her throat, Julie reached out to touch Reagan's arm. "Please don't go."

"My part in this is finished. I wanted to help you find the truth, and hopefully, you now have some peace." His thumb brushed across her cheek. "Take care, Julie."

Before she could say another word, he opened the screen door and stepped outside.

As she stood paralyzed in the doorway, Heath

came up beside her.

"You'd be an idiot to let him go." He scratched at his scruffy, brown beard.

"What?" She swung to face him.

He winked and smiled. "You heard me. Don't be stupid. Reagan loves you. He'd do anything for you. Don't let that kind of love slip away."

Heath's first loyalty was always to John. His advocacy represented John's blessing. She took off running, not caring if the whole neighborhood thought she was crazy, and intercepted Reagan before he opened his car door. "I was wrong," she blurted. "About everything."

Reagan slowly turned to face her and raised his eyebrows. "Well, I don't hear that every day."

Nice to see his playful nature again, after all this time. She searched his face, wanting to find any traces of the love he'd once had. "Are you—" she stammered and stared down at her bare feet. "Did you find someone else?"

A brief laugh escaped him. "No, Julie. I haven't wanted to be with anyone but you."

Relief replaced fear, and she almost sagged. "I don't want you to leave. Stay with me, please. Give me another chance."

Reagan shook his head. "I can't love someone with my whole heart and only get part of them in return." He reached for the door handle.

Blood pounded in her ears. Julie blocked him with her body. He may be twice her size, but he didn't stand a chance against her will. At that moment, she was an unmovable force. "I'm not letting you leave without a fight. You want my whole heart, well…here. I'm offering it to you." She took his hand and held it over her rapidly beating heart.

A slow smile emerged onto Reagan's face. "Well, looks like I've got myself a little warrior."

"You can laugh at me all you want, Reagan Harrison, but you will hear me out."

He raised his hands in mock surrender. "Okay, okay. First, give yourself some time to digest what you just learned. Spend some time with Heath. He's a good man, and I think he needs your support as much as you need his. Call me tomorrow, and then we'll talk."

"No. I'm not calling you." She smiled with the knowledge of what she had planned. "You're meeting me. I'll tell you the time and place. Oh…and wear comfortable shoes. We're going for a hike."

Chapter Twenty

While Julie drove over to Maple Street, she reflected about yesterday's events and her long conversation with Heath. He shared his struggles since leaving the Army, his constant nightmares, and survivor's guilt—all symptoms of his PTSD. Julie offered her forgiveness, explaining she didn't hold him responsible for John's death. He provided the best medical care available at the time, and she knew her husband willingly gave his life to protect his team.

He promised to keep in touch. Heath had been John's best friend and part of her family. They'd said a tearful goodbye, and he left for Texas to start a new life as a civilian.

Following the hurricane of emotions, Julie had finally found peace. The story Heath told her had been heart-wrenching to listen to, but it provided her with the answers she needed. Finally sealing shut a long-exposed wound.

As she approached her destination, her heart skipped a beat at the sight of Reagan standing next to his sports car. She parked behind him and exited her car. Her gaze absorbed every single detail—his tousled hair, the blond stubble covering his jaw, and the shorts and shirt that showed off his athletic physique. Her body certainly had its own reaction to seeing him.

He walked over to greet her. "What's with the

shovel?" He pointed to her hand.

"This is not a shovel, it's a garden trowel. You'll find out soon enough." She led him toward the trees and onto the path.

"Where are we going?"

"My, my…aren't you full of questions." She laughed, even though her insides were a hive of nerves. "There's someplace special I want to take you." She grabbed his hand, loving the connection, and they walked silently through the woods until the clearing came into view.

The young grass swayed back and forth with the gentle breeze. Plump, green buds adorned the branches of the trees, ready to burst forth with life.

Moving into the field, she picked a yellow flower and twirled it between her fingers. "This field is very special. John and I came here a lot when we were in high school."

Reagan glanced around them and began to retreat, tugging her hand. "Why did you bring me here?"

"When I moved home to Timber Lake, this place held a mystical power over me. At first, I was afraid to come here because reliving those memories would be too painful." She glanced at the beautiful nature surrounding her. "Then, I found myself seeking comfort here. I wanted to feel John's presence."

"I don't understand, Julie. I thought you wanted to give us another chance?"

"Just hear me out, okay?" She shifted her body to face him. Her pulse raced with anticipation. "Two nights ago, I had a dream. I was here with John. He told me that I needed to open myself to love again. After he disappeared, I was so scared, but then you came for me.

You told me to choose. I could stay here and hold onto my sorrow or go with you. You showed me the way home."

Julie strengthened her hold on his hand and looked deep into his eyes. "I want you, with my whole heart and soul." She wasn't too proud to beg. "Please forgive me. Don't leave."

In one swift motion, his mouth covered hers. All the hurt and anger fell away like leaves of an autumn tree. Their kiss fastened her soul with his—a lock softly slipping into place.

When they finally pulled apart, Julie reached to the ground and retrieved her trowel. Then she pulled the blue stone bird out of her pocket. Walking over to a patch of wildflowers, she bent over and dug a small hole.

Reagan knelt beside her as she worked.

I love you, but the time has come to let you go. With a deep, steadying breath, she placed the bird inside the hole and covered it with dirt, packing down the ground with several pats. Each move released her regret. The pain of the past had been buried. She was ready to take the first step toward the future.

"Why?" he asked.

"I needed to say goodbye." She wiped away a tear. "Now, I'm ready to start a new life with you by my side."

"Marry me." He cupped her face in his hands. "I want us to build a wonderful life together. I already have your ring."

Did Reagan really ask her to marry him, or was this just a trick of her imagination? She pinched her arm and smiled at the stinging sensation. Excitement blossomed inside her. Dreams really did come true. "Yes." What more was there to say? "Nothing would make me happier." As she left the field, she turned one last time, saying farewell to her past. Once on the wooded trail, she enjoyed conversing with Reagan. While they'd been apart, she'd missed out on so much time with him.

Returning to their cars, Reagan refused to let her go. He hugged her with so much enthusiasm, she was afraid she'd pop.

"I don't want to be apart from you for one more minute." He rested his chin on top of her head. "I'd marry you right now if I could. You'd have my last name, and we'd be a family. We could start working on a little brother or sister for Aiden. That kid needs a sibling."

Another baby. What a wonderful idea. "Sounds like fun." She peered into his blue eyes, which sparkled. He must have read her mind. Julie's smile turned into a huge grin. Right now, she'd agree to anything.

"Vegas," they both blurted out in unison.

With that decisive statement, she took the final leap. "I want to be your wife by the end of the day."

He held her in his arms and gave her an enthusiastic spin. "You go home and pack an overnight bag. I'll go grab a few things from my house and make the travel arrangements. Be ready to go in an hour."

****

Six hours later, Julie rested in the back of a black limo, moving down the Vegas strip. The spacious interior was dimly lit, soft music played over the speaker system. Reagan handed her a glass of champagne and she took a sip, and then reclined in the soft leather seat. She gazed out the window as the flashing neon lights brightened the night sky.

"Welcome to Vegas." He held her close. "The city that never sleeps."

"Good, since we're having our wedding ceremony in the middle of the night." The thought of their impromptu nuptials made her giggle. When she'd told her mom and Chrissy about what they planned, they were surprised but thrilled. When Reagan arrived at her house, he'd slipped a gorgeous diamond ring on her finger.

Before boarding the plane, Reagan pulled her aside. "We could wait. I don't want to cheat you out of your dream wedding. I'd throw you the biggest, most extravagant wedding if that's your wish."

"I just want to be your wife. I don't need anything else."

By the time they got on the plane, Reagan had all the arrangements made. Amazing, that with enough money, a person could make the impossible happen.

Now, snuggled together in the rear of the limo, they made the short drive across the strip, finally arriving at a two-story, flagstone church. Their chauffeur opened the door, and Julie stepped out into the warm night. With the city lights behind them, the dark sky opened to reveal a sparkling sea of diamonds.

Reagan took their bags and escorted her to the entrance of the building.

A tall, balding man in a navy suit greeted them, ushering them inside.

She was shown to her dressing room, and then shooed away Reagan so she could change into her wedding gown. Inside the space, a beautifully simple dress hung before her, another gift from Reagan. The guy had good taste. She'd have to remember to thank his mom and sisters one day.

Fifteen minutes later, she stepped out of the room. Her garment was light and airy, made of ivory gossamer. Its narrow straps attached to a delicately beaded bodice, flowing to a pool of fabric at her feet. An elderly woman waited to take her to the pastor and her groom. She was handed a bouquet of yellow roses mixed with white jasmine. A sweet and heady fragrance filled her nose.

As she approached the chapel, she walked on air. The doors opened for her, and she stepped out onto an outdoor stone patio. Thousands of white twinkle lights hung in the trees, which lined the narrow walkway. The space glowed with soft illumination. Had she stepped through a magic portal into another world? *Canon in D Major* played in the background, and the scent of flowers filled the air.

Reagan stood by the stairs, which led to the white gazebo.

He might be her second husband, but he'd never be second place. Loving Reagan had expanded her heart. And his love filled the emptiness inside her, making her once again whole. When she reached him, she took his hand and climbed the three stairs to enter the gazebo.

"You've held my heart since the first time I saw you." Reagan brushed his fingertips down her arm. "I knew you couldn't resist my charms forever."

Julie laughed, fighting back the tears building in her eyes. "As charming as you are, I'm here today because of another gift you've given me. Something I thought I'd lost forever."

"And what would that be?" He turned with her to

face the minister.

"Hope," she whispered. Her pulse quickened with the swell of emotions inside her. Someday, she'd give him a gift as precious. "You've given me hope."

Epilogue

"Come on, kid," Reagan called as he walked down the upstairs hallway. "We need to leave soon." Looking inside Aiden's room, he saw him lying on the floor, feverishly coloring on a piece of white paper.

"I'm almost done, Dad," he said in a breathy voice. "I want to give it to Mom."

"Sure, come downstairs when you are done."

Aiden's bedroom was three times the size of his old room at Julie's house and filled with everything a young boy could want. A large set of windows overlooked the back yard and lake.

He went into his own master bedroom and grabbed the bag Julie had asked for. His room had undergone a transformation over the past months as well. Long gone were the framed sports jerseys and wildlife pictures. Instead, the bedroom was filled with feminine touches. Multitudes of throw pillows covered their king-size bed, high heel shoes were scattered on the floor, and sitting on the nightstand was Julie's latest romance novel. As he came down the hall, he met Aiden with the homemade card in his hand.

"I'm ready. Do you think she'll like it?" He showed it to Reagan.

"She'll love it."

Aiden ran to the mudroom to grab his coat and put on his shoes. They moved into the garage, and Aiden got buckled into the seat.

A few years ago, Reagan would have considered fatherhood an unwanted complication. Now, having left his carefree bachelor days behind, he found family life an even better fit.

"Why can't we take the fun car?" Aiden pointed at the red sports car.

He glanced at his son in the rearview mirror. "The fun car doesn't handle very well in the snow. I want to get you to Mom safe and sound." As they pulled out of the icy driveway, Reagan's gaze was drawn to the American flag blowing in the strong January wind. He and Julie had erected the flag pole in a small flower garden in their front yard. A metal plaque resting at its base read:

In loving memory of Sergeant John Richard Ellis
United States Army Special Forces
His sacrifice will never be forgotten

Twenty minutes later, they arrived at Timber Lake General Hospital. Eagerness took hold as he led Aiden through sliding doors. When they got on the elevator, they rode to the fourth floor. As they exited, a large "Maternity" sign greeted them.

"Do you think the baby will like me?" Aiden scrunched up his nose.

"She'll adore you." Reagan gave his small hand a reassuring squeeze. "You're her big brother."

"What does she look like?"

"Just wait and see." Reagan chuckled at his impatience. Yesterday, he'd been the one who'd been impatient, when Julie awoke him at three in the morning to tell him she'd gone into labor. He'd quickly jumped into action, running to the guest room to wake up Mary, who'd been staying with them for the past week. That panic—he'd never felt anything like it in his life.

Julie had been as calm as Reagan was nervous. Her reaction at going into labor shouldn't have surprised him though. She'd gone through this once before.

Coming to the door to Julie's private maternity suite, Aiden quietly stepped inside. Reagan followed him in and was struck by the scene before him. In the bed sat the glowingly beautiful woman he was lucky enough to call his wife. She was wrapped in a soft white robe and held a tiny pink bundle.

****

"Aiden, come meet your new baby sister, Hope Catherine Harrison." Julie raised the baby in her arms.

Aiden climbed onto a chair, which was adjacent to the bed, and peered into the blanket.

Sleeping inside was his sister. Julie brushed the soft strawberry blonde curls that topped Hope's tiny head, and then kissed the small hands resting on her cherub face. She inhaled the sweet smell of baby.

"She's so small," he whispered. He reached out, tentatively touching her hand.

"She's small now, but she will grow fast. Hope has her father's appetite." Julie gave Reagan a gentle smile. How many other of her father's traits would Hope be lucky enough to inherit? "Would you like to hold her?" she asked Aiden.

"Can I?"

"Wash your hands, and go sit in the rocking chair," she instructed.

Aiden did what he was told. Reagan picked up the baby and tenderly placed her in Aiden's waiting arms.

A huge grin spread across Aiden's face.

"See," Reagan said. "She loves you already." He looked over at Julie. "I hate to leave you on Saturday."

His never-ending devotion warmed her. "You'll be here to take us home tomorrow, and my mom is staying with us for a while longer. Plus, your family is coming soon, so I won't have to lift a finger the whole time you're gone. Just go win the playoff game and come home to us. Hope won't change too much in two days."

He sat on the bed and rested his head on her shoulder. "I love you."

"I know." She brushed his hair with her fingers.

Aiden glanced at his parents, snuggled on the bed. "Dad, when we watch the game, I'll tell Hope what's going on. That way she knows what a super Dad you are."

"Thanks, buddy." He smiled at Aiden, who was gently rocking his sister. Raising his head, he kissed Julie softly. "Just think...this little girl was the reason you got so sick on our honeymoon. I'll never forget our trip to Belize. Besides enjoying time with you in a tropical paradise, I learned I'd be a father. Or should I say a father, again."

Hope started to fuss, and Aiden glanced up with big, round eyes.

Reagan came over to take the baby, swaying back and forth in an effort to soothe her. Aiden started singing a lullaby.

"You know, with the two of you watching her like a hawk, she'll never keep a boyfriend." The picture they made was adorable. Julie laughed.

Reagan's and Aiden's jaws dropped.

"My daughter will never be allowed to date."

"Okay, okay, relax. I love you both for being so protective of our sweet, little Hope." She watched as her husband and son fussed over the baby, and she felt an overwhelming joy fill her heart. Thinking about the difficult path, which had led her to this moment, made her appreciate her family even more. No longer would the past sorrows and heartache interfere with her present happiness. She was here, with her wonderful family. Living for today, living for the future.

A word about the author...

Laurie Winter is a true warrior of the heart. Inspired by her dreams, she creates authentic characters who overcome the odds and find true love.

She keeps her life balanced with regular yoga practice and running. When not pounding the pavement or the keyboard, she's enjoying time with her family, who are scattered between Wisconsin and Michigan. Laurie has three kids and one fantastic husband, all who inspire her to chase her dreams.